DIRTY ADDICTION

DIRTY SERIES BOOK 2

ELLA MILES

FREE BOOKS

EllaMiles.com/freebooks

Want to get my full-length romance *Not Sorry* for **free**?

Want to get my **free** bonus novella—*Aligned: Ever After*?

Want to know when I put my books on sale for **free or 99 cents**?

You can get all of the above and more goodies here:
EllaMiles.com/freebooks

READING ORDER

Dirty Obsession (Dirty Beginning, a teaser novella, included in Obsession)
Dirty Addiction
Dirty Revenge (Coming June)

PROLOGUE

NINA

One year.

That's how long Eden has been gone.

Taken.

Stolen.

That's how long I've been living my life, blissfully ignorant while I was enjoying my new life with my new love, she was going through hell.

One year.

That's how long Matteo has had her.

Matteo used to be caring. A man that I even loved, although never as much as Arlo.

But Arlo and I leaving changed him. Hardened him again. And now who knows what he is capable of.

One year.

That's how long Eden has been with Matteo.

Was she beaten?

Tortured?

Raped?

Or did she soften Matteo's heart, the way Arlo softened his with me?

One year is a long time. I'm a horrible friend for not realizing she was hurting. She needed me, and I wasn't there. I'll never forgive myself if Matteo hurt Eden.

Eden's strong. She'll survive another few hours until Arlo and I get to Italy to rescue her. Arlo didn't want me to go. He wanted to go alone. But there was no way I won't be there for my friend, now that I know she needs me.

Eden's strong, but I know how being stolen affects people. Makes you addicted. To getting better. To proving you haven't changed. To life.

But sometimes, you get addicted to the darkness and let it consume you. With no hope to escape.

1
───────

EDEN

My life is perfect.

I have the perfect body, which I work hard to keep in shape every day.

I have the perfect condo with an oceanfront view in Los Angeles, California.

I date the perfect guys. They are all impeccable gentlemen, taking me on fancy dates and treating me like a queen in the bedroom.

And most importantly, I have the perfect job.

"Will the defendant rise for sentencing?" the judge asks, staring at the accused and his lawyers.

I look over at Ivan, the suspect and soon to be prisoner, with a smirk on my face. I toss my hair back and hold my head high as the monster stands before the court for judgment. He's a terrifying man. The kind of man who can just glance at you and strike fear into the deepest confines of your soul. His entire body exudes evil and dark. Even the suit his lawyers bought for him doesn't hide his cruelty.

They could have put him in a bunny costume, and it wouldn't have hidden the monster inside him. The dark suit he's wearing reflects the darkness of his soul. His hair is shaved short, revealing the tattoos inked into his scalp. The long jacket sleeves can't contain the tattoos, nor the scars, that blanket his arms and hands. But it's not only his general appearance that makes him menacing. It's the glare in his eyes, the arrogance in his strut, and the vulgar venom in his speech. Everything about him makes it clear he doesn't give a shit about anyone but himself. He'll hurt anyone who dares to cross him.

Right now, he's terrified. He no longer stands proud and strong, like no one can touch him. His body trembles a little as he stands and his bottom lip quivers. He tries to hold back the tears staining his bulging eyes. He knows he's lost. He knows he's going to prison for the rest of his life at the very least, or he's going to die on death row.

This is my favorite part. The part where the bad guys realize they're not untouchable. They are weak. And by locking them away, I'm saving countless other souls from these evil savages.

"Ivan Shaw, on the count of murder in the first degree, this court has found you guilty."

I cock my head to the side as I stare at Ivan. Gazing at him as the single tear rolls down his cheek. I watch as the handcuffs go around his wrists and he is lead out of the courtroom. Before he's pulled out of the courtroom entirely, he turns his head and gives me one last dirty, sullen stare, his face shining red and jaw clenching. But it does nothing to intimidate me. In fact, it warms my insides to see him dragged away, never to see freedom again.

"You're fucking amazing," Jules, my assistant, says next to me as she begins gathering up the files of papers we had laid out across the courtroom table.

I put a couple of the files into my briefcase and snap the leather case shut. "I'm not that incredible. My work is important, so I have to get it right. If not, a man like Ivan could go back out on the streets and kill dozens of other innocent people. I'm the last line of defense to ensure he doesn't hurt another person."

Jules smiles and shrugs. "You're still freaking awesome. Ivan left no evidence. His men were utterly loyal to him. The fact that you got one of his men to flip and give you the gun used to commit the murder, with Ivan's fingerprints all over it, is astonishing. No other lawyer would have gotten anyone loyal to him to say so much as a single syllable against him. Any other lawyer would have lost the case."

Exhaling, I turn and walk out of the courtroom with Jules on my heels. She's young and inexperienced, but she's well on her way to becoming my mini-me. I hope to train as many people as I can to do my job, so we can apprehend more evil creatures and protect this city.

"How do I look?" I ask before exiting the courtroom, preparing myself to face the reporters outside.

Jules scrutinizes me up and down, peering down my dark red skirt and jacket, up to my pin straight black hair, and across my face to examine my makeup. "You're flawless and perfect as usual. Not a lipstick smudge or glisten of sweat visible."

I nod. "Good."

Plastering a smug expression on my face, a warning to all other convicts out there that I'm coming for you and I'm going to win, I step out into the lobby of the courtroom. The flashes should blind me, but I'm used to it by now. Bristles from the microphone booms brush against my cheek. The attention should make me uneasy, but instead, I find it as easy as talking to a close friend.

"How were you able to lock away one of LA's worst criminals, abating the police and court system for decades?" one of the reporters asks.

I stare directly at the camera that is pointed at me. "I surround myself with the best team, and I have dedicated my life to making our world a little safer. I'll do whatever it takes to ensure the bad guy goes to jail every single time. Ivan Shaw was a villain. It may take some time, but in the end, good always conquers evil."

"This case seemed impossible. How were you able to convince the key witness, in this case, to cooperate with you?"

I turn my head towards the next camera. "Because impossible doesn't exist. Not really. Every one of these people are human. They all have wants and desires of their own. No one wants to go to prison for the rest of their lives. No one wants to be responsible for the criminal going free. So it's a matter of having a heart-to-heart conversation with someone, human to human. After that, the witness was more than willing to talk."

I glance around all the reporters. "I'll take one more question."

"What's next? You prosecute more cases than anyone in the state. Are you going to take a much-needed vacation?"

I laugh. "I'll take a vacation when all the bad guys are locked up, and there are none left to terrorize this city."

I start walking again, and the reporters reluctantly part for me, still firing off questions despite me saying I was only taking one more question. I walk fast in my stiletto heels, keeping ahead of the reporters and Jules who are trailing behind me.

I don't like admitting it, but I like the attention winning a case brings. I like the afterglow and the feeling that I did something helpful for the world. I feel like a rock star, and hopeful that maybe, this was the time I locked away the last criminal. Tomorrow I'll wake up and sleep in, instead of getting a call about yet another murder that happened while I slept. This will be the time I never get that call. All of the horrible people will have somehow been eradicated from the world, or at least my small part of it.

But I know it's just a dream, a fantasy. Tomorrow I'll wake up to a phone call asking if I want to take another case on. I know I will accept the new case because this is my life, and despite how hard it can be, it's also precisely what I want for my life. I have a perfect record when it comes to defeating wicked, cruel beasts, and I don't plan on giving up the reins anytime soon.

I walk out of the courtroom and over to my red Ferrari. I climb in and roll down the window to talk to Jules one last time before I head home.

"Do you want to get a drink or something tonight to celebrate?" Jules asks.

"Sorry, but I have —"

Jules rolls her eyes as she crosses her arms and leans against my car. "You have a date with one of your Mr. Perfect's, don't you?"

I grimace. "Am I that predictable?"

"Yes," she huffs. She glances over at the reporters who are now busy interviewing the families. I look away, unable to watch the families. I don't feel sorry for the criminal's family. As for the victim's family, I can never do enough to get the haunting, sickening feeling to leave my stomach.

"You should take some time off Jules."

She smirks. "I will if you will."

"It doesn't work that way. I'm telling you as your boss to take next week off."

"And what happens tomorrow if you accept a case for the second most evil person in the world, after that bastard, and I'm sitting on the beach somewhere?"

"Then I guess I'll have to do the initial groundwork without you. Now go. Have fun tonight, and go spend some time relaxing on the beach this week. Turn off your phone and the world, and enjoy life away from all this." I wave my hands out motioning to the courthouse and the chaos surrounding it.

She nods slowly, pulling out her phone. "I'll turn my phone off as soon as I hear about how your date with Mr. Incredible goes tonight. You know I love hearing all the juicy details."

I laugh. "No, you can hear about them when you come back."

She pouts.

I laugh again, and snatch her phone from her hand as she squeals. I turn it off before handing it back to her.

"I mean it. Keep this thing off so no one at work will bother you for a week."

"Fine."

She will probably turn it back on as soon as she is out of eyesight of me, but I can hope at least one person in my office is going to get a much-needed break from this life.

I can't take a break. I couldn't live with myself if I took a break and someone went free because I wasn't here leading the charge to lock the criminal up. Jules is still young and doesn't have the responsibility of the world on her shoulders. She should enjoy herself.

She walks back to her car a few aisles over as I start my own car and drive off. Blasting the radio as I drive home, I try to drown out my thoughts and forget about work so I can enjoy my hot blind date tonight.

I was set up by Jack, a guy I work with. My blind date's name is Saul. He's a businessman, doing something with real estate, hotels, and condos. From what I'm told, he's smart, a gentleman, and a hottie. Exactly what I'm looking for tonight. He's taking me to one of the newest and hottest restaurants in LA. It will be nice to sit back with a cocktail, delicious food, and hopefully interesting conversation with a sexy man to ogle.

My mind wanders to my usual thoughts whenever I'm not focusing on work: *Nina*.

I haven't heard from her in weeks. She usually checks in at least once a month and lets me know that she's safe and Arlo is still treating her well. Because if he's not, he knows I'll come for him and lock him up like I do all the other criminals.

But every time Nina calls, she seems happy, no, better than happy. She acts like herself, like this is where her life was leading her all this time. So as much as I want to go to Arlo and knock his balls clean off his body for what he did to Nina, and for now making her live a life on the run, away from her friends and normal life, I won't. Because I love her and she loves Arlo. Despite all his faults, I do believe now he will do anything and everything he can to love and protect Nina.

A few minutes later, I park the car and get out, say hello to my doorman, Larry, and grab the mail before I head up to my sprawling condo on the fifth floor.

I throw the door open to my expansive home, walk over to my sound system and turn it on. Blaring music makes me feel less alone. I don't have any pets or roommates, no one to keep me company. I prefer it this way. I like having my own space and the freedom to spend my evenings how want.

It's also one of the reasons why I stick to dates. I like being alone. I don't care about settling down anytime soon. I don't want a live-in boyfriend or a husband. Work keeps me plenty busy. I date one night a week.

My date gets one shot with me, and no matter how much we connect or how good the sex is, that's all I'll ever give him. I don't want to get attached. I don't him to develop feelings for me either, so I follow my simple rules. One man, one date, once a week.

I stretch, wishing I had time for a quick yoga session before my date but I don't. I pour myself a glass of red wine and then head to my bedroom to find a suitable dress for tonight. I strip down to my black lace bra and underwear. I always wear sexy underwear, even when I'm the only one who is going to see it, especially on days I'm in court. Racy lingerie makes me feel strong and confident, which I need in the courtroom.

I dig through my closet and find a simple black dress with plenty of sex appeal between its short length and low-cut front, giving off the vibe that I expect sex tonight and lots of it. I get dressed and touch up my hair and makeup in the mirror. I consider curling my hair but think better of it. I don't want him to think I'm trying too hard. That's not what tonight is about. If he thinks I'm trying hard, then he'll think I want to go on a second date. I don't.

I apply another coat of red lipstick as I hear a knock on the door, faintly from behind my blaring music. I glance at the clock on my phone; he's early. One positive strike for him already. Carrying my wine and phone with me, I head to the living room and turn off the music on my way to the door. We have plenty of time to have a drink together first before heading to dinner.

I open the door with an intriguing smile. My skin flushes, my lips part, and my knees grow so weak I have to grasp the door-frame to remain standing when I see how ruggedly handsome my date is. He has shoulder-length dark hair, a scar across his cheek that makes him look a little dangerous, but nothing compared to the men I prosecute. His body looks strong and fit beneath his simple black T-shirt and jeans. He appears to be way underdressed for the restaurant he told me he was taking me to tonight, but maybe I'm the one who's overdressed. There is also something familiar about him that I can't place.

"Would you like to come in and have a drink before our date tonight?" I ask Saul. I rake my teeth over my bottom lip letting him know how much I appreciate his body and charming appearance. Jack did an excellent job setting us up.

"I'd love to come in."

He steps inside, taking up space like he owns the place as he walks. I shut the door behind us and rush forward, leading him into my kitchen.

"Is red wine okay or would you like something else?" I ask, my voice raspy as I speak. I swallow hard, trying to remedy my voice.

He scours the room, but I have no idea what he's looking for. "Red wine is fine."

I suddenly feel nervous, my hands clammy, as I begin pouring him a glass of wine. I'm used to dating powerful, strong men, but this man is different. He walks around commanding attention, demanding my eyes to stay on him and he's barely said anything or hardly even looked at me. I'm used to sharp dressed men that give me flowers and complements, place their hand on the small my back, or link our fingers together.

He does none of these things. But yet he requires everything of me.

He walks over to the colossal windows spanning the entire length of the wall, looking out over the ocean. I walk over to him and hold out his glass of wine to him, my hand shaking slightly. "Here you go."

He takes the glass from me, lifts it to his mouth, and takes a sip before spitting it out.

He eyes the glass suspiciously. "You call this wine? It's disgusting."

I snort and raise an eyebrow as I take the wine glass back from him. "Sorry, I don't have much experience with wine, so I usually buy whatever cheap wine is on sale. I think I have some whiskey if you prefer?"

He shakes his head. "I don't think I trust your taste in whiskey either."

"I guess you'll be the one picking out the wine at dinner tonight."

He reaches out and tugs gently on one of my strands of hair. "Do you always straighten your hair like this?"

I nod. "Why? You don't like it?" I open my eyes wide and give him an 'I dare you to say you hate it' stare.

"No reason. I used to know someone who wore her hair very much like yours. It suits you well."

"Thank you. Although, straight is a trendy hairstyle. I do have a close friend who wears her hair very similar to mine. People would call us twins, or at the very least, sisters because we were so much alike."

"And what is your friend's name?"

"Nina."

"Would Nina like to go on a double date with us to dinner this evening?"

I shake my head. "No, she doesn't live here."

I swear he frowns at the news, but then again, he seems always to be frowning or grimacing or glaring. He doesn't seem like a happy, relaxed person. He seems stiff and far too serious.

I'm one to talk. I spend my whole day being serious. Maybe his work is similar to mine, and he has to take it seriously. I can understand why it would be hard for him to relax, even on a date.

"Shall we head to dinner?"

"Sure, that way we can get you a proper drink," I say smiling at him, hoping he will smile back.

He doesn't; he continues to stare at me like he has seen a ghost or something.

A knock at the door startles me, and I turn.

"Maybe it's the doorman delivering a package or something?" I say, walking toward the door after setting my wine glass down on the kitchen counter.

I open the door and see a charming man standing in my doorway in a suit, holding a modest bouquet of daisies. He grins at me as he approvingly checks out my tanned legs and cleavage.

I wince, holding the door open. "I'm sorry I think you have the wrong condo."

"You're Eden Collins, right?"

I nod. "And you are?"

"I'm Saul Lewis. Jack set us up on a blind date tonight or did I get the wrong day?" He glances behind me to the man standing in my living room.

"Wait, you're Saul?"

He nods.

"Can you show me your ID?"

He raises an eyebrow, reaching into his back pocket for his ID and handing it to me. I read his name across the top of his driver's license. Saul Lewis.

I storm back to the living room, leaving Saul standing in my doorway.

"Who the hell are you and what are you doing in my home?"

I cross my arms over my chest and give him a glare I only reserve for the worst of the criminals I prosecute.

He chuckles. "I'm surprised you don't recognize me, sweetheart."

I stare at him a second longer, and then I do. "No..."

He cocks his head to the side flashing me a grin I immediately hate. "So you do remember me. That's good; it means you'll help me."

"No, get out of my condo Matteo. Now."

He takes a sprawling seat on my leather couch instead, a couch that seems small with his muscular body dwarfing it.

My eyes fly open at the audacity of him to come here, let alone sit down on my couch, after what he did to my friend. Nina may have forgiven him, but I don't. I've barely absolved

Arlo, and that's only because she loves him. I can't forgive Matteo. Besides, now he is in charge of the Carini company, so I'm sure he's done far worse things than any of the men I lock up on a daily basis.

"Should I come in or what?" Saul asks from the doorway.

"Yes, come in."

Saul walks inside. "Do you need help throwing this guy out?"

"No, I can handle him."

I turn my attention back to Matteo. "Unless you came to tell me something's happened to Nina and Arlo, I don't want to hear about it."

"Actually, I'm here to find out where they are. They call you. You know exactly where they are. So tell me, and I'll be on my way."

I hate myself for finding him attractive for even a minute. I hate myself for wanting anything to do with this monster.

"Why do you want to know?"

"Because I need my brother's help."

I search his eyes. "Liar."

He smirks, leaning forward, his eyes glued to me. "Fine. Because Arlo stole something from me and I want it back."

My heart sinks. "Nina. You want Nina back."

He nods.

I smile. "You're never gonna find them."

"And why not?"

"Because I don't know where they are. Yes, they call me and let me know they're safe every once in a while, but they never tell me where they are. Just that they're safe. They never tell you where they are either. Arlo is better than you at this sort of thing. They'll be able to run and hide from you forever."

A pinched expression crosses his face as he stares at me, then at my date, and back to me again.

"I don't think I'll have any trouble finding them," Matteo

says, standing up from my couch and walking toward Saul. "Enjoy your date. Don't let her pick the wine." He's at my door in seconds, while I'm still staring at the couch, confused as to what the hell's going on.

"Where are you going?" I snap out of my stupor.

He stops short of the door, turns, and smirks at me. His eyes grow venomous.

"I'm letting you have one last date before I take you."

2

EDEN

I'M STUNNED as the door slams shut.

He's gone as quickly as he came. He struck fear into my heart and disappeared into the night leaving me with a thousand questions and no answers.

I close my eyes and crack my head side to side before deeply exhaling as I let all of the air out of my body. Calm. I need to remain calm. Now I wish I had had time for that yoga session to help relax me.

"Eden, what's wrong? What's going on?"

I ignore Saul. I can't handle his questions right now. I don't even have time to deal with my own fear. The only thing I can worry about is how to keep Matteo from kidnapping me.

There's a reason Nina and Arlo ran. Matteo was one of those reasons. He may be Arlo's brother, but I know what he's capable of. He's ruthless and will do whatever it takes to get what he wants.

I'm desperate for a solution and fast. I need a way to get rid of Matteo.

Nina. I rush over to the counter where my phone is lying and pick it up, ready to dial the number I memorized by heart. A number I'm only supposed to use in emergencies. Matteo coming back and threatening to steal me is unquestionably an emergency. I unlock my phone and begin dialing the numbers 376...

I stop.

I can't call Nina.

I try to swallow the lump in my throat. The one person who could help me is the one person I can't call. The one person who understands Matteo better than anyone. The one person who knows what Matteo might be planning.

All I know is I don't trust Matteo. I would be putting her in danger.

And if I tell Nina what is going on, she will come back. She will want to fight. And I can't put her through something like this again. She's happy. And even if I was able to convince her not to come back, Matteo could be tracking my calls. He could figure out that I know how to contact her. He could use the information to discover where she is. And I won't help him find her. I won't risk Nina's life no matter the cost.

Matteo didn't tell me why he wants Nina. But I doubt his intentions are pure. Nina told me almost everything. Matteo loved her as much as Arlo. She made her choice. She chose Arlo, now Matteo has to live with it. I don't want to imagine what battle might ensue if he was to find her.

I don't trust Arlo much more than I do Matteo, but Nina is as safe as she can be with him. Matteo can't find them.

Heath. I can call Heath. He is the only other person who might understand. He went through all this with Nina, and as much as I hate to bring him back into this world again, he is the only option I have.

I find his contact in my phone and dial the number. I hold my phone to my ear as my fingers drum across my granite countertops. I listen to one ring, two, three...

"Come on Heath, answer your damn phone."

Four rings... It goes to his answering machine.

"Call me when you get this. ASAP. It's an emergency."

I slam the phone down hard on the counter, not caring when the small crack forms in the corner of my phone. *Stupid phone.*

My whole body shakes. I'm not afraid Matteo's going to take me. For one, I won't let him. But I'm petrified of what would happen to Nina if he stole her from Arlo. She wouldn't survive being ripped from the love of her life. So I have to stop Matteo.

"Eden?...Are you okay?" Saul says as he walks over to me and carefully places his hand on my shoulder.

I exhale deeply again, letting everything out. I try to find my tranquil, happy place, but his unsteady hand shaking my entire body isn't helping.

"Thank you. I'm going to be fine." I step away, causing his hand to drop from my body.

"You want to tell me what that was about?"

I turn and try to make my eyes brighten at him as I force my lips to smile. "No. It was nothing important."

He looks away as he rubs his tidy hair, making a mess of it. Sweat glistens on his forehead.

"What do you want to do now?"

I pause before answering. "Go out to dinner on our date and then whatever you had planned afterward. I want to forget about all this." I don't mention that I'm more desperate than I was before to have him. For him to fuck me and make me forget about what just happened. I want him to take me to a restaurant and then fuck me in the bathroom halfway through dinner.

"Okay," he smiles at me. He holds out his arm, and I take it, trying to focus on him as he leads me out of the condo and out to his waiting Volvo. He opens the door for me like the perfect gentleman he is, and I climb in as he goes around to the driver side. He starts up the car and turns on the radio, drowning out the silence.

"Do you like Asian food? This restaurant I'm taking you to does this fusion thing between Asian and Mexican."

Normal conversation. This is exactly what I need.

"I love Asian food."

He reaches over and takes my hand in his, holding it softly. I let my hand rest in his, despite how clammy his hand is.

I'm going to pretend like Matteo didn't walk into my life. I'm not going to run as Nina did. I'm going to stay and fight. All running did for Nina was stall the inevitable anyway. She ran and was still stolen. And in the meantime, she lived a life of fear.

I'm not running. I'm a smart, intelligent woman. I'm skilled enough to take on this asshole and win. I won't be taken.

The restaurant is impressive. It's the kind of restaurant where you sit on the floor on pillows, and they bring out food on sizable trays. The food was clearly thought out to blend aspects of Asian and Mexican cooking, with some dishes bringing a sweet heat of Korea and others the full-on spice of a jalepeño. The chef apparently had deep roots in both of the cultures, and it shows.

Saul does his best to keep the conversation light and moving, but we don't have much in common, and I'm far too distracted to be able to focus on much of what he is saying.

"Have you taken self-defense classes before?" I ask, unable to take my mind off the fact I may require his help tonight.

Saul clears his throat and blinks rapidly. "No."

"Know how to shoot a gun?"

"No."

"Know how to evade someone who is following you in a car?"

"No."

I sigh.

"But I do know how to order delicious wine. The kind that will make you turn up your nose at anything less."

My cheeks flush, and I readjust my legs loving the sound of his voice and the promises of more. "I could drink some fabulous wine. And I promise no more talk about self-defense or guns."

He reaches his hand out and holds mine again. Somehow his palm seems to have taken on even more moisture. I try my best to ignore it.

"Good, I may not own a gun, but I do know how to call the police."

I nod, and repeat to myself: *I won't let Matteo make me afraid. I won't fear him.*

I push away all thoughts of Matteo and enjoy my meal with Saul. I drink fabulous wine and eat delicious food. And I let ideas of all the ways that I want Saul to fuck me creep in like I would on any other date. His hands may be clammy, and the words that leave his mouth may be dull, but when he moves, I can see his biceps flex beneath his suit jacket. When he does grin, it reaches his deep blue eyes, inviting me in. And I have noticed his cock straining against the zipper on his pants more than once tonight. I do not doubt that he's incredible in bed.

I take the last bite of my chocolate dessert, savoring it slowly in my mouth before I swallow it down. I moan a little at the richness and glance over at Saul staring at me like he wants to eat me for dessert. I glance down at his erection that is straining against his pants. My lips part. I can't wait.

"You had your fun. Now tell me where Nina and Arlo are or I'm taking you with me."

I don't have to turn around to recognize that it's Matteo standing behind me.

"No."

My eyes cut over to Saul, whose eyes are bulging up at

Matteo. Saul's scared shitless. *Why couldn't I have been set up with a Navy SEAL or something?* This man is utterly useless to me.

Matteo places his hand on my shoulder, gripping it firmly, letting me know that he's in control. I grab his hand, zeroing in on his pinky finger, and twist hard, ensuring that it breaks.

"Son of a bitch," Matteo says, pulling his hand back from me to tend to his wound.

I stand up and turn to face him with a set jaw and my chin high.

His finger is bent backward in a way that no finger should bend.

"You bitch. You broke my finger."

"I did."

"Do you know who I am? I'm a monster now. King of everything evil. Your little tantrums won't protect you from my army."

I smirk. "I put away monsters every day. I can handle you." I pick up my purse and turn to Saul. "We're leaving."

Saul stands and hurries past us, not bothering to wait for me. *Some gentleman he is.* I follow after him, Matteo won't be far behind.

I always knew that there was evil in this world. I just didn't realize evil would ever come for me.

3

MATTEO

DAMN, this woman.

My finger stings like a bitch. You'd think I'd be used to the pain, but I'm not. Living the life that I do, puts me in dangerous situations every day. But that's what my men are for, taking bullets for me. I rarely, if ever, have to deal with the agony myself. It's only a broken finger, but it still hurts like hell.

I've only ever broken a bone once before. When Arlo and I were fighting as teenagers, trying to prove who was better, stronger. He won, of course, breaking my jaw with a hard punch in my face, knocking me out cold.

I never expected Eden, of all people, to be the one to break one of my bones. I'll make her pay for it, of course.

I need Nina. I thought I was okay when she chose Arlo. I thought I could live without her, but I can't. She haunts my dreams and forms my nightmares. Everything makes me think of her. Everything makes me want her. She tortures me, and she's not even here. I'm addicted to her. I can't be apart from her.

And my idiot brother needs to be punished for what he did. I don't care that he's my brother. As the new leader, he needs to know that there are consequences to crossing me, whoever you are. For taking her from me. For abandoning me when I need him the most. I thought I could always count on him. I was wrong.

"Sir, are you okay?" a waiter asks, staring at me with wide eyes at my broken finger. His bright face changes to green, and quickly shuts his mouth to keep from puking. His eyes never leave my finger, despite the vile that's I'm sure is forming in his throat. It's like I'm a car crash on the side of the road that people can't stop staring at once they start, despite how unsafe it is to stare.

"Does it fucking look like I'm okay?"

His face is now red as he stands there, wholly incompetent.

"Get me a Band-Aid, or preferably a first-aid kit. Now," I growl.

The boy runs off toward the restaurant's kitchen. I have no clue if he's going to return or not. But he only has about a minute of my patience before I storm back there myself and find what I need.

He returns in a few seconds. He may be a fool, but at least he's fast.

I plop the first aid kit down on the table and sit down, popping the lid open. I dig through it, throwing band-aids aside, not caring about the mess I'm creating on the floor until I find the gauze and tape I am searching for.

I tape my pinky to my ring finger for support, ensuring that my little finger is aligned correctly and not flopping around everywhere.

"You should have a doctor examine that," the waiter says, turning green again.

I glare at him as I stand and he shuts up. At least I'm still able to intimidate him.

I thought Eden would come with me easily. I thought a

simple threat would be enough to convince her to do whatever I wanted. I was wrong. This requires a more thorough plan.

I start walking out of the restaurant, ignoring the disgusting smell wafting off the food and the cheap wine sitting on every table. I have to steal this woman for no other reason than to show her what first class food and superior wine is.

Focus. I need a plan. I didn't bring backup. I didn't think I would require assistance. I wouldn't use it if I had it. This is personal. I want to do this alone.

I walk outside and down the sidewalk the three blocks to my car. Eden creeps into my mind as I walk.

I was dumbfounded by how similar her appearance is to Nina when she opened the door to her condo. So astounded, I thought she was Nina for a second. Her skin is the same olive color. Her hair long, dark, and straight. Her eyes just as piercing.

But my mind likes to play tricks on me when it comes to Nina. Eden, of course, isn't her. But they are best friends. They lived together. I'm sure Nina's told Eden everything. I doubt the similarities end with their appearance. Eden now shares the same fate Nina did. Eden will be captured the same way the Nina was.

I throw the door open to my convertible and calmly climb in, enjoying the smell of the leather seats. The car is brand-new. I bought it for this trip. I don't like sharing cars, and I can afford the more expensive things in life, even a new car for my single day in the US. I fire up the car and pull out of my spot, chasing after them. I pull out my phone and begin tracking Eden's phone. She may be feisty, but she's not smart enough to realize that she needs to get rid of her phone. The app on my phone instantly finds them. They are about ten blocks away, headed in the direction of her condo.

I start driving fast, weaving around car after car as I catch up to them. Each minute that passes I get closer and closer. Adrenaline rushes through my muscles as I drive almost automatically. My brain doesn't operate the car, my excitement does. The sooner I take Eden, the sooner I take Nina back and get to punish my brother.

My hands remain unshakeable as I speed through another red light. My heart beats steadily, my breathing relaxed, when I almost crash into an old Volkswagen Beetle that's driving far too slow in front of me. I dart out into the next lane and speed around it, not bothering to flip off the driver as I should. I've chased after someone in a car hundreds of times before. This is my life.

I see her douchebag of a date's car two in front of me. He thinks he's fancy driving in his Volvo S90. It's a ridiculous car, for men who are too weak to drive anything faster. His driving could use some work. I shouldn't have been able to catch up to them as quickly as I did.

I make a hard left turn, followed by two rights, looping around the block to get in front of them and stop at the light at the intersection. I lurk in the shadows of the building, waiting for them to stop at the light, perpendicular to where I sit. They do, and then I wait. I watch them from my seat in the car, talking to each other, having no idea the danger they are in. Having no clue that I hide feet away from them. Ready to take them out.

I don't know what kind of man she's dating, but he's definitely not worthy of her. He can't even protect her from a villain like me.

I keep my eye on the light and watch as it turns green for them. I step on the gas, slamming into his side of his car.

Our airbags go off, knocking the wind out of me for a second, but I'm determined. It does nothing to stop me. I want Eden, and I want her now. I'm tired of the games. I throw open my door and give myself a once-over before I examine my car. It barely has a scratch on it, while his shitty car took the brunt of the force. The entire front half is smashed in.

I walk toward the driver side of the car, knowing now my target should have been Saul, instead of Eden. If I understand anything about her, I know she will protect her stupid date. She'll put herself last.

I throw his door open and grab his arm, pulling him out of the car as I take my gun out of the back of my pants and aim it at his head.

"Now, let's try this again," I say, staring at Eden.

Her eyes bulge as she undoes her seatbelt and pushes the airbag down out of her face.

"Don't hurt him."

Her voice is slick and unwavering as she speaks without a drop of fear.

I smirk, my plan will work.

"Do as I say and I won't kill him."

She inspects me then her date. "I'm sorry," she mouths.

She throws open her door and runs.

"Damn it." *What's wrong with her?* She doesn't give a shit about her date.

I throw him hard against the concrete road.

"You can blame Eden for this." I shoot him squarely in the leg to keep him from coming after me. He has a fighting chance of surviving, as long as I didn't hit any major artery running through his leg. *I might need some help cleaning up this mess after all.*

I start running after her. She won't run far before I catch up with her. I'm far too impressive of a runner, and I'm far too motivated to not catch up with her. Her only hope is if there happens to be a police station or some place of sanctuary she can run to and hide inside.

But she seems to be out of luck. I see her turn a corner and I run after her, a second behind. She is fast, but not quick enough. I make a mental note not to underestimate her speed in the future.

She feels me catching up to her and turns to glance behind her, only to see me feet away. She darts down another road, leading her out toward a four-lane street filled with cars zipping by. She's trapped.

I slow my jogging down a little. She has nowhere to go. She won't be able to cross the busy street without getting hit by traffic. And there is nowhere else for her to hide.

She hesitates, staring out at the cars whizzing by her and then glances back at me.

I smirk.

She darts out into traffic, because, apparently, she'd rather die then get taken by me.

Shit.

I run after her, dashing out into the traffic. One car stops, honking their horn emphatically. She won't get so lucky a second time. I catch up with her, grab onto her and pull us out of the way of another speeding car.

We both lay on the cold concrete, my arms still around her, panting hard as the rush of adrenaline continues to beat wildly throughout our bodies.

"You're welcome."

She tries to climb out of my arms, but I hold her tighter to my body, enjoying having her warm body pressed against mine.

"What? You aren't grateful?"

"No."

"But I saved your life."

"You saved my life only so you could steal me, and use me against my best friend. That's not saving me."

"It's better than what you did to your date."

She scowls at me. "If I had gone with you, you would've killed him anyway."

"That's where you're wrong. If I give you my word I won't kill someone, then I won't."

"Will you kill me?"

"Not today."

She doesn't hesitate. She knees me hard in the balls, giving her enough time to free herself while I wrap myself around my wounded manhood.

She's good. But I'm better. I jump up, run the few feet after her, and grab her arm, twisting it hard behind her back.

She cries out.

"Now that I have your attention again, you will do what I say, or I'll break your arm, which trust me, from how much agony my finger is in, you won't recover from rapidly."

"You're a monster."

"I know."

I walk her back toward where my car and her date still sit, him bleeding out over the concrete.

I smirk at the weak man lying on the ground. "How does it feel that this incredible woman wasn't willing to save you?"

Her date glares back at me, too broken to even fight back with words.

"Should I kill him now since he means so little to you?"

"No, you wouldn't."

"I would and I will."

She pants hard. She makes the mistake of looking at the what is left of her date.

"Save him, and I'll cooperate."

"No, you won't."

But I walk her forward to him, still holding her arm behind her back.

"Take off your shirt," I say to him.

He squeezes his eyes shut, like that will make me disappear.

"Shirt off now," I bark again.

"Listen to him," Eden pleads.

He reluctantly removes his shirt, and I turn to Eden. "Now, take his shirt and tie it above the wound as tightly as you can."

I release Eden, keeping the gun firmly to her head as she does what I say. As soon as she's finished, I use my gun to slap him as hard as I can in the head, knocking him unconscious to the floor.

"Why did you do that?" she screams, trying to wake him up with her pathetic shakes of his shoulder.

"So he wouldn't follow us or remember any of this conversation to tell the police."

I grab her arm again, pulling her up from his limp body as I take out my phone and dial 911.

"911, what's your emergency?"

"There's been an accident at the corner of 7th and South Olive." I hang up.

"I kept my word. Now get in the car and cooperate before I change my mind and kill you both."

4

EDEN

MATTEO SPEEDS OFF, away from the accident. Away from Saul.

I glance into the side mirror at Saul's car shrinking smaller and smaller as we speed away, until it all but gets lost among the other cars driving by. Regret instantly fills my soul. *How could I have been so heartless to have let Matteo shoot Saul?* I needed to save myself. I needed to save Nina. *But will I ever be able to live with myself if Saul dies?* If he dies, it's *my fault.*

Matteo turns the corner, and I'm no longer able to see the car or Saul.

"He's going to die, isn't he?" I stare out the window as buildings whiz by, narrowly registering what's happening to me. All I can think about is Saul.

"He'll survive if he's strong enough."

I turn toward Matteo, who is whistling to himself as he loosely grasps the steering wheel. He's acting as if nothing happened. Like he didn't just shoot a man in the leg and leave him bleeding out on the sidewalk, most likely to die. Like he's not currently kidnapping me. In fact, the entire car appears that way. His convertible hardly has a scratch on it. And when I take a deep breath, I smell the fresh new car scent, when it should reek of death and gloom.

"How do you know that?"

"Stop worrying about your date. You didn't seem concerned with him before, by the way you ran off instead of trying to save him."

"That's because I didn't think you would shoot him. And I wasn't thinking about him, I was thinking about Nina."

He rapidly steps on the gas, accelerating as we go around another corner. I grab onto my seat to attempt from slamming my head into the side of the door.

"Relax, he'll survive. I missed all his major arteries, and if the emergency system is halfway decent around here, the paramedics are already at his side providing medical services. And as long as it doesn't take them hours to drive him to a hospital, he won't bleed out before they save him."

"How do you know you didn't hit any major arteries? You're not a doctor."

He rolls his eyes. "Because he would've been dead by the time we got back to him and blood would have been pouring out of his leg."

I'm not sure if I believe him. It sure as hell looked like a lot of blood to me. I'm not sure he knows anything about gunshot wounds, although he's probably been shot dozens of times before, so maybe he does.

But I also know that he is willing to tell me whatever he thinks I want to hear to get me to cooperate. He's right about one thing; I won't be cooperating. I plan on running again the next chance I get.

I rest my hand on the door handle in case he decides to stop, and I can make my escape.

"Don't even think about it."

"I'm not thinking about anything."

He shakes his head and punches the gas. My body slams against the door as he swerves around cars and goes the wrong way down a one-way street. I close my eyes and pray we don't hit anything, and simultaneously hope we do crash and die so this will be all over.

"I'll never slow down enough for you to be able to jump out of the car and run, so remove your fucking hand from the door."

My hand slips off the door, bracing myself again as he continues to speed and curse. I have to be more careful at revealing any part of my plan to him in the future. He's done this before; he's going to be able to spot what I'm planning before I carry it out. I have to make sure I don't give him any signs or clues that I'm going to bolt again. Not even a tiny hint with my body.

"Where are you driving me?" I stare at him, demanding an answer to my question but doubting he'll give me one. I'm sure the less I know, the better, in his mind.

"Italy."

My mouth drops a little when he answers me. He's taking me back to his home. I'm not sure why I didn't realize what his plan was before. I thought he would hold me captive in a hotel room, or an empty warehouse somewhere where he could torture me to find out where Nina and Arlo are. It would end with either me escaping or with a bullet through my head. Apparently, though, that's not the plan.

Italy. He's taking me back to Italy. So many memories and emotions pour through my head as I think of going back to a country I both love and hate. I love because it was the last time I got to be free.

I always thought I would do something creative, bringing more joy to the world with art and imagination. I enjoy painting and studying history. Architecture. Everything beautiful.

A life of art and creativity was the path I was headed down in Italy, and it was the last time I did things solely for the love of it.

But Italy is also where I lost my best friend. Her life changed forever, and so did mine. I realized I couldn't do things for the love of it anymore. I needed a more significant purpose. So I went to law school and then started prosecuting bad guys. I've been fulfilling my new reason to exist every day since.

We arrive at the airport far too quickly. He takes me to a private airfield, not LAX. He drives through the security gate, past the armed guards who merely open the gate without asking for ID, because apparently they already know who Matteo is. He continues right up to a plane I assume he owns and parks a few feet away.

I can't leave with him. If he takes me to Italy, I could end up trapped for weeks. Or dead. I need to escape. Now.

He undoes his seatbelt and pushes the door ajar. I undo my seatbelt and throw my door open wide and sprint as fast as I can in the opposite direction of the plane.

I don't have a plan. I move as quickly as my body will run, away from Matteo. I will hopefully find someone who can help me. A police officer, someone in the military, or any person with a car who will stop and drive me far, far away from here.

I sense him behind me. I'm a runner and in shape. I'm fast; he's faster. I hoped catching him off guard for a second would allow me enough of a head start to escape. But I was wrong.

His arms wrap around my body as he tackles me to the rough tarmac below. My face hits the ground with a thud and scrapes harshly across the tarmac while the rest of my body is stricken with the force of his body.

"You don't know when to give up, do you? You're mine. I'm kidnapping you, and there's nothing you can do to deter me. Fighting won't help, it will only earn you more punishment later."

I struggle against his arms, trying frantically to smash free, but his arms tighten more around my arms, making it impossible for me to make any of the moves I learned in self-defense classes over the years. I can't physically break free, but I can convince him of all the reasons he shouldn't do this.

"You can't take me. I never take a vacation or miss a day of work. Tomorrow morning when I don't show up for work, my boss will call and try to find me. My friend, Jules, will call the police when she can't reach me. I already called Heath and told him you are here and to contact the police if anything happened to me. You won't be able to get away with it. People will start searching for me; the police will become involved, maybe even the FBI. They will hunt you down and put you in prison for the rest of your life."

He laughs as he stands up, pulling me to my feet and twisting my arm behind my back. I try to move, but I can't wiggle free without snapping my arm in two. Maybe the pain of breaking my arm would be worth it to be free.

"I'm not too worried about the police or FBI. They can't touch me. And we all know how well Heath was able to save Nina. You do have a point though; I don't want people searching for you until I'm ready for them to find out you're missing."

His eyes rake over my body. "Where is your phone?"

"In my purse, back in Saul's car."

His hands travel over my body. Into the pockets of my pants as he searches for a phone that doesn't exist. Then his eyes burn into my chest.

"No," I say.

His hand reaches down the top of my shirt and over my breast, softly grazing my nipple as he forages for my phone. I squirm beneath his fingers, partially because I want his hand to stop invading my personal space and partly because I want to know how it would feel for him to touch me for real.

"I guess you weren't lying." He removes his hands from my shirt, reaches into his back pocket, and pulls out his phone, handing it to me.

"Call work and tell them you're taking an extended leave of absence. That you found out your mother has cancer and you will be taking care of her. And you won't be back anytime soon."

I smirk. "No."

He reaches into the back of his pants and aims the gun at my head. "Leave the message, or I'll kill you."

I stare at the gun. I should be terrified, but I'm not. "You won't shoot me. You hardly shot Saul, and you had no use for him. *Me*, you have use for. You won't kill me, or even harm me."

He glares at me as his nostrils flare and his face turns red with rage. He places the gun back into the back of his pants. "Do it, and I won't look for Nina for one week. She gets seven more days of safety."

Damn it. How was Matteo able to figure out my weakness so quickly? One week is a long time. In a week, I could find a way to escape. In a week, I could find a way to warn Nina and make sure she stays safe forever. In one week, I could kill Matteo.

"How do I know that you'll keep your word?"

"Because I'm an honorable person. I keep my promises."

He holds out the phone. I take it, not needing to consider his offer any further. I dial the number for my work. I realize as soon as it goes to voicemail I could change course. I could tell them Matteo took me and to look for me in Italy. I could save myself. But Matteo would still take me, and Nina would still be at risk.

"Hi, this is Eden. I'm calling to let you know I will be taking an extended leave of absence. I was in a car accident tonight. I'm fine, but it shook me up a little bit, and it made me realize I'm not living my life. I need a vacation. I've been working too hard for too long and not enjoying life. I don't know how long my absence will be, but I'll contact you when I'm ready to return. In the meantime, I'll be using all my vacation days I saved over the years. Jules can inform you of anything you need on my past clients. The other prosecutors should be able to handle new cases, since I closed all my current cases." I press end.

He holds out his hand, and I toss the phone back.

"You didn't do what I said."

"My mom died years ago; your plan wouldn't have worked."

He twists my arm again and walks me toward the plane, then up the stairs onto the lavish private jet. I've never been on a plane this nice before. There are leather chairs and couches everywhere. A small kitchen and bar area toward the back and doors I assume lead to bathrooms or possibly even bedrooms all the way in the rear.

I don't understand why it takes me this long for it to hit me again that I'm being stolen and I have to do everything I can to fight back. I turn, planning on elbowing Matteo in the nose as sharply as I can with my elbow, but he blocks me and grabs my other arm.

"I'm not going to deal with you fighting me all the way to Italy. I have work to do."

"Too bad, because that's exactly what I plan on doing."

The jab pierces my skin without warning before the needle burns into my neck. I don't have a chance to react.

"No, I think you're going to take a very long nap."

My body grows weak and tired in his arms. The bastard drugged me. But it will do nothing to prevent me from fighting again the second I wake up. So unless he plans on keeping me sedated the entire time he has me, he better be prepared for a fight.

———

My head pounds as my eyelids flutter wide. I'm groggy, my entire body aches, and my mind can't make sense of why I feel like I've been run over by a train.

I attempt to raise my head up, but the cloudiness is enough to knock me back down against the bed, my head hitting the soft pillow. My headache is so intense that even the pillow makes the thumping in my head worse.

Instead of raising my head up, I look around the fancy room with just my eyes. I'm lying in an oversized king-size bed made of shiny black wood, covered in a light gray comforter. The bed matches the dark dressers scattered throughout the room. I glance over to the expansive windows that are covered with opaque shades, giving me no clue to what time of day it is or where I am.

I glance over at the two picture frames sitting on the nightstand next to me. One of Matteo, Arlo, and what I assume is their sister, Gia. Nina has told me about her, but I've never met her. The other is a picture of Nina. I reach over and pick up the frame. My hand shakes as I struggle to hold onto the frame. She appears so happy in the photograph. I don't know when it was taken or whose picture it is. *Am I in Arlo's room or Matteo's?*

It would make sense if this were Arlo's room before he left. He loves her. But if this were to be Matteo's room, I don't understand why he would have a photograph of Nina. *Is it love or hatred he feels toward her?*

I set the frame back on the nightstand with uneasy hands. Still lying on my back, I work my way to the edge of the bed, let my feet dangle off the end, and finally, I gradually push my body up into a sitting position.

My eyes flicker shut as the pain and dizziness overwhelm me. I rest on the edge of the bed for much longer than I want. I want to run. I want to find out what's going on and why my memories are so foggy.

I try to remember how I got here, but I can't. I try to recall why I feel so shitty, but I have no idea. *Is Nina waiting for me in the next room? Or is something more sinister happening?* The only way to find out the answers to my questions is to stand up and walk out of this room. A room that is more like a gloomy cave than an actual bedroom.

I lean forward, over the end of the bed, until my feet touch the floor. Then, I slowly get to my feet using my arms to help push me up. I grab a bedpost to maintain my balance as I take a few steps forward, ensuring my legs are strong enough to carry me before I let go. I walk cautiously and deliberately, focusing on the walnut wood door. When I make it to the door, my body collapses against the doorknob and smooth finish.

I don't ever recall ever enduring such exhaustion in all my life. Not even after all the nights staying up studying to pass my board exams for law school. I've never felt this tired. I take a deep breath, trying to fill my body with oxygen and energy.

I force my body off the door enough to reach the doorknob. I expect to have to walk several more feet before I find another person on the other side of this door. But when I pull it ajar, Matteo is standing in the doorway looking at me.

"Surprised you were able to walk this far out of bed."

I narrow my eyes, scolding him. But then I get a whiff of what he is holding. Some type of soup. A delicious tomato-based broth I instantly want in my stomach. My stomach growls at the thought of food and my mouth waters, already able to taste it in my mouth from the smell alone.

"Sit down on the couch," he says, clearly noticing my hunger lust.

I glance behind me and see a living room on the other side of the bed, connected to a small kitchenette area by a door. I clumsily walk to the soft cushions, because I don't have any other options and because I seriously want that soup. My legs give out several feet before I make it to the couch, so I prepare myself for impact on the floor. Matteo grabs my arm at the last moment before my body hits the ground.

"Jesus, you're one determined woman," he mutters under his breath as he pulls me upright again.

Determined, yes. Determined to get that soup into my stomach as fast as possible. He guides me to the couch where I plop down, my body giving out the moment it feels the cushions on the back of my legs.

"Here," he says, placing the bowl of soup into my hands. "Eat, and you'll feel better."

I lift the spoon slowly to my lips and pour the creamy liquid down my throat. The soup is silky, creamy, with a hint of sweetness, and some flavor I can't identify. It's mainly a thick broth with a few soft noodles and tomatoes, but primarily liquid, as to make it easy to swallow. It's simple, but the most delicious thing I've ever tasted.

My growling stomach eases a teeny, tiny bit, but it's going to take me a long time to eat this entire bowl of soup and give my stomach the satisfying, full feeling it's seeking.

I lower my hand again to scoop another spoonful and lift it to my lips. This time, as the liquid goes down, my stomach burns. As mouthwatering as the soup tastes, my stomach no longer agrees.

"I'm going to be sick."

Matteo jumps off the couch and races across the room for a trashcan, but I can't wait.

"I'm going to be – "

I grab the towering decorative vase sitting in the center of the coffee table and scoot it towards me seconds before the contents of my stomach come back up. There's not much left in my stomach, but whatever was inside dispenses into the shiny gold vase.

"Jesus, Eden," Matteo says, holding the trashcan he went to retrieve in his hand.

"What happened to me?" I dry heave, grasping the vessel like it is my most valuable possession.

Matteo unhinges my hands from the vase filled with my puke and carries it out of the room ignoring my question and leaving me with the empty trashcan. He returns less than a minute later with a glass of water, a warm washcloth, and two pills in his hand.

"Clean yourself up and take these anti-nausea pills, they will help you keep the food down."

I take the washcloth from him and wipe my face before I set it down on the coffee table. Then I pop the pills into my mouth, swallow, and down the entire glass of water.

My eyes suspiciously cut to the soup sitting on the coffee table. I should try eating it again, but I don't want to vomit.

My hunger wins out over my fear. I try picking up the bowl with my hands. I manage to lift it an inch before it slips out of my trembling hands and hits the table with a thump, spilling a couple of drops onto the table's flawless surface.

Redness flushes my cheeks. I can't even lift a fucking bowl I'm so weak. I grab the spoon with my still unsteady hand, while I lean over the bowl. I scoop some of the broth onto the spoon and lift it to my lips more slowly than before. The liquid finally touches my lips, and I quickly swallow. I wait for my stomach to growl or burn again, giving me any sign that food is settling well in my stomach. It doesn't.

I smile. Success.

Now on to another spoonful.

"Fuck this. We'll be here all day," Matteo says, snatching the bowl of soup away from me.

My eyes protrude from their sockets as I glare at him. I may not have the strength to do much damage to Matteo, but I will use every ounce of strength I have left to attack him for taking away the only thing giving me any comfort.

"Sit back," he commands.

I do, but only so I can see his pupils when I tell him off.

He puts the spoon down on the table and holds the entire bowl of soup up to my lips.

"Drink."

He tilts the bowl, and the liquid gradually pours into my mouth and down my throat. He continues to feed me until all the soup is gone. My cheeks begin to warm, my head becomes lucid, and my stomach no longer aches for food. Even just moving my arms is manageable compared to before.

He sets the bowl back down. "You should climb back in bed and sleep."

I nod and stand, my legs still wobbly and weak.

Matteo doesn't have the patience for me. He scoops me up in his arms and carries me back to what I now assume is his bed. He places me down and pulls the covers back over me, but that's as far as his chivalry goes.

"Sleep."

My eyes drift closed, following his command. None of this makes any sense. The photograph of Nina. Matteo taking care of me. My body so incredibly weak. I can't process what's happening in my still foggy head. My body, nor my mind can deal with solving the problem. What I need is sleep. It's the only thing I can think about.

———

I open my eyes, and everything becomes clear.

Matteo stole me.

He knocked me out. He pretended to care about me when I was at my weakest.

I don't know how long I've been asleep, but I won't stay his prisoner. My feet hit the floor, I sprint to the door, and throw it wide to see Matteo standing there again like deja-vu.

He smirks. "Video cameras," he says, answering my unspoken question and explaining how he knows I was out of bed.

This time, when I confront him, I'm not decrepit. This time, I remember what he did. I punch him in the nose, making sure to cause the most impact to a sensitive area, as my self-defense classes taught me all these years. I don't wait to see the blood spurting out. It isn't the first time I've broken a man's nose before.

I bolt down the hallway, barefoot. He must've changed my clothes because I'm dressed in one of his T-shirts that scarcely covers my butt and underwear. I should've put regular clothes on first before I tried to make my escape, but it's too late now. I'll run barefoot as long as it takes to reach my freedom.

I round the corner and see several men standing in the hallway. They end their conversations and gape at me. I keep running, managing to slip past them and down another long corridor. This hallway has a door at the end with light shining around its edges. Could it lead outside?

I beg my legs to move faster. They do, but it's not fast enough. A man steps out of one of the rooms lining the hallway and blocks my exit.

I turn around, preparing to race the other direction, but the men I passed earlier are now storming after me.

I'm trapped, but I won't go down without a fight.

My legs are moving swiftly, preparing to slip through the men's grasps again.

I run fast past the first, but the second grabs my arm. I knee him in the balls and keep running.

I punch the next man I see and hear his nose crunch, the bones breaking.

Almost free.

My arm jolts me back as one of the men grabs hold of it. He ducks as I try to punch him, the same way I did his friend. He puts me in a headlock before I have a chance to attack. I bite down hard, tearing through the flesh on his arm until I taste blood.

He lets me go, but only for a second before four hands are on me, grabbing my flailing arms roughly.

"Where do you think you're going, bitch?" One of them asks.

"The cunt bit me. I can't wait to see what Matteo does to her," another says, staring at the wound on his arm.

I may not have escaped, but I caused damage. That's a start.

They drag me back down the corridor and out to the living room where Matteo is sitting, waiting. He has an ice pack pressed to this nose and a whiskey in his hand. His entire body tenses when he sees me.

I smirk. At least I made him bleed. He may have won now, but I'll make him suffer over and over and over again.

"Do you want us to lock her in the dungeon?" the man whom I bit asks.

"No, I need her to talk. She won't talk in the dungeon."

"The cunt bit my arm, she deserves severe punishment."

"I agree."

He stares at me intensely.

"Maximo, bring me some shackles."

The man whom I bit lets go of my arm and galavants away. "With pleasure."

Matteo stands up, dropping the ice pack to the ground, and walks toward me. My arms are still spread wide, away from my body held by the three men left.

"You have two choices, Eden. One, I drug you again and lock

you in the dungeons until you learn to behave. Or two, I chain you to me so you can't run and you start talking."

Neither seems like a good option.

"Which do you choose?"

"Chained."

He nods. Maximo returns with the shackles and hands them to Matteo. He bends down and shackles my legs so close together I know I won't be able to do much more than shuffle my feet. I, indeed, won't be able to run. He then connects my right wrist and to his left wrist with another shackle.

"You can't win Eden, so stop trying. The only way you can earn your freedom is by giving me, Nina and Arlo. If you attempt to escape again, or hurt my men or me in any way, you'll remain medicated and unconscious the rest of your time here. Understand?"

I nod.

He gives his men a look, and they let me go. My instinct is to bolt over and hurt Matteo. Punch him in the face, rip out his heart, snap his neck. However, I don't want to spend the rest of my time here drugged, even though he's bluffing. He won't allow me to endure my entire time here in a coma because I would be of no use to him. I don't doubt he would at least drug me for another night though, and that could result in several days in bed recovering.

"How long have I been here?"

"Too long," he answers before he walks away. The handcuff on my wrist pulls, and I struggle to remain even with his long strides as we walk down the hallway, my feet shuffling as rapidly as I can move them in the chains.

"Slow down."

"No."

He jerks me into, what I assume, is his office before he takes a seat behind the desk, not offering me a place to sit. I'm left either standing, leaning against the wall, or sitting on the floor. I decide to conserve my energy and take a seat.

I study him as he makes phone call after phone call, hoping to gain some useful information I can use against him. All of the calls are boring, none of them giving me any insight into a way for me to escape. He mostly talks numbers, men, and how many weapons are to be sent to various clients.

I sit on the floor for at least an hour with nothing to do but to listen to him talk on the phone. I try to figure a way to get out of this, but I come up empty.

I close my eyes, deciding I'll rest while he works.

My body is jerked awake as he strides out of the office giving me no warning. My eyes fly open, and I scramble to my feet.

"You could at least give me some warning when we are going somewhere."

"No, I can't. You need to learn to behave and maybe then I'll treat you with some respect."

He walks into a small bathroom, and I have no choice but to step inside with him.

"Really?"

"Don't act like you don't want to drool over my cock."

"Gross." I turn up my nose.

He undoes his pants and pulls out his penis to take a piss. And I admit I can't help but take a quick peek. His cock is long and thick, more substantial than I expected it to be. I try to keep my thoughts pure, but I can't help it. Any woman's mind would immediately think of what a cock like his is capable of doing.

He zips his pants and washes his hands smirking at me in the mirror while I frown again.

"Where are we going next?"

"Going for a run."

My eyes widen. "You can't be serious?"

"I always go for a run every day."

"I can't run with the shackles on my feet and no shoes on."

He walks down the hallway dragging me behind him without another word. I realize we're heading back to his bedroom and I smile a little.

We step inside, and he locks the door, trapping us inside together. He unlocks the shackles on my arm and legs.

"I think you'll find the clothing and shoes you require to go running in that closet." He motions toward a closet opposite of the one he heads to.

I walk over to the closet and step inside, finding a whole wardrobe of women's clothes. They all look like they could fit me. I don't ask how or why, but I see a pair of shorts, a sports bra, and a T-shirt. I change into them quickly, along with some tennis shoes I find in my size. I change as fast as I can because I know the second he's ready, he'll put the shackles back on, regardless if I'm ready or not.

I step back out into the main bedroom in time to see him slipping a shirt over his rippled body. I notice a few tattoos covering his chest, but otherwise, his body is flawless.

He puts one of the shackles on his wrist and then looks at me with an impatient glance. I hold out my hand, offering to behave, because it would be nice to stretch my legs outside and breathe some fresh air. If this is the only way I get to do it, fine.

He snaps the shackle on to my wrist and leads me outside.

I close my eyes and inhale deeply, letting the air and warmth take over me.

But I'm jerked forward as Matteo starts running, giving me no time to warm up. He's faster than me, so I have to push myself to prevent myself falling to the ground and getting dragged.

The path he jogs is beautiful. Through the forest behind his house, a trail he has clearly carved out for himself and no one else.

We jog for a long time until my legs and lungs burn, but I don't complain. For one, I have a great view of his ass as he runs. And as much as I hate to admit it, he has a great ass. And two, I get to push myself and work on gaining speed and strength so someday I can outrun him. And three, I can bask in the warm sun.

As we return to the back of the house, a buzzing sound makes Matteo stop and pull out his phone.

"Yes?" He pauses. "You still haven't found my brother and Nina then?"

"Fine." He hangs up the phone.

I strike him on the back, frustrated.

"What was that for? And just when I thought you were learning to behave."

"What about our deal? You promised if I left those messages at work, you wouldn't go after Nina and Arlo for at least a week."

He pulls out his phone again and hands it to me showing me the date.

"You have been here two weeks."

My mouth drops open. *Two weeks.*

"How did you keep me alive for that long unconscious?"

"IVs. The medications I gave you seem to have had a particularly strong effect on you."

I look up, needing to know an answer to my question desperately. "Why? Why do you want Arlo and Nina? Why do you have a picture of Nina in your bedroom?"

"Because Arlo owes me for leaving. He's my brother. He is supposed to stay and work for me, but he left, abandoning me without a word or a goodbye."

"And Nina?"

"I love Nina. I want her back."

"You're lying. You're saying that so I'll eventually tell you where they are. You don't love Nina or care about your brother. How can you love someone that hurt you?"

His eyes shoot straight into mine as his lips pull back.

"I guess you'll find out if it's possible. Could you ever learn to love me despite how I've hurt you?"

"No. Could you if I hurt you as badly as you have hurt me?"

He shrugs. "I guess I'm a more forgiving person than you are."

He stares past me as he leads me back inside. I don't believe he loves her. He's not capable of love. He doesn't even know what love is. Matteo is evil, and I won't ever tell him where Nina is. Even if it costs me my life.

5

___

MATTEO

I NEED to shatter the shield around Eden.

I need to demolish her will to live so that she will tell me anything I want.

I need to find Nina and Arlo, now.

My heart has turned to ice with them gone. I have power now. I control the entire Carini empire along with hundreds of men and money at my disposal. *What good is having all this power if I can't use it, especially to deal with the one matter I care about?*

Getting Nina and Arlo back is about so much more than claiming the woman I love and punishing my brother. It's much, much bigger.

My alarm clock goes off, but I don't need it to wake me up. I rarely need an alarm clock, but I've been struggling to sleep even more since I took Eden. I climb out of bed and stretch before I dress in jeans and a dark gray T-shirt. I walk over to the small living room in my quarters where Eden is snoring on the couch.

She spent the last three days handcuffed to me, stuck following me everywhere. Her dreams are the only thing that gives her the illusion of freedom. I can't have her in my bed though. I like having my own space. And I haven't had a woman in my bed since Nina. My insomnia would get worse with her in my bed anyway.

So instead, she sleeps on my couch with her leg attached to a hook on the floor I had Maximo create to ensure she wouldn't run off or try to shoot me during the few hours of rest I actually get at night.

My head jerks back every time I see her lying on the couch in the morning when I come in. It isn't the only part of me that is drawn to attention at the sight of her. My cock quarrels with my brain for me to fuck her.

Soon. Very soon.

Eden doesn't normally seem like the kind of woman who would allow herself to let her guard down when her enemy is so close. Vulnerability is seen as a weakness to her, and she will do anything not to appear fragile. Either she's too exhausted to stay awake, or she doesn't believe I'll hurt her while she's out.

"Wake up sleepyhead," I shout, grabbing the couch and shaking it violently like I have the last two mornings.

She drops off the couch, the weight of her body crashing to the floor with a smack.

"You bastard."

"Just a bastard today? I must be growing on you then."

She bares her teeth at me as she stands up and lunges at me, trying to can grab ahold of me and cause any damage she can. But like every other morning, the chains take her by surprise, and she's pulled back to the ground.

I smirk, as her round ass hits the floor again. "You're not a very fast learner, are you?"

She pulls against the restraints, trying to pummel me. "I learn just fine. I've learned how much of a heartless ruler you are. I've come up with a dozen ways to kill you. It only takes one night of forgetting to lock me up. One time to get careless with the knives or the guns, or for me to find a way to pick the lock. That day will come soon. That's when I'll murder you."

"And that's when my men will kill you."

"It will be worth it." Her eyes taunt mine with a smugness that I want to wash away with my cock down her throat.

Patience, I remind myself.

I place the shackles back on both our wrists, joining her to me. I can't decide whether I love or hate tethering her to me. I love having the control over her, but I hate having her around me all the time. It's as much of a torture to me as it is to her. She's starting to mess with my head.

Today is when the real fun starts. Nina is Eden's weakness, but there are only so many ways I can use Nina against Eden. Eden has to have more than one fault, so I plan on finding and exploiting them to my advantage.

I turn and start walking out the door, not giving Eden any warning. She's relatively used to my abrupt changes by now, and can keep pace with me effortlessly. She's starting to anticipate my moves before I make them. Probably because I have a routine she has already learned.

Today that ends.

I sneer back at my little slave. Her face is bored and restless. Her body tired. She has no idea what's about to happen to her.

I walk into the dining room. A long rectangular table stretches across the center of the room, able to hold two dozen people, underneath the antique chandelier, which sparkles brightly overhead. Half a dozen men are at the table already eating breakfast, ready for their daily orders from me.

I walk to my usual spot at the head of the table, and Eden follows. She ordinarily takes a seat next to me at the table, but not today. I snap my fingers and motion for my two closest men to claim the seats next to me. Even when Eden isn't here, they rarely sit next to me. I like being alone in my thoughts in the morning.

They pick up their breakfast plates and move down until they are occupying the two chairs on either side of me. I take a seat knowing there's nowhere for Eden to sit. The chain, attaching us, isn't long enough for her to sit in any of the other open chairs at the table.

I wait for her to complain or make a snarky comment, but she doesn't. Apparently, she's going to pretend I don't affect her when I clearly do. I crawl under her skin like no one else.

She's giving me a dirty look, one that I'm sure is meant to display her hatred for me. It does. But her cheeks are flushed, her lips slightly parted, and, every so often, she wets her bottom lip. She can pretend to hate me all she wants, but she can't deny her body craves mine. She's an uptight woman used to getting her way, but I have a feeling after one kiss she's going to be putty in my arms.

"Here's your coffee, sir. Would you like your usual omelete?"

"Yes, Emilia," I say, lifting the coffee to my lips.

My servant turns her attention toward Eden. "And what would you like for breakfast?"

"I'd love –"

"She won't be eating or drinking anything."

Emilia fidgets with the bottom of her apron as her eyes cut from Eden to me. I'll have to make sure that Emilia doesn't try to sneak Eden food.

"That'll be all," I say, dismissing my servant.

Emilia runs off to fix my breakfast, and I wait for Eden's reaction.

Eden doesn't say anything to me. She pretends I didn't deny her food. She pretends I didn't refuse her a place at the table and make her stand behind me like a dog. I was cruel before, but she hasn't seen my dark side yet. Her silly plan of acting like I don't affect her won't work.

She can act tough now, but I'll break her. I have to find the right button to push. We'll see how well she does without nourishment. I give her three days, at most, before she starts begging me for water, bread, even scraps off my plate. Especially in her weakened state.

Emilia returns with my breakfast. Her eyes dart to Eden before she scurries off again.

My men continue to eat silently at the table, occasionally snickering or glaring at Eden. They too realize that today is the day the real fun begins. Today is when we get Eden to talk, no matter what it takes.

"Were you able to confirm the shipment for Thursday, Maximo?" I ask.

"We ran into a few complications, but we plan on using force tonight. I think it can be done."

"Good. Once that's dealt with, we can move on to more important things like finding Nina and Arlo. After tonight, I want at least half the team searching for them.

"And as an added incentive, if you find Nina and Arlo before Eden discloses their location, I'll make sure a substantial bonus awaits you in your next paycheck. I'll even let you participate in helping me teach Nina and Arlo a lesson for running."

Maximo laughs, and it soars through the room. "We'll find them long before Eden speaks a syllable." His eyes eat up her body, which attempts to hide beneath the thin T-shirt she's wearing.

A low growl escapes my throat. A warning. Maximo stops looking at Eden.

My jaw slowly unclenches, and my vein stops throbbing in my forehead. I don't understand why it annoys me that Maximo leered at Eden. After my cock claims Eden and she spills their whereabouts, he can fuck her all he wants. All I want is to find Nina and Arlo.

Maximo shouldn't have dared to check her out. I rub my neck trying to release the tension he caused. Maybe my anger reared up because he's now my number two since Arlo left. I want Maximo to be entirely loyal to me, not pining over some woman.

I look to Dierk on my left. "You up for the task, Dierk?"

"Absolutely."

"Good. I need all of my best men on this. Now everyone get the fuck out of here and start working."

The men immediately stand and file out of the room, leaving whatever remains of their food on their plates.

Eden immediately sinks into the chair next to me that Dierk had occupied.

"I thought you love Nina? I thought you wouldn't hurt her?"

"I do, but we tend to punish those we love the most. Nina chose my brother over me. She made the wrong choice."

"Your plan isn't going to work. I don't believe that you love Nina. But even if you do, you don't deserve her. Arlo does. He has kept her safe for this long."

I shake my head minutely. "Nina hasn't told you the truth about her stay here, has she?"

Eden's pupils bore into mine as she crosses her arms and leans back in the chair. "She told me enough."

"Let me fill you in on the details she didn't tell you. I saved her life and protected her, just like Arlo did. I healed her body countless times. I provided medical treatment and nursed her back to life. So don't tell me I don't deserve her. I can protect her better than Arlo can."

"Your plan won't work," she repeats.

Her stomach growls, and I grin. "I think my plan will work fine."

I take another bite of my omelete chomping on it vulgarly, taunting her with the food in my open mouth.

Her hand darts to Dierk's plate and snatches the biscuit he left. She shoves the entire thing into her mouth, chews rapidly, and swallows before I have a chance to do anything else.

I lean forward, grinning at her. "You think you won?"

She nods.

"You lost. You showed me you have a weakness. You're not used to going without sustenance. It may take a few hours longer actually to crack you, since you took a bite of food, but you'll still break. You'll tell me where Nina is. You'll betray her, and you'll have to live with yourself forever because of it. I give you three days, tops, before you beg me for food. You're scrappy, but not strong enough."

She huffs and reaches for my omelete. I grab her wrist stopping her.

"I hope you enjoyed that biscuit, because it's the last bite of food you will get."

It doesn't take three days for Eden to break.

In fact, it's been almost two weeks, and she hasn't so much as cracked. She's not even close. I've tried food deprivation. Somehow, I know she is getting food from someone. Emilia is the most likely culprit, but I can't prove it.

Eden should be close to death's door. Instead, her legs simply move a little slower when I pull her behind me, her stomach rumbles a little more frequently, and sleep is more necessary.

I tried sleep deprivation, keeping Eden up for days at a time, but losing sleep did not affect her. She became delusional, her words slurred, her body slowed. It was impossible for her to think, much less talk to me, and yet she refused to give up their location.

I threatened beatings. I threatened to rape her. But it didn't scare her. Probably because she thinks I won't follow through with my threat. She thinks she looks too much like Nina for me to beat her.

Nothing works.

It's because I haven't tried the one thing that I know will.

Torture.

I wanted Nina to like me still, instead of despising me, when I got her back, but I'm running out of options. It's time to turn into the monster Eden thinks I am.

She's currently tied to the couch while I shower. I needed some time alone to think, but my hand falls on my cock, stroking it as I let Eden's body saturate my thoughts.

Her dark hair, still smooth and silky despite not washing it in weeks. Her flawless, smooth skin that my hands are about to mark. Her perky breasts with nipples that will harden, despite how hard she tries to hide her attraction. And her tight cunt that will be torn between trying to push me out and drench me, as it pulls me back in.

My erection hardens and lengthens in my hand, ready to take Eden. I smirk as I turn the water off and step out of the shower and out into the living room, not bothering to dry off or even clothe myself.

She doesn't notice me at first or even glance at me. Her eyes are half shut. Her body limp on the couch.

I clear my throat. I want Eden to look at me. I want her to feel terrified about what I'm going to do with her. I want to see the change in her eyes before I rape her.

Her head turns, and her lips slowly drop open. Her eyes go straight to my dick, but I can't tell if she's turned on, disgusted, or indifferent.

I growl. I need to feel Eden's suffering. *Soon enough, I will.*

I walk to her, grab her neck, and climb on top of her, water dripping down onto her. My body presses against hers, and the only thing separating us is my shirt she's wearing and her panties. I clench her throat with my hand.

"This is your last chance, baby. Tell me where to find Nina."

She squeezes her eyes shut, and her lips move, but nothing comes out.

I loosen my grasp.

"No." Her lips curl up into a smile.

I'm not a good person. I've raped plenty of women before. She should believe my threats.

I snarl.

I tighten my hand again watching as the blood drains from her face.

"You're so much prettier when you can't speak."

She doesn't move beneath me or struggle at all. She still thinks I'll stop. I won't.

My other hand ducks under her shirt, running up the length of her body savoring the smooth skin on her belly and up to her hardened nipples. Her body wants me, despite her hatred of me.

"You want me, baby." I flick my thumb across her nipple.

Her cheeks flush, and I loosen my grip on her throat, taunting her. Letting her deny her cravings if she wants, but she can't.

Her head jerks to the side as she bares her teeth and sinks them into the flesh of my hand. I grab her jaw, prying her mouth off my hand before slapping her across the face.

She huffs, breathing heavily in and out as the sting spreads across her face. She's angry now and is finally going to fight back. Good. I need her fighting to find out exactly how strong she is.

"You're nothing more than a rapist. I don't want you. I could never want someone that hurts me as you do. My body is human. It responds automatically to a man's touch. It doesn't mean anything."

I rip her panties down and plunge two fingers inside her, feeling the wetness and spreading it out between her legs so that she can feel how wet she is for me. Her arms fight against my body trying to push me off, but she's barely fighting at all. I've pissed her off, but not enough to become desperate.

"You feel that baby? You're so wet. Wetter than you've ever been before. Aren't you?"

I grab her chin and turn her head toward me. "Answer me!"

"I hate you." Her nostrils flare with each exhale. Her body is tense beneath mine as she does everything she can to keep me from penetrating her shell.

"I'll take that as a yes."

Her hands fight against my chest, trying to get me off. One of her nails sinks into a sensitive spot in my back, releasing a deep growl from my throat. I grab her wrists and lift them above her head, holding them with one hand as she struggles beneath me.

"Last chance. You can stop this beautiful. Tell me where to find Nina, and I'll spare you."

She bites her lip, forcing herself to keep her mouth shut. I don't scare her enough. Even the thought of me raping her isn't enough for her to give up her friend. She's a saint. I'm about to make her feel like a sinner.

I grab her thigh with my free hand and pull her leg wide, as my cock sinks between her legs pulsing at her wet entrance.

I tease her, letting the head of my cock push inside her sex and watch her eyes darken. With rage. Anger. And pleasure.

It's been a long time since she's had a man between her legs and her body is practically pulling me further inside.

I wait three seconds for her to change her mind.

One.

Two. My cock slips further inside.

Three.

My cock drives into her, feeling every inch of her slick interior. I could stay here forever, fucking her.

Her hips buck underneath mine, trying to get free. But all it does is allow me to descend deeper. I close my eyes, letting my body enjoy hers for a moment, before I start tormenting her again until she's crying and willing to give me whatever I want to make me stop. So many different ways and places I could fuck her, make her suffer.

Nina.

No, she's not here. I'm fucking Eden, not Nina.

I close and open my eyes trying to make Nina go away but I can't.

"I chose you, Matteo," Nina says, looking at me with big sad eyes.

"No, you chose Arlo."

She shakes her head. "I chose you..."

Knocking, followed by shouting, brings me back to reality and the dream slowly fades.

Eden is lying beneath me, her eyes wide with concern.

My bedroom door opens, and Maximo sticks his head in. He immediately turns his head away when he spots the two of us.

"Sorry boss, but we need you. We lost three men in a gunfight. Clive and Erick were trying to sell weapons on our territory again and—"

"I'll be right there. Drive the Rolls Royce around to the front, and I'll meet you there."

"Yes, sir," Maximo says, sticking his head back in for half a second to catch another peek. His face flushes red, and he smirks before he runs off to do what I commanded.

"This will have to continue later."

I stand up and release my hands from her, although her leg remains chained to the floor.

She exhales like she has been holding her breath this entire time, while I walk to the bathroom where I left my clothes to shower. I grab my underwear and slip it on, not bothering to wash her slickness off of me. I put on my jeans and T-shirt before grabbing my gun from the counter and stashing it in the back of my jeans. I glance in the mirror.

I punch it without thinking. My knuckles split as the glass digs deep into them. Rage is all my body registers; the pain doesn't even exist. I'm pissed that Maximo interrupted us, but also mad that even if he didn't, I wasn't strong enough to finish torturing her. Nina is messing with my head. I'm not strong enough to abuse her as I should. I didn't do enough to break her. My cock barely touched her. I have to rape her, make her fear for her life. It's the only way.

It's because you're such a pathetic little bitch, my father's voice rings in my ear.

He still has a fucking hold on me even though he's no longer in power. He's gone, or as good as gone. Last time I checked on him, he was recovering in a physical therapy center in Scotland.

I walk back to Eden who is pretending to sleep on the couch so that I'll leave her be.

"Get up."

Her eyes open thinly, but she doesn't move. I grab her arm and jerk her up, tired of her games. I unshackle her, not bothering her to shackle her back to myself. Instead, I twist her arm behind her back and lead her out my bedroom, down the hallway, and down the stairs to the darkest place in the mansion. The dungeon.

"What's going on?"

"I have work to do, and I'm tired of your games. I know that you've been getting food elsewhere. And I know that the food and sleep deprivation aren't doing enough anyway. It's time for Plan B."

"And what's plan B?"

I throw her to the dungeon floor and pull out the needle filled with drugs that will knock her out for at least twenty-four hours.

"No." Her eyes grow big and her body trembles, just enough to be noticeable. She's more afraid than she was a moment ago when my cock was buried inside her.

I should be focused on pushing the needle into Eden's neck, instead of cooking her. All I can think about is her gorgeous lips and beautiful cunt wrapped around my dick.

It gives Eden a chance to run to the door I locked behind me. She grabs the doorknob and shakes it fiercely, trying to pry it open, but it doesn't budge. I march toward her with the syringe in my hand.

"No."

"You don't have a choice. You either tell me where to find Nina, or I'll jab this needle into your neck. You'll stay passed out for hours. Weak and incapable of defending yourself if any of my men decide to get frisky with you. You won't even remember if I raped you or not."

She stares at the needle, and for the first time since she's been here, I can truly see the fear. This is her Achille's heel: being unconscious. But I don't have time to deal with her now. Maybe after getting knocked out again, she'll be ready to talk, but it's clear she is not willing to speak now.

I plunge the needle into her neck as she cries out. She tries to push my hand away, but she only fights for second before her body collapses to the floor.

Her lifeless body is lying on the ground, and I can't help myself. I pick her up and carry her to the bench in the corner of the room. It's not much more comfortable, but at least she's off the dirt. I shouldn't have touched her. I should have left her in the dirt. I don't know why I moved her.

Because Eden is so much like Nina, that's why I.

I walk out of the dungeon and pull the gun I always keep in the back of my pants out as I head to my car. It's time to kill some motherfuckers for daring to cross me.

6
———

EDEN

MY EYES FLUTTER open and the same familiar headache throbs in the back of my head like last time. My stomach heaves and the dizziness and grogginess consume me. My muscles ache like I just finished running a marathon. Last time I didn't know what was happening to me, but this time I do.

Matteo knocked me out with drugs.

I take my time sitting up, so I don't vomit like last time. I lie in bed for several minutes as my eyes adjust to the light and my body gets used to being awake before I try to sit up.

I don't know how long I was out. Hours? Days? Weeks? It doesn't matter. I don't have access to a calendar or phone telling me what day it is. I can hardly keep track of how long I've been here when I'm conscious.

I very carefully sit up in Matteo's bed. Careful not to move too fast, so I don't get sick.

Surprisingly, I don't feel like throwing up when I sit up. I felt much worse last time. So either my body is getting used to the drugs, or he didn't give me as much as last time.

I close my eyes, trying to regain my strength before I stand

65

up. Darkness and cold overwhelm me in one memory. Matteo's black eyes before he locked the door, leaving me in the filth.

The dungeon. I remember.

He locked me in the dungeon unconscious and left me there all alone. I don't remember why he was so angry. What did I do to piss him off enough to do that to me again? He's a horrible person; he doesn't need a reason to do monstrous things.

I know one thing: I will do anything not to get drugged again. Well, anything short of telling him where Nina is. But I need a plan.

I thought I had one after Matteo tried taking food and sleep from me. I thought when I found a way to get food and defy him; he would give up and realize I was a dead end. Apparently, he hasn't given up yet.

I need help. My lips curl up. I've made one ally here. I can make plenty more. Eventually, I'll have enough allies to escape or fight back. Maybe I'll find more allies as I did with the first...

———

My stomach rumbles again for the hundredth time today. I've never gone so long without food. It's only been three days but the way my stomach heaves, it feels like torture. If I don't get some food in my system soon, I'm going to become delirious, and I'll tell Matteo whatever he wants.

"I have to go meet Maximo and sign a deal for a weapons trade for next week. Watch her." Matteo undoes the shackle on his wrist and hands it to Dierk who hesitantly attaches it to his arm.

"What am I supposed to do with her?"

"Make sure she doesn't run. And if she tries to, beat her."

We both stare, as Matteo walks away from us, both thinking this is some sort of a joke. He hasn't left me alone with anyone since I got here. He's only worked at his home office. Today, though, he either needs to leave or having me around is getting on his nerves. Matteo is a loner; he likes to be left alone in his thoughts. We don't converse a lot when I'm around; he doesn't like the company. I think I remind him too much of Nina. That, or he's a grumpy ass for no reason.

When I get out of here and talk to Nina again, I need to ask her what happened when she was here. Because apparently, she did a number on Matteo.

My stomach growls again and Dierk gawks at it, like a stomach making noise is a foreign concept to him.

"You hungry?" he asks.

I nod.

"Let's get you some food then. I could eat, too."

I try not to react. My eyes gloss over, and I smile politely. But my heart is beating fast in my chest. My feet are jittering at just the thought of food. And I can't keep my lips from curling up. Matteo forgot to tell Dierk he isn't supposed to feed me or let me sleep. If I play this cool, I might get to eat.

My stomach is going to give me away, though. It's booming loudly now at the thought of getting fed. I try to calm it down by holding my belly gently, but it can't be calmed.

Dierk turns and starts walking toward the kitchen at a much slower pace than I'm used to following Matteo at. I don't like it. Especially not now, when I might be getting food.

We finally make it to the kitchen, after what seems like hours have passed. Lines at Disney World have moved faster than Dierk.

"I'd like a Turkey sandwich with fries," he says to Emelia.

He looks at me, waiting for me to give Emelia my order as well.

"Same," I say, though I really want a Turkey sandwich, fries, a burger, tacos, and a milkshake. I try to act like I haven't eaten in hours instead of days.

The woman's eyes bulge while I stare at her, biting my lip hard, begging her with my entire body to not give me away. To fix me food and not question if she should be feeding me or not.

I don't know how Matteo treats his staff. I've never seen him treat the men who work for him poorly. The worst I've seen him do is raise his voice slightly when he was frustrated with them. I've never seen him hurt them or threaten to kill them or something. But for the most part, I've never seen any of the men who work for him do anything that would deserve punishment. They practically worship him.

I'm not sure if the regular house staff would be immune to any discipline if they were to fuck up. If this cook got caught giving me food when she knew I wasn't allowed to eat, what would Matteo do? Dock her wages? Fire her? Beat her? Or kill her?

I don't know the answer, and I hate making this woman take the risk, but I'm desperate.

She nods and turns toward the grill to start preparing our food.

Dierk turns, takes a few steps, and waits for me to follow him until we are standing side by side. He doesn't go to the main dining room as I expect. Instead, he walks past it to another room, which I realize is an office.

"You okay eating in here? I like having some quiet time to think before things become crazy at night."

I nod, happy not to have to eat in the dining room where any number of people could walk in and remind Dierk he's not supposed to be feeding me.

He slowly walks me over to the small table in the corner of the room where two chairs are seated around it.

He pulls out my chair for me like we are on a date or something.

I smile at him as I take my seat. I try not to let his simple charms eat at my heart. There is a high probability this is all an act. Like a good cop, bad cop routine. Dierk is going to treat me nice so that Matteo can treat me like crap later and I'll let something slip.

"What do you do?" he asks.

I snort.

His eyes wide and his mouth parts questioningly, like he doesn't understand why I could find what he said funny.

"You're serious? I'm a slave in this house, and you want to pretend we are friendly strangers chatting for the first time?"

He rubs his neck with the hand tied to me. He stares at the chain like he's seeing it for the first time and realizes what it means.

"I'm sorry." His eyes show the sadness of the world as he speaks. He leans forward in his chair placing his hands in his lap. "I'm sincerely sorry. I know you don't understand, but I am."

I frown. Dierk can't be serious. I distract myself with the office filled with ancient wood, worn like it was made in a different time, as is the entire house. It looks old-fashioned and regal. The mahogany desk takes up most of the space in the room, leaving enough room for a bookshelf and this small table.

"This is your office, right?" I ask.

He nods.

"Then I don't think your sorrys mean very much. You decided to work for the devil. So you are just as culpable for what happens to me as he is."

A knock startles me.

"Come in," Dierk says, staring at the door past me.

Emelia comes in, carrying two plates of food and my stomach churns. The dizziness in my head aches, knowing soon it could be gone. Soon I might be able to walk straight without swerving. Soon, I might have some strength back.

"Can I bring you anything else?"

"No, thank you," Dierk says.

The woman leaves.

It takes everything inside of me not to dig into my food, stuffing everything on my plate into my mouth in one scoop.

"I know you're hungry. Eat."

I hesitate and peek at Dierk, even though I know I shouldn't. I need to eat as he said.

"You know?" my voice trembles, thinking this is some twisted game.

He nods. "I know Matteo isn't feeding you."

"But you're allowing me to eat? What game are you playing? The food's poisoned or something, isn't it?"

His lips fall, and his body seems to hunch over a little.

He reaches onto my plate, stealing one of my fries and popping them into his mouth. He chews and swallows before I'm satisfied.

I can't wait any longer. I dig into my food as Dierk nibbles on his fries.

"Why? Why be nice to me?" I ask, my mouth full of my turkey sandwich.

He stares out the large window out into the forest below.

"Because I know what it feels like to be hungry."

My mouth drops open a little. Dierk seems to have transformed into a young boy in seconds.

"I went without food many a night when I was a kid. I watched my mother starve to death. My sister cried herself to sleep every night because she was in so much pain from the stomach aches. No one should ever be hungry."

I swallow down the turkey, along with the lump in my throat.

"Thank you."

He nods. "I know Matteo wants you to tell him where Nina is. He still loves her, but he deserves better. She loves Arlo; she will never love Matteo. He needs to move on and do what's best for his family."

I shovel the rest of the fries into my mouth and Dierk places the rest of his food on my plate.

"Matteo is a caring, devoted man. He's just lost. He's always had his brother. He doesn't have the confidence to operate on his own. He hasn't found his place in the world yet."

I frown. "I don't think Matteo's a very caring man."

He takes a deep breath staring at me. "Maybe you're right. Maybe he isn't a kind man. I don't know. I took this job in high school to put food on the table and ensure my family never goes hungry again. But

I can say Matteo is a better boss than Enrico was. That doesn't make Matteo a saint; it makes him better."

"I guess," remembering all of the horrible things Nina told me about Enrico, Matteo's father.

"Now, tell me about yourself. I might as well get to know you if I'm risking getting fired for you."

I wince. "You could get fired because of me?"

He shrugs. "Maybe. If Enrico was in charge, yes. No one has gotten fired since Matteo took over. But probably."

"You shouldn't have risked it." I don't want another family hurting because of me.

He laughs. "You say that now you have a full belly again. I couldn't sit back and watch you wither away."

"You're prolonging the inevitable. Tomorrow Matteo will start starving me again."

"He'll try, but he won't be able to, not when I'm sneaking you food."

I smile. "Thank you. I wasn't sure there was a kind person in this house."

"There are a lot of nice people here. There are a lot of bad people too, though. Now, what do you do for a living when you aren't here?"

"I prosecute the bad guys and lock them up in prison."

He grins. "I guess you were right. You do have a better judge of character than I do. Any chance you will spare me when this is all over with?" He wiggles his eyebrows, and I laugh.

"What makes you think I will make it out alive?"

"Because you are strong and resourceful. And despite Matteo being cruel, he's not the worst kind of monster. He won't kill you. Heck, he can't even beat you or rape you as he wants. He's desperate to get answers about a woman he loves, you're the only lead he has to find her, and the best he can do is deprive you of food. I'm pretty sure he left you with me because he knew I couldn't resist feeding you. He's aware of my past."

I think for a minute, letting Dierk's view of Matteo in, but I'm not sure it's true. I think Matteo hides his plans from everyone he doesn't fully trust.

"You don't have a clue where Nina and Arlo are?"

He shakes his head. "Not a clue."

I grin. "I will spare you once I escape."

———

Dierk said Matteo has a soft side, that Matteo has some warmth in him, even if the evil hides it. Looking around at where I woke up, I'm beginning to think Dierk might be right. I was drugged in the dungeon, but he didn't leave me there. Instead, he brought me back to his bed.

When I was unconscious, did Matteo sleep next to me in bed or did he sleep on the couch and give up the bed to me? I'm guessing from how I was lying in the middle of the bed, I slept in the bed alone. So he gave up his bed for me, again.

His weakness is Nina, I know that, but could I also be his weakness? I remind him of her, so maybe I can find a way to use that to my advantage. All I know is I won't let him drug me again. I'd rather he starve me. I can't handle giving up substantial portions of my memory.

The door opens, and Matteo steps in, but only to make his presence known as his eyes focus on me.

"Come on. Breakfast is getting cold."

I raise an eyebrow. "Breakfast?"

"Yes, starving you only works when my staff doesn't feed you behind my back."

My heart races. "Your staff didn't—"

His face tenses, and his dark eyes protrude, threatening me. I stop.

"I'm not asking you to rat out who it was. I don't care. I know my employees are loyal to me and I can understand how a woman like you could manipulate them into doing what you want. Now get the fuck up and let's go."

I stand up abruptly, forgetting I'm still weak and need to move slowly. My knees give out, and I grasp for the post at the end of the bed, hoping it will keep me upright. I miss. I prepare for impact, my arms outstretched to catch myself. I don't hit the floor though; Matteo's arms snatch my wrists, holding me up.

He searches my eyes. "Why do I do this?"

I swallow down whatever emotions are creeping up in my throat. Matteo doesn't have to explain himself. I know what he means. *Why does he keep protecting me? Why doesn't he let me fall to the floor? Why does he care at all?* I don't know the answer, but I have a feeling it's the same reason I haven't stolen a knife from the kitchen and jabbed it into his throat while he sleeps. Something unexplainable stops me.

He lifts my body up into his arms, carrying me like a baby. My head instinctually rests against his firm chest. I breathe in, and the chills all over my arms cause all the tiny hairs on my arms to stick up straight.

He notices the goosebumps on my arms and carries me to his closet, before pulling a sweatshirt off one of the hangers. He gently places me down on the bench on one end and holds the sweatshirt above my head. I lift my arms up, and he places it over my arms and head, pulling it down to my waist. He walks back over and pulls a pair of yoga pants off the shelf and bends down in front of my leg. He puts one foot into the pants, then the other, and helps me shimmy them up my bare legs until the pants are on.

I feel much better now that I'm clothed. I don't know why Matteo always has me sleep in my underwear and one of his t-shirts.

"Why?" I ask, confused why he dressed me.

He stands up, seeming taller somehow, and lifts me back into his arms. "You look like Nina, and I like taking care of people. It's a curse."

I frown. He could have fooled me about the taking care of people. He only takes care of me after he drugs me and I literally can't function without him. Dierk is twisted if he thinks Matteo is warmhearted.

He carries me down the hallway to the dining room where two plates of food are already sitting in front of our usual seats.

He leisurely drops me into my seat. None of his men are seated at the table. I glance out the window behind him and realize it's the middle of the day, not morning.

"How long have I been out for?" I ask.

"A few hours. I gave you a much smaller dose."

I exhale. Only a few hours. I'm not sure if I believe him, but I need to if I'm going to keep my sanity.

I start shoveling the eggs and toast into my body without waiting for him to permit me. Despite having at least one hearty meal a day for the past couple of weeks, I'm still starving, especially after not having eaten for however long I was out.

Matteo stares at me, not touching anything but his coffee.

I try to ignore him, but it's impossible to ignore his presence. He's just sitting there, but I can't enjoy the eggs I'm putting in my mouth because all I can think about is him. What he wants, what he's thinking.

"What are you doing?" I ask, my mouth jammed full with toast.

He shakes his head, ignoring my question.

I keep eating. I'll need it to regain strength for whatever ridiculous plan he is scheming next. I watch him out of the corner of my eye, and I can't help but notice he's different. Tired. Worn down.

His eyes are bloodshot like he hasn't slept in a week or is

high. His clothes are ragged like he hasn't showered or changed in days. I notice the spots of dirt and blood scattered over his shirt and jeans. It's not a lot, but enough to make him look like he's been through hell and back.

"What happened?" I ask, staring at the blood. I don't know if it is his or someone else's.

He doesn't answer. Instead, he glances past me like I'm not here.

Strange. He usually answers all of my questions. Today though, all I get is silence.

I don't like silence. I know from experience when the men I prosecute become quiet and stop talking, that's when things start happening. They make one last desperate attempt to get what they want. And it's never pretty. Someone ends up hurt or dead.

I need to keep Matteo talking. I need him to go back to the old Matteo, who was solely focused on Nina. He requires focus to keep him going. And I need him to keep his sights on getting Nina back to stay alive long enough to escape.

I eat the last drop of runny eggs with the last piece of bread, sopping up every last drop. I lean back in my chair trying to remain relaxed. Food in my stomach makes me calmer. But it won't last, not with this Matteo.

The old Matteo was predictable, this man sitting at the table next to me is erratic. He's dangerous. A flip has been switched, and I'm not sure how to turn the switch back off.

I have to change my plan. I have to do something daring for a chance to get out of here.

"I'll tell you where Nina is, but I have some things I need in return."

He doesn't move. He doesn't react. This is the one thing he claims he wants above everything else. The thing he kidnapped me for, but he doesn't care.

"She's in Monterey Bay, Jamaica."

I wait for him to answer. For his eyes to grow big or him to grin so widely he can't contain it. Or for him to smirk and let me know he realizes it isn't true. He doesn't do any of these things. He sits in his chair like I don't exist.

I glance around. No one is in the dining room. Most of Matteo's men are gone or are hanging around in their offices or the living room. *If I got up and walked out, would anyone stop me?*

I consider it for a second before I realize it's a stupid idea. Far too risky. If Matteo were to snap to and realize I ran off, he would probably kill me when he found me.

"Did you hear me? I told you where to find your precious Nina."

Nothing.

"Matteo!" I slap him on the cheek. It feels good to have my hand hit his rough face, even though my arms are weak and the hit was more of a light slap. So light that it didn't even make a satisfying sound when our skin touched.

It does earn me a growl and a glare.

I smirk. "Glad to bring you back to the living. Did you hear me?"

"Yes. I'm not deaf."

"You could have fooled me."

"I heard you, but it wasn't worth responding to. It was a lie. We both know it. You want some of your control back. You want to know what's going on so you can try to get one step in front of me. Well, guess what sweetheart? Not everything revolves around you and Nina. Sometimes, I have more important things to worry about."

I wrinkle my brow. "Like what?"

"Nothing that concerns you. You need to shut up. I need to be alone right now, and even though I can't be alone because I have to babysit you, I can at least pretend in the silence."

"You could let me go if you want to be alone."

"I said, shut up!" His voice beams, bouncing off the high ceilings and walls so loudly I'm sure anyone in the house could hear him.

"No."

The anger rolls off his body, but there's something else mixed with it too. I'm playing with fire, but maybe figuring out what is going on is the key to gaining my freedom. I need to know everything I can about Matteo. It's the only way I can be free.

Matteo shoves his uneaten plate of food in front of me.

"Eat. I know you are still hungry and if your mouth is full, maybe you'll stop fucking talking."

Damn it. My stomach aches at the sight of more food. I could use more nourishment. Who knows when my next meal will be.

But it's a distraction. I know that. But it's a diversion that is going to work.

I dig in, filling my belly. It will only work temporarily, and then I'll be back to questioning Matteo every second until he starts speaking.

"Matteo Carini, it's been a long time," a deep voice bellows through the dining room.

I keep shoveling in food as I turn in the direction of the man who has entered. It's not a man I recognize, but I haven't met all of the men who work for Matteo.

"Not long enough," Matteo answers.

The man chuckles and walks over and takes a seat opposite me and next to Matteo. He leans back in his chair, ignoring me completely as he stares at Matteo.

It gives me a chance to study him. He's well dressed in dress pants and a buttoned-down shirt. It fits his body perfectly, like it was handmade for him. His hair is gelled and his face cleanly shaven. He doesn't look like the rest of the men who are employed by Matteo. They wear clothes to make them look as menacing as possible. Dark jeans, shirts, and jackets. Items they can quickly move in and store weapons in. Not suits meant for an office.

"Your sister is ridiculous," the man says, leaning back in his chair.

Matteo glares at the man. "Careful," he warns.

"What? We're friends. And you know how your sister can be. I came by to ask her to go with me to the ball my family is throwing."

"Just because we are friends doesn't mean you can say anything bad about my sister because she turned you down."

"I didn't say anything mean. I could have called Gia a bitch or cunt or something."

Matteo is going to kill him. They don't appear to be friends to me.

"What do you want Armas?" Matteo growls.

Armas grins at Matteo's foul mood. "You know what I want. The same thing I've wanted for the past couple of years."

"Gia will never go out with you."

"Why not? She should. I'm handsome, charming, have almost as much money as this family. I'm your best friend, so we already have your blessing to date."

"You don't have my permission to date my sister. Not that it matters, because she will never date you."

"Not without some help. Come on Matteo, put in a good word for me."

"And why would I do that?"

"Because we are friends and I have saved your butt plenty of times."

Matteo narrows his eyes. "When? Because all I ever remember you doing was running when I needed your help."

Armas laughs. "They were shooting at us. What was I supposed to do?"

"Stay and fight like a real man."

"And get killed? No, thank you. Where is your brother anyway? He's the one who usually saves your ass."

"None of your business."

Armas cracks his neck side to side. "Why won't Gia go out with me? She is going to my family's ball anyway. You all are. So why won't she go with me?"

Matteo shakes his head. "You are clueless. She won't go out with you because she's in love with another man."

Armas laughs like it's the most ridiculous thing he's ever heard. "You can't be serious. She doesn't fall in love. She's a Carini. Carinis are ruthless, uncaring, and controlling. They don't deal with things as simple as love."

My eyes burn into Matteo. It's not true. Arlo is definitely in love. He gave up his whole family, his entire life to live a life on the run with Nina.

Matteo doesn't mention Arlo. Apparently, no one in town knows Arlo is gone or the reason.

"Well, call it lust then, but Gia is still hung up on the last guy that took her out on a date, so forgive her if she isn't interested in letting you take her out."

Armas sighs and leans back in his chair until his feet go up on the table. As he does, he notices I'm in the room for the first time. A creepy smile slinks up on his face as he gawks at me.

"And what's your name, beautiful?"

I shovel in the last bite. "Eden." I stare at him cautiously, letting him know not to mess with me.

Armas looks to Matteo. "Seriously? You have a slave? I thought the stories were only rumors."

Matteo shrugs. "When will you learn all of the rumors are true?"

Armas cocks his head to the side. "Well, well, it's my lucky day then."

"I don't know why? You have no luck," Matteo says.

Armas turns his head toward me. "You can give me some luck by letting me borrow your slave tonight. It will help me get over your sister."

Matteo crosses his arms across his chest. "And why would I do that? She's mine."

I swallow hard, not sure about this exchange at all or what I want to happen. For one, I want both men to stop referring to me as a slave. And two, I don't know whose side Armas is on. If he takes me, maybe I can convince him to help me escape. But if not, then I want Matteo to win. Matteo, I understand. Matteo, I know what to expect from him. Armas would be like starting all over. And he might have no problem hurting me unlike, Matteo.

"Because you owe me. And I know your little secret."

"What secret is that?"

"You just told me to trust the rumors. And the rumors are Arlo fell in love with the last slave the family brought home. He's run off with her." He cuts his eyes to me. "I have a feeling this new slave has a lot to do with fixing your little problem. But she doesn't appear too broken to me. Let me have my fun, I might be able to help you, and I'll promise to keep your secret."

Matteo growls and grabs Armas by the collar of his shirt. "Don't threaten me. You know what I'm capable of."

"Not threatening, simply offering my assistance."

Paul, one of Matteo's men, enters the room.

"Sorry to interrupt. There has been another attack," Paul says.

"I'll be right there," Matteo says, dismissing Paul.

He waits until Paul has disappeared before he gets up from the table and jerks Armas back in the chair.

"Babysit her for me, I have to go," Matteo says, walking away.

I watch him walk away from me, and I'm not sure whether to be happy or terrified. With each step he takes, I think he's going to stop, turn around, and tell Armas to go to hell. I think he's going to say I'm his slave and no one else has permission to touch me. Matteo isn't the kind of man who can share easily. He likes being in control.

But he doesn't stop. He doesn't turn around. He doesn't say another word. He leaves me alone with a man who claims to be his friend, but from the short exchange I witnessed, I know he is anything but his friend.

Matteo's gone, and I'm left with a man who is a stranger. I don't know what he wants from me. I don't know what drives him. I don't know what his weaknesses are. I don't know anything about him. I need to tread carefully.

"How long have you known Matteo?" I ask, trying to make light conversation. It might give me some clue to who he is and how to survive until Matteo gets back or better yet, escape.

He smirks. "Since the day I was born. Our families are both rich, old, and know each other well."

"So you sell weapons too?"

He chuckles. "No, we only meddle with legal things. Our family sells wine."

"So you aren't as rich since you don't do illegal things?"

His eyes narrow. "I guess not."

"Are you and Matteo truly friends? Because it seems there is more to your friendship than either of you are saying."

"Does it matter if we are friends or not?"

I shrug. "No reason. I might be able to help you if you are more enemies than friends."

He leans across the table with a smirk on his face. "Oh, yea? And how could you help me?"

"I've been here a month or two now, and I've overheard plenty of secrets I'm sure could help you take Matteo down."

He laughs. "No secrets I don't already know."

"I know his weaknesses. It's how I've ensured he hasn't touched me or hurt me."

He leans back in his chair again and folds his arms across his chest while he raises an eyebrow. "Really? He has a slave he never uses?"

I nod. "He is using me to get his brother back. Help me escape, and you'll cause him more pain than you can imagine."

He stands up and walks around the table to my side and leans against the edge of the table.

"I have a better idea."

I bite my lip and tuck my matted hair behind my ear. "And what's that?"

"I'll fix his problem."

I narrow my eyes not understanding until I see the gleam in his eyes. His eyes darken, his grin widens, and he licks his bottom lip like he's about to devour the most delicious meal he's ever tasted.

"I'm going to rape you."

7
___

EDEN

Rape.

I've known it was a possibility since Matteo forced me onto his private plane, but I always thought I would be strong enough to stop it from happening. I've taken self-defense classes. I'm smart and know how to find people's weak points and exploit them. I thought I would be able to escape long before anyone even attempted to rape me.

Matteo thought about raping me. I saw the glimmer in his eyes every now and again. He couldn't do it, or at least I don't remember him doing it. Something held him back. I can't rely on the same thing happening with Armas. I don't know him, but from the way he's devouring me, I think he's far more evil than Matteo has ever pretended to be.

I swallow hard.

"You're not going to rape me."

His grin widens. "You're a spitfire, huh? I'm going to enjoy this."

"No, you're going to be sitting with a bag of ice on your balls for a week, recovering from your wounds."

He purses his lips together as he studies me up and down. I

83

don't look like much, not in my weakened state, but it doesn't matter. Let him think I'm delicate and incapable of anything; it will only make it easier for me to escape.

I have to take him down. Matteo is gone, along with all of his men, dealing with whatever latest attack. If I can get past Armas, then I might be free.

I try to decide if I should wait for him to grab me or strike first. My blood is pumping, already full of adrenaline. My legs bounce, and my mouth dries. I feel the fear, but mostly the excitement, at the possibility of being free.

Free.

I never thought I would be begging to be released. I never thought I would have to struggle for it, but that's what I'm going to do. And when I gain it back, I'm going to fight every day to ensure every other innocent, kidnapped person is freed and stays that way.

I can't wait for Armas to try and take even more from me. I have to run. Now.

I ball my hand into a fist, and then I jab it forcefully into his neck as hard as I can. My arms are weaker than usual, but the adrenaline and determination make up for the disability.

He grabs his throat as he struggles to breathe.

I jump out of my chair and start running. I don't shoot out the back of the house. I know what awaits me back there. An immense forest and rolling hills that lead nowhere. I'd be sprinting for days to get to anyone who could help me. I don't have the strength to flee more than a few hours at best.

Instead, I race toward the other side of the house, which leads out to the garage. I need a car if I have a chance to escape.

My legs stumble as I run, like they are going to give out at any moment, but I don't let the fear of falling consume me. Instead, I allow it to drive me forward. I let it fill me.

The fear of failing. The fear of giving up. The fear of what would happen if Armas caught me. The fear of what will happen to Nina if I don't stop Matteo from finding her. I let it all fuel me to make my legs move faster.

I don't know if it's enough. I know I'm not quicker than Matteo. Armas appears fit. He doesn't look like he's had a day of manual labor, unlike Matteo who gets his hands dirty protecting his business on a daily basis. Armas is used to sitting in a corporate office building, away from the action. Hopefully, my fitness will be enough to outrun him.

I don't turn around or glance behind me to see if I'm right. I keep moving, running fast.

I haven't been to the garage. I don't know if Matteo keeps the keys in the cars or nearby. I don't even know how many cars he has in the garage, or if there are any left, but it's my only hope.

I turn down another hallway and see the door at the end that I think leads to the garage.

I can make it.

My feet carry me faster as I fly down the hallway. I grab the door, hurl it open, and flip the light on.

I pause for a single breath when I see more than a dozen cars in the expansive garage. I'm clueless when it comes to cars. I don't know how expensive they all are or how fast they go. I run to the nearest one and fling the door open, begging for the keys to be inside.

Please, please, please.

The car doesn't have a spot to slide the key in. Instead, it has a button you use to start the car. I have no clue where to search to see if there is a key somewhere in the car or not.

I push the button and exhale deeply when the engine roars to life.

I press the clicker at the roof the car, and the garage door opens.

I step on the gas and speed out of the garage, clipping the side mirror of a black car parked near the exit.

I remember the long driveway that leads off the property and I know I'm not anywhere near safety yet, but getting the car makes me feel unstoppable. There is nothing Armas can do at this point to stop me.

The driveway curves and I see Armas. He's standing in the middle of the driveway, his red sports car sits behind him parked sideways across the gravel. Hundred-year-old oak trees line both sides of the road.

He's blocking my exit. There is no way out, except to run him over.

I smirk.

I don't have a problem killing him if it means my freedom. I'll hit him with my car first. Then I'll take his car if that is what I need to do to get out of here.

I step firmly on the gas making my intentions known. Armas can move or get killed.

He turns to his car, opens the back door, and grabs a woman by the arm, jerking her out. He holds her by the arm next to him in front of his car.

I squint trying to get a better look at the woman and realizing it's one of the cooks. She made me breakfast most days. She probably has a family; people that love and depend on her.

Shit.

I keep my foot on the gas, hoping if I play chicken with him long enough he'll move her out of my path. As my car inches closer, I know in my heart, he won't. I'll have to run them over and kill them both if I want a shot at getting free.

Damn it. Damn it. Damn it. I hit the steering wheel trying to figure out what I should do.

I swerve the car just before I hit them, stomping on the brake. The car doesn't stop. I was going too fast.

I squeeze my eyes shut, not wanting to see the tree the car is about to crash into.

My body slams forward, the airbag deploys and launches my body backward, and the air is knocked out of me for the second time since Matteo entered my life. I've never been in a car accident before, and it makes me never want to ride in a car ever again.

All I feel is pain as the airbag slowly deflates. Pain in my head, my stomach, my leg. I should get out of the car and start running, but I can't. I can't move, the pain is intense.

Instead, I have to wait for Armas to come to me. I try to think of what my next plan is and how I can cause the most damage. But at the moment, I'm out of ideas. The self-defense classes I took never covered how to defend yourself against someone when you've spent your night drugged and were in a car accident where you couldn't physically move.

I hear twigs breaking and leaves crunching, his presence looming nearer and nearer.

I close my eyes, pretending I'm anywhere but here. I'm back in my office going over a new case. Or I'm in the courtroom after winning a verdict.

I can't.

I hear the door pop open, and I'm brought right back to reality.

"Good thing I like my women feisty."

I gradually turn my head to him, and give him my worst death stare. "Go to hell."

He grins. "I think I'll fuck you first."

He pushes the airbag down and reaches over me and undoes my seatbelt. He grabs my arms and starts yanking me out of the car.

I cry out.

"My. Leg. Is. Stuck." Each word comes out with a cry of pain. Like somehow talking is making the torment in my leg worse.

"Stop being dramatic and get out of the fucking car," Armas says.

"I can't," I cry again, trying to wrench my leg loose. I glance down and realize the front of the car has smashed in and trapped my leg. There is no way I'm going to be able to get it out, not without damaging my leg or something that can cut the metal.

He grabs me by both shoulders and begins tugging me violently, trying to get me out of the car.

I cry out again. "Stop! My leg is stuck, you idiot!"

"I don't give a fuck." He pulls forcefully, and my skin scrapes across the jagged metal as he heaves me loose.

We topple to the ground.

I don't wait for the agony to stop or to catch my breath. I get up and try to run. My left leg works fine, but my right leg is useless. I collapse to the ground after only a few strides.

I've never broken a bone before, and I never want to again. The pain is fire, burning throughout my entire body. It overwhelms me. I can't budge it. I can't think. I can scarcely exist.

I stare down at my useless limb. I have a huge gash on the top of my shin where blood is spilling out. Not fast enough I'm worried about dying, but enough to warrant going to a hospital to have it cleaned and stitched up. The laceration looks awful, but the damage is much deeper in my leg. My leg is red and swollen. Broken, possibly in multiple places.

My eyes drift up, and Armas is standing over me. His eyes are the darkest I've ever seen, his lips curled up into an evil grin, and his face hot with desire.

My arms start moving as I attempt to crawl away. It's a useless endeavor, but I can't lie here and let him take me.

"You don't give up, do you?"

I ignore him and continue crawling away, despite every movement feeling like I'm getting thrown on a fire and then stabbed repeatedly. *Who knew breaking a bone burned from the inside out?*

My head is jerked back as he grabs my hair.

I scream.

A tear trickles out of my eye, overcoming my effort of doing my damndest to keep in. I hate crying in front of these monsters, but crying is the least of my worries.

He starts dragging me across the rough, gravel road. I strive to grab him to right myself and soften the aching.

I can't move fast enough.

Every pebble, every rock, every stick. I feel it all. And each one is like a knife being thrust into the most sensitive parts of my body.

If Matteo were here, I would be pleading with him to jab me with his needle and give me the drugs to knock me out and make this go away. I would rather give up control than be in this torment for one more second.

He pauses when we get to his car. I glance around for the women whose life I saved when I swerved and hit the tree instead of her. She should be here thanking me or on the phone with the police helping to rescue me, but she is doing neither. She's loyal to Matteo, like everyone else here is.

My heart turns dark. *I should have run her over. I should have saved myself.*

No.

I can't let them win. I can't become as evil as Matteo and Armas are. I will find another way to save myself.

He opens the back door, and tugs savagely on my hair forcing me up onto my healthy leg while my mangled leg dangles uselessly.

"I can't wait to get you back to my place."

The car ride to his house is long.

Either because he lives far away from Matteo's mansion or because I'm in writhing pain. But as long as it is, I wish that the car ride would never end. Because I know what is coming when the car finally stops and as much suffering as I'm in now, it will be nothing compared to the torture I will be left with when he rapes me.

I can come back from a broken leg, but I've prosecuted too many rapists. I've met with their victims. Once brutality like that happens to you, you're never the same. For some, it makes some of them stronger. Others debilitated and timid. Either way, it always makes them afraid. Fearing other people. Scared of the violence. Terrified of life.

I don't want to live life afraid of getting raped again. I've spent the entire trip trying to come up with a plan. Some way to escape. I've tried finding a way to fix my leg so that I could run, but that would be impossible even with the best of equipment. I need a doctor.

I'm surprised that Armas was okay with me bleeding all over his fancy leather seats. I guess he feels kidnapping me so that he can rape me makes it worth it.

I've tried thinking back to all my training about how to defend myself against an assaulter, but even if I'm able to do some damage to him, all my instruction was around the fact that I could temporarily injure my assailant while I ran away to get help.

I can't run.

And there is no help coming.

Armas may not be as rich as Matteo, but judging by the mansion buried deep in the woods that the car stopped in front of, Armas has plenty of money. Money buys loyalty and silence.

No one is going to help me.

Armas steps out of the car and slings my door open. I kick with my uninjured leg, trying to fend him off. Adrenaline takes over and helps with the pain.

He seizes my leg, and I fight in his grasp. He yanks my leg, and I'm pulled out of the car. I crash to the ground, not registering much of the new pain. My head hits the door, which should add a headache to the list, but a headache doesn't even register on my pain scale.

"You are just what I need."

He smirks.

Bile rises in my throat as he undresses me with his eyes. He's sick.

I won't let him win.

I narrow in on his crotch and kick with all my might. I hit my target, but it's not enough.

He laughs, a high-pitched annoying sound. He takes a step back as he snaps his fingers.

My eyes search around him, to see who he summoned with the snap of his fingers. A butler? His dogs? I could handle either.

Two men, in dark suits, start running toward us.

Damn it. I can now spot a guard anywhere. Even well dressed guards.

Both men cower by their master's side. He glances down at me, and they both automatically reach down and clutch my arms. I try unsuccessfully to get them off for only a second before they stand me up. I balance on my good leg while I glare at Armas.

"I thought you only dealt with legal things? What would you need men like this for if you were on the straight and narrow? They are experienced in handling women if all they needed was a look to grab me."

Armas steps forward, standing inches from me, now that he

has his men to hold me back and I can't do anything to harm him.

"I said my business was lawful; I never said that I wasn't a monster."

"You're a coward. You won't even face me alone. I've got a busted leg, and you still couldn't take me alone."

My stomach churns looking at his devilish grin.

"Don't worry. I'll have you *alone* soon." He glances at the man on my right. "Take her to my bedroom and make sure she's secured with handcuffs."

The man's eyes widen as he stares down at my leg. "I'll confine her, but I don't think it's necessary. She's not going anywhere."

Armas glares at the man, who is going to be punished later for daring to speak out against him. "You need to use the thick handcuffs. She's not as broken as she looks. She will do every-thing she can to escape, even when there is no hope left."

The man nods and both men start pulling me into the house while I hop on one leg, attempting to keep up instead of getting dragged again.

They pull me inside the house, and I'm overtaken by the smell of sweet flowers. The whole house has vases of fresh flowers everywhere, sitting on almost every hard surface.

A woman lives here. There is no way that Armas would think to have flowers in his house if he lived alone. A tiny glimmer of hope flickers in my heart. If I can find the woman and convince her to help me, then I might have a chance.

I glance at the man that thought it was pointless to tie me up.

"Does Armas live here by himself?"

"Yes."

I frown, not sure if I believe him.

"Ow," I moan. My injured leg hits the bottom step as they start leading me up the stairs.

The men pause, giving me a moment to catch up with them. I do my best to lift my wounded leg up.

"It seems like such a big house for him to live here all alone. And I've never heard of a man that has so many flowers."

The man chuckles. "Trust me. He lives alone except for the staff. The flowers were supposed to be for Gia, but —"

The man stops when the man to my left clears his throat and gives him a look.

I sigh.

The men start moving quickly again, and I struggle to keep up. My leg hits more stairs than I can tolerate and when we reach the top, I collapse in their arms.

They don't let me rest though. It's like a flip has been switched and gone are the men that didn't want to bring me additional pain.

I have no energy left. Nothing left in me to fight with.

I let them drag me, despite the stabbing pain, down the hall-way, and into a bedroom.

I can make out the bedroom from behind the dark spots that have formed in my field of vision. There is a bed and some other furniture, but I can't make out what color the items are or any details.

My heart palpates so loudly in my chest that I'm sure both men holding onto me can hear it and feel it. My body trembles in their arms. I blink rapidly trying to clear my head. I'm desperate to figure out a plan to get out of here.

But no matter how many times I blink, my eyes don't uncloud, my head doesn't focus, and the pain doesn't leave my body.

The men start dragging me toward the bed, and I dig the heel of my healthy leg into the ground, trying to stall them until I can come up with a plan. Once I'm tied to the bed, I will have no hope of escaping.

The men exchange glances and pick me up off the floor entirely.

I thrash in their arms determined to escape. They hold my arms and legs tightly, making it almost impossible to kick free. I move my head over to bite them on the arm, but I'm too slow. One of the men grips my head and holds it still.

I can't move.

I can't do anything to prevent this from happening.

"Please, you don't want to do this," I beg. I can't use my body, but maybe I can remind them that they have a soul. That they don't want to work for a devil like Armas.

One man laughs.

"You think we care?"

I bite my bottom lip to keep it from trembling. "Yes, I know you do. I've been held captive for weeks now. I know when a man has a heart or not. You both do. Help me escape. Find the kindheartedness inside you. I'll give you whatever you want if you do."

The second man snickers.

"We don't need your help. We get paid handsomely for the work that we do. Mr. Espocito is a fair employer, better than Mr. Carini. He doesn't ask us to risk our lives as Mr. Carini does. We deal with wine shipments and security. Occasionally, he asks more of us. Things you might call evil and wrong. But it's not wrong. We've learned that bitches like you always deserve what is coming to you."

My eyes widen at the smug expression on his face. *How could I think he had a heart?* No man in Italy has a soul. No one can save me. All these men want is money. They will do anything their masters command of them for it.

They carry me to the bed and toss me down, not caring that I scream when they do. A sharpness shoots from my leg up to my spine as the soft bed hits it, but it feels like a sharp knife instead.

My head is light, and the room spins around, making it impossible for me to fight, as they start holding down my arms and legs. I feel the familiar cold of handcuffs going around my wrists, as my arms are jerked above my head and attached to something. I don't even bother testing the strength of the metal cuffs. If they had used floss to tie my arms up, I still wouldn't be able to break through. I'm that weak.

Metal goes on my left leg, and my right leg is spread wide, but I don't feel the cold I'm expecting.

I stare down at the man looking at my broken leg. He's hesitating to put the last cuff on. He knows it's useless, but his boss commanded it, so after a few seconds of hesitation, he puts it on and attaches my leg to the bed.

I grimace as my broken leg is pulled tight like every other one of my extremities.

The men leave without a word. I close my eyes as I hear the door slam shut.

Sleep. I've never wanted to sleep so much in my life. My body needs rest to attempt to start healing. Maybe if I fall asleep, I'll sleep through the whole thing and have no memory of the rape.

Rape.

The thought of the word causes my stomach to flip in my body. I'm sick. This can't be happening.

I try to take a deep breath, but I can't. My body won't relax. It's on heightened alert. Blood races through my body as my heart pumps way too fast. Nerves fire off, alerting every inch of my body to stay awake and ready. Alerting me that something dangerous is about to happen.

The door opens, and Armas appears in the doorway.

I narrow my eyes at him, as he walks to the edge of the bed. I will not let him see my fear or pain. I may not have a chance of escaping, but I'm going to leave with as much of me intact as possible.

His hand runs over my wound, and I do everything I can to not flinch, but my leg twitches involuntarily trying to escape the discomfort.

He smirks. "It hurts, doesn't it?"

My lips tighten. I won't answer him.

He shakes his head, as his hand trails up my injured leg over my sex and across my stomach to my breast. He squeezes it tightly, attempting to invoke another reaction out of me.

I'm stoic. I don't move. I act like he is shaking my hand, nothing more.

He exhales as his eyes roll back in his head like my reaction is turning him on. "I'm going to enjoy this far too much."

My lips frown before I have a chance to stop them.

His thumb glides up over my lips, and I try to bite him, but he pulls his fingers away before I have the opportunity to.

"I can't believe Matteo hasn't touched you yet. It seems like such a waste."

"He has touched me," I say, hoping if I can convince him Matteo has already had a turn with me, he will lose interest. I doubt it will work, since I already told him he hasn't touched me, but I have to try.

Armas is right, though, about me being lucky so far. I don't fully understand why Matteo hasn't raped me or beat me yet.

His hands move back down to my shirt and rip it in two, revealing my bare breasts. His eyes burn into my plump breasts, before he bends down and takes my nipple into his mouth.

I cry out, and my back tries to sink into the bed, away from his sharp teeth, as he nibbles harshly on my nipple.

"No, he hasn't touched you. No man has been with you for weeks. If Matteo had touched you, you would already be broken.

You're the opposite of lost. You are more alive than any woman I've ever had the pleasure of tying up in my bed.

"But don't worry, the hope you feel deep in your belly will soon be gone. I'll shred every bit of attachment you have to this world until you are begging me to die, only then will I return you to Matteo."

He's going to keep me alive. That's the only words I focus on. He doesn't want to kill. He can't kill me, or Matteo would kill him.

Matteo still thinks that he can crack me and convince me to tell him where Nina is. I'm beginning to believe that Armas might be part of that plan. Once he's done with me, he's right though, I'll be begging for death, and I'll give Matteo whatever he wants.

Blood pours out of my lip, into my mouth, as I bite down on my lip while Armas takes my nipple in between his teeth again. He's cruel, treating me like an object that he can do what he pleases with.

He removes his shirt to reveal his muscular body. He has a fit body, but it's nothing like Matteo's. I close my eyes, hating myself for comparing his body to Matteo's. Both men are evil. The fact that they both have hot bodies is irrelevant. It doesn't make me want to fuck them.

Hands tighten around my neck so that I can't breathe.

"Open your eyes."

I try to hold out, but I need to breathe.

I open my eyes.

"Good girl."

He stands back and pushes his pants and boxer briefs down. "Like what you see?"

I turn away in disgust.

"Look at me bitch," he says, as his hand grabs my neck again, forcing my head to turn back to him.

He smirks. "You like my body. Your pussy is begging to feel a man again."

He's insane. There is no way I could feel anything positive about this man, not even lust. My leg is shattered thanks to him. My body is tied up, and he's about to rape me against my will.

I spit in his face. His hand crashes against my face. He doesn't slap me like I was expecting. His fist was tightly balled as he punched me.

Dots. All I can see are black spots, no matter if my eyes are open or closed. My head throbs so severely that I don't want to move it. I don't even want to think.

His hands are at my pants, and my body trembles, as he rips my pants off.

I'm naked. Exposed. I've never felt so vulnerable in my life. Not even when Matteo kidnapped me. This man is going to rape me. Nothing is stopping him.

I try to squeeze my legs together, but his hands grip my thighs, pushing me wide, while his body settles in between my legs. I can feel the head of his erection pushing at my entrance, and a tear trickles down my cheek.

My arms thrash against the restraints, but I'm tied up so tightly that I can only wiggle them an inch.

My body tries to twist away from him, but his hand crashes down on my chest, putting his entire body weight on my chest.

I can't breathe. I try to move my lungs up and down to let air in, but I can't. His hand is pressing down too hard.

I stop moving. I stop trying.

Only then does he let his hands up enough so that a little air pushes into my lungs.

I don't want the air anymore. I want to stop breathing, stop living. I won't survive this.

No.

He doesn't get to win.

I will survive this.

My eyes fly open. He's going to have to look me in the eye when he rapes me. He's going to see the anger that he's causing instead of the pain. He'll see the rage that he created, and he'll know that I will spend the rest of my life coming after him. That I won't let him rest until I've hurt him like he's hurt me, and then I'll kill him.

I swear I see a bit of hesitation and fear in his eyes when he sees the fire in mine when I open them, but it's probably my imagination.

I need him to fear me to get through this. I need to fight him. And if I can't do that with my body, I will with my eyes. I'll let him know what's coming to him when I get out of these restraints. Matteo used to be my number one target, but now it's Armas.

His head drops, and he slobbers down my neck. It's because he can't look me in the eyes, the coward.

He thrusts his cock inside me with his face still buried in my neck. It's probably a good thing that he's not looking at me though, because I can't stay strong now that his cock is inside me. My eyes water and I close them to keep the tears in.

He groans as he sinks deeper, while tears burn my eyes.

He won.

I may eventually get free and kill him, but right now, he won.

"You're mine, bitch. You're nothing but a slave. You're going to spend the rest of your week tied to my bed so that I can come fuck you whenever I want. You are going to be black and blue. By the end of the week, your body will be begging for my cock."

His cock thrust in and out of me and my insides burn, my stomach aches, and vile shoots up my throat.

I hate him.

I hate him more than all the criminals I've locked up. Armas is the worst. I will make him pay for what he's doing to me.

My eyes gloss over as I try to pretend I'm anywhere but here. I try to imagine myself in the courtroom. My brain won't go there though.

I try to imagine I'm on a beach, the warm saltwater stinging my eyes, and that's why they cry. But my mind knows it isn't real.

I try to imagine Nina. I pretend we are back in college and are about to head out for a night of drinking and hitting on boys. But it only makes the tears come faster, because if I can't save myself, how am I going to protect Nina?

My mind goes to Matteo. His dark locks, his intense gaze, his sculpted body. I want to blame him for this. If he hadn't stolen me, then I wouldn't be here getting raped.

But I don't hold him responsible. Because going back to him is going to feel like a sanctuary compared to where I am right now.

8

MATTEO

It was a false alarm.

The men thought they were being set up and about to be ambushed. But they weren't. Instead, the client they were delivering weapons to changed the location and snuck up on them to try to keep their secrecy.

I had a stern talking with the client to let him know we won't be working with him again. We set the rules, not him. He doesn't get to change the location of the drop. We do. What he did was unacceptable and put everyone at risk.

We have been under attack numerous times lately. It's put everyone on edge. I know it's Clive and Erick behind the attacks.

They are still upset about us taking Nina from them. And they are testing me. I'm the new leader of the Carini family, and they want to find out what they can and can't get away with. They are trying to push me and take over some of my turf.

I won't let them. Soon, they will find out I'm more ruthless than my father when it comes to protecting my own. I will need to go on the offensive to prove it to them and end this nonsense.

My phone buzzes in my pocket, as I walk back from the wooded area to where my car is parked along the street.

"Yes," I answer, snapping harder than I mean to. I'm in a foul mood. I don't know what to do with Eden and having to deal with this idiot only made my temper worse.

"Sorry to bother you, sir. I wanted to let you know we saw Armas drive Eden off the grounds and I thought you'd like to be aware."

I growl.

"How could you let this happen?"

He doesn't answer. I already know how. I left one guard, and I've threatened them all with their lives when only one guard is on duty to never leave the premises if a Carini is still in the house. Gia must be home. She needs protection. It's my fault for calling my men here to defend our turf, without leaving more behind to protect what's mine.

I end the call, shove the phone back into my pocket, and I run to my car. I hop in, speeding off as my wheels squeal against the pavement.

Thoughts of what Armas could be doing to Eden right now cloud my head. His lips on hers. His dick inside her tight cunt, making her cry out while he breaks her.

All the things I wanted to do to her and barely got a taste of. Things that I could never entirely go through with myself.

I thought it was what I wanted. I couldn't break Eden myself so why not let Armas do the dirty work? But now that it is happening, it's not what I want.

And I need to teach him a lesson for thinking he could take what's mine off my property. He knows I'm going to retaliate for breaking my rules.

I'm not far from his house. Assuming that's where Armas has taken Eden. Maybe I can save her before anything happens.

I press my foot down all the way on the gas, my car speeds up, and I hit the apex of each of the turns that weave through the woods. I shouldn't drive so fast, not on these roads. But I push my limits to get to his house faster.

Ten minutes. That's how long it takes me, when usually it would take more than twenty. The gate to Armas's property is closed, but it's nothing my car can't handle.

I rev the engine, going full speed again, breaking the flimsy lock on the gate as my car bursts through it. I don't stop until my car is right outside the side door leading into the house.

I jump out of the car and draw my gun. Armas doesn't deal with weapons or anything illegal, but he has security guards who wouldn't have any difficulty shooting me. I didn't bring any backup of my own. I considered it, but I don't need the help. And I don't want any witnesses for what I decide to do Armas. My men have no problem with torture or killing, but they may give my actions pause when it comes to innocent rich men who could have been their boss instead of me.

"Sir, Armas is busy at the moment. If you'd like to come back later, I'll let him know you came by," one of his security guards says, coming outside.

God, he needs to train his men better. You shoot first, ask questions later.

He didn't notice my gun yet, so I let it hang in my hand casually to my side.

I smile as I walk up to him like I want to give him a message to deliver to Armas. When I'm a foot away, I draw my gun again aiming it at his head.

He puts his hands up in surrender.

I shake my head. *Idiot.*

"Where is Eden?"

"Who?"

"Don't act dumb. Where is Eden? The woman Armas stole from me this morning. I know he brought her here."

The man stares down at my gun like he's never had a gun aimed at him before.

I roll my eyes. You never hire someone who hasn't at the very least had a gun aimed at them. Preferably you want someone who has been shot before. That way you know they understand the risks and are adequately trained.

I see another man step out, out of the corner of my eye. I shoot him in the chest without a second thought. The man drops to the floor.

"How many other guards does Armas have?"

The man's eyes cut to the man lying lifeless on the floor behind him. "It's just the two of us."

"Don't lie to me or I'll kill you, like I did him."

The man swallows. "I'm not lying."

"Good. Now, where is Eden?"

He glances up. "She's upstairs in Armas' bedroom. It's the third bedroom on the left."

I smirk. "Good boy." I strike him hard in the head with the end of my gun. His body falls to the floor as I race inside. I cough on the intense flowery smell when I enter his house. If he doesn't rape her, he's going to smother her to death with the scent of roses.

I take the stairs two at a time as I climb up the grand staircase. The staircase swerves, taking up most of the space in the entryway. It's meant to be magnificent, the centerpiece of the room, but I have three staircases that trump this one in size and stature.

I get to the top of the stairs and intently listen as I slink down the hallway as quietly as I can. I don't want Armas to know I'm here until I want him to know.

I don't hear anything as I walk down the hallway counting the doors as I go.

One.

Two.

Three.

I grab the doorknob as I lean against the door listening.

Nothing.

I draw my gun ready to kill in a second if I need to.

I push the door open. The room is dark, I flick on the lights, but I already know what I'm going to find. Nothing. It's empty.

The bastard lied to me. I should have killed him.

Eden screams.

I turn and run toward her screams. The fourth door. I kick the door open without thinking about anything other than getting to Eden as fast as possible.

Armas is on top of Eden when I enter the room. He doesn't even turn his head to me. Either because he didn't hear me enter, or because he believes I'm a member of his staff, who is coming to check on him and will quickly leave.

My eyes go to Eden. All I can see though are her arms and legs tied to the bed. Her screams and cries pierce my heart, begging me to protect her.

I respond, running to the bed without thinking. I may not be any better than Armas is, but if anyone is going to lay a hand on her, it's going to be me.

Stowing my gun in my waistband, I grab Armas by the neck and fling him against the far wall as easily as I would tossing a ball. I'm much stronger than he is, and in my pent up state, he's not a match for me at all.

Anger.

Rage.

Pain.

The emotions alight deep in my belly and spread like fire through my entire body when I see Eden. I've never been so mad in all my life. I've never felt such rage. My body is red, my arms shake, unable to keep my frustration inside.

Eden is tied to the bed by her arms and legs with shackles to the frame of the bed designed with loops to attach rope or chains. It's clear Armas has done this to women before.

She's naked. Nothing I haven't already seen plenty of times before, but seeing her now makes me ache, my cock throbs against the zipper of my jeans. It makes me want to finish the job that I didn't get to finish.

It's been a long time since I've had a woman. Months. Usually, it isn't a problem, but when I look at her body, I'm tempted to pull out my cock and fuck her right here, right now.

Her eyes look straight at me, but she doesn't react. She doesn't think this is real. She thinks she's dreaming I came and saved her. She must have been desperate to get away from Armas to be fantasizing about me protecting her.

I expect her to look broken, lost, gone. But her eyes don't show that. She still has hope and fight. Her body doesn't seem beaten, other than some redness on her breasts. He's barely fucked her or touched her. No more than I did before.

My eyes continue to inspect her body until I see her leg.

Her entire leg is red and swollen with black and blue bruises all up and down it. But the coloring isn't what has me concerned. There is a large gash on the top of her shin still actively bleeding and filled with dirt and debris. It looks bad. Most likely broken.

Red. It's all I see and feel as I turn from Eden to Armas, who is smirking at me in the corner of the room. He slowly gets to his feet, wiping the blood off his forehead. I must have caused the blood when he I threw him across the room.

"Jealous much? I was having a taste and helping to break her in so she would be ready for you." Armas continues to smirk as he stares at Eden on the bed.

"She wasn't yours to touch."

He cocks his head to the side as his eyes stay locked on Eden, looking at her like he wants to devour her.

"You left her with me. You gave me power to do what I pleased with her when you left. What is she to you that you would be this upset anyway? She's only a slave."

My fist pulls back and then makes contact, hard, with the side of his jaw. His face whips around and I can see redness forming where my fist hit him, but it's not enough. Not nearly enough.

His eyes darken when he looks back at me, holding his face. He doesn't dare try to fight me back. I've kicked his ass before, and I'll kick it again.

"What the hell man?" he says.

"Eden's mine." My fist hits his face again, and this time it knocks him off balance enough so when I hit him again, he falls to the floor.

I can't think of anything other than causing him as much agony as possible for what he did to Eden. He touched her. Raped her. And broke her fucking leg. He doesn't deserve to keep breathing.

I punch him again and again, each strike harder than the previous. He holds up his hands trying to block my punches at first, but eventually, his hands fall to the side as does his body.

I can't stop though. I have to make Armas pay for what he did to Eden. I don't understand why I feel this way. Eden is nothing to me but the key to getting Nina and Arlo back. But my stomach is in knots and my body filled with rage as I pound into his flesh over and over.

My fists are raw and bleeding, but I don't feel the pain. Only the anger. It consumes every muscle in my body, so all I can do or think about is making Armas pay.

Eden groans and I stop.

I turn to her immediately, ignoring the bloody, lifeless mess on the floor in front of me.

I run to her body and cradle her head in my hands.

"Matteo? Are you really here?" she asks, her voice trembling.

I nod. "Yes, I'm getting you out of here."

She rapidly blinks like she's trying to make me go away by blinking, but when I don't, she smiles enough to melt the anger that has taken over me.

She pulls on the shackles holding her down on the bed. My eyes go to the bedside table where I find the key. I grab it and unlock each shackle, moving quickly and efficiently.

Her eyes stay with me each time I move, her eyes narrowed like she doesn't understand what I'm doing.

She doesn't have to understand. I don't even understand what I'm doing. She can't stay here. And I won't let anything like this ever happen again.

When I've removed every single shackle from her extremities, I help her sit up. Then I gather a blanket draped over a chair in the corner of the room and wrap it around her body.

She winces when the fabric touches her leg.

I scoop her up as gingerly as I can in my arms.

"What are you doing?" she asks.

"You can't walk. I'm getting you out of here and taking you where it's safe."

I expect her to argue with me, that my own home is no safer than this place is.

She doesn't.

Instead, her head falls against my chest as her body shakes gently in my arms. The adrenaline now controlling her body has no place to go, making her tremble.

I hold her tighter against my body, ensuring she can't see Armas's dead body as I take her out of the room.

My gun is still tucked into the back of my pants as I leave the room and run down the hallway and the stairs. It's not the smartest move I've ever made, but I doubt Armas has many more guards on duty. And if he does, I don't expect them to be any smarter or more adept than the other guards I ran into.

I stare intently at Eden as I carry her out of the house, not understanding what spell she currently has over me. My erection is still stiff in my pants. My body still aches to toss her in the back of the car and rape her, now. But something stops me.

The need to take care of her. To heal her. Help her.

That's my biggest weakness. I can't stop helping others. And I'll most likely hate myself for taking care of her instead of taking care of my own needs.

Rescuing her made me a target. I shouldn't have messed with one of the wealthiest families in Italy. Now I'll have to deal with the rest of his family once they find out what I did.

I get to my car, but it barely has a second row. I start to put her in the backseat, but I don't want to let her go. It's not far back to my house, but for her, it will seem like an eternity in her condition. And I want to keep an eye on her leg to make sure she's still awake.

I reach into my back pocket and pull out my cell phone while I hold her with my other arm. Even when she is dead weight and barely able to hold herself up, she's still light in my arms.

I dial the number for Maximo.

"Yes, Matteo."

"I need you to get to Armas' place with an SUV as fast as you can and bring someone with you to drive back the sports car."

"Is everything okay, sir?"

"Yes, hurry."

"I'm five minutes away."

I end the call and pocket my phone.

Eden's eyes flicker, and I can't help but stroke the hair away from her face. I've grown soft. It's only because she reminds me so much of Nina. That's not true, because, besides her looks and strength, she is the opposite of Nina.

Nina was soft and caring. She cared too deeply about others and was obsessed with Arlo and me. Eden is harsh. She's faced the cruel world before, and it's made her icy and closed off. She doesn't care about others as much as she cares about protecting Nina and herself.

She swallows as she stares at me and I swear I see her blush a little as her eyes rake down my body.

"How are you feeling?"

"My leg hurts a lot."

I nod. "And everything else?" I ask, unable to ask if he left permanent scars when he raped her or if he even got that far. I couldn't tell from where I was standing or when I pulled him off her. I didn't leave scars when I touched her, but I'm not sure if it's because she has no memory of it or because I didn't go far enough.

She purses her lips together as she takes her time answering me. "I'll heal."

My stomach churns. Armas did rape her; she's just not telling me. Most likely, she doesn't want to admit it to herself either. She'll have to face it eventually. But in the meantime, I'll play along and pretend the only problem that needs healing is her leg.

Maximo drives up, stopping feet from me. I pull the back door open and slide her body inside before I climb in after her. I let her head rest in my lap.

One of the men runs to my car to drive it home, while Maximo starts driving us toward my house.

The car hits a bump in the road, and Eden moans loudly, louder than I expected.

"You okay?" I ask.

She doesn't answer right away. "Yes," she finally breathes. "The pain is getting worse for some reason."

I stroke her hair. "The adrenaline pumping through you, that helped you survived, is leaving your body. It was masking some of the pain."

As we speed around another corner, she closes her eyes and winces. A tear rolls down her cheek and then another, despite her eyes being shut tight. Her face is turning redder every second. Her body shaking faster in my arms trying to distract her from her agony.

There is nothing I can do to comfort her, except hold her.

"Do you..." she starts and then stops as the discomfort overtakes her.

"Shhh. Try to relax. We will be back soon."

I glance down at her wound to make sure the bleeding hasn't gotten worse. It hasn't. I considered tying a tourniquet around it but decided against it, when I knew how much torture it would cause her, and the bleeding wasn't strong enough to warrant it anyway.

There is nothing I can do to help her until we get back and I have the proper medical supplies to help her.

"Do you have any of the drugs you've used to knock me out on you?" she asks, her voice stronger than before.

My eyes widen, and my heart stops. She wouldn't ask me if she wasn't desperate for relief. She's made it clear how much she hates it when I knock her out. The lack of control makes it impossible for her to handle when she wakes back up.

"No, I don't have any on me."

She lifts her head a little and turns to look at me, her eyes imploring me for solace.

"Please, I'm begging you, please help me. Knock me out. Make me forget. Make the pain go away. I can't stand it."

I swallow hard, uncomfortable with the way she's looking at me when I know there is nothing I can do to alleviate her pain.

"You can dig through my pockets if it makes you feel better, but I don't have any of the drugs on me."

Her tears stream down her face as she realizes she's going to have to wait for painkillers.

"Make the pain stop. Please. I know you know how."

I've seen plenty of people in pain before. Hell, I've caused most people as much or more suffering than she is currently dealing with. I've heard their cries for me to bring them relief. And the only way I ever did was with a bullet through their head.

She looks at my pants and her hands claw at my waist searching for the gun she knows is stored there.

Damn it.

She's more fucked up in the leg then I realized. Or being raped by Armas screwed up her head worse than I thought it did.

She wants me to kill her. I won't let her give up so quickly.

"I'm not going to kill you!"

She stops, her face stoic like I slapped her.

"I don't want you to kill me."

"You don't? Then why do you look like you've given up and you are reaching for my gun?"

"Because I want you to knock me out as you did to Saul. Make the pain go away until you get me some pain medication. If you don't, I'm going to chew my leg off to make it stop."

I smirk and don't tell her chewing her leg off would only make the pain unbearable.

"Please," she begs.

Knocking her unconscious will make her suffering worse later. That healing will take longer. My heart is too infatuated with her at the moment to disappoint her, so I keep quiet.

I don't use my gun like she wants me to. It wouldn't take much to knock her out. Not in her current state.

I look over to Maximo, making Eden follows my gaze to him. I wait until her head is turned to him and then I hit her hard across the back of her head. I catch her as her head drops into my arms.

Maximo looks in the rearview mirror, judging me with his eyes, but he doesn't say anything.

I stroke her cheek again, pretending she fell asleep instead of me striking her.

"Is she going to be okay?" Maximo asks.

I nod. "She's going to be better than okay."

"Do we need to go to the hospital first? We can go to Dr. Pietri; he won't question it. He owes us."

I stare down at Eden's leg for a long time. I'm sure it's broken. A woman as strong as Eden wouldn't cry in pain like that at anything less than broken. It's probably shattered.

I know how to treat most wounds and ailments. I've healed most of Arlo's injuries without any issues. I'm not sure if I can repair Eden's leg if it is broken in more than one place and requires surgery.

She could never walk properly again if I don't take her to the hospital.

But I can't. I don't want to give her up. She may think I'm her savior at the moment, but I'm not. I'm still a monster.

"No. Take us home."

Maximo doesn't question me again. He knows the decision I made might lead to her death and he doesn't care. Eden is mine to do with what I want. I stole her. Saving her was only to reclaim her as mine, not because I cared or have a heart. She'll realize soon enough when she'll never be able to walk again. At least I won't have to worry about her running away from me.

9

EDEN

MY EYES FLICKER wide as the sharp pain in my leg wakes me up. My head is pounding, telling me not to dare move my head off the pillow. I've been drugged enough times now to know the familiar feeling. Although, this time it's different. Achier than before.

Matteo.

He's hovering over my leg; his hands gloved as he inspects it. He stops when he sees I'm awake. He takes the gloves off and tosses them to the floor as he sits on the edge of the bed.

"How are you feeling?"

"Like I was in a car accident and raped."

He winces when I say the word rape. I don't understand why he would care. That's why he left me with Armas in the first place, so he would rape me and do the dirty work Matteo was incapable of doing.

"So you remember what happened?"

I close my eyes as the images start flooding back. Me slamming my car into a tree, Armas taking me to his place and raping me, Matteo rescuing me, and then striking me in the head as I asked.

I rub my head on the back and find the bump that has formed.

He narrows my eyes. "Still happy I knocked you out?"

"Yes," I say, despite the agony I'm in now.

He turns from my eyes to give my leg his attention again.

"It's bad, isn't it?" I ask.

He doesn't respond. Instead, he moves down the length of the bed until he's resting next to my leg.

"Can you move your toes?"

My eyes widen at his request. I don't want even to try to move a single part of my leg.

"That's what I thought." He peers back into my eyes trying to tell me something he won't tell me with his words.

I swallow hard as a lump creeps up my throat. My mouth runs dry as Matteo stares at me like I'm the most important thing in his world.

"It's broken."

I bite my lip to keep from smiling. He thinks he's delivered me bad news, but it isn't something I didn't already know. And telling me I have a broken bone is nothing when I was just violated by a man. Had his mouth on my skin. His cock inside me.

"I guessed that."

He nods.

"Can it be fixed?" I ask, hoping he will offer to take me to the hospital or at least bring a doctor to me. For one, it gives me a tiny chance at escaping from Matteo. Although, at the moment, I don't feel like running. Him rescuing me from my nightmare gave me a little bit of hope and respect for him. And two, I would love to have a working leg again, and the only way that can happen is with a doctor's help.

"Yes, but it's going to be painful." He gives me a warning look.

My heart thumps wildly in my chest as I bask in his eyes. I could get lost in them forever.

I shake my head. What's happening to me? I must be feeling guilty for him saving me, that's it.

"A doctor?"

He shakes his head. "No, your leg doesn't need surgery. It was a clean break. It needs realigning, the wound cleaned up and sewed shut, and plenty of rest. Your body will do the rest."

I stare at him wide-eyed. It's the second time he's shocked me with his knowledge of medical information. But I don't know whether I believe him.

"Do you trust me?"

I smirk.

He grins. "That's a no."

I nod.

He turns his attention to my leg.

"But I don't have much of a choice, do I? Either trust you or die."

His face scrunches like he smelled something rotten "Yes, you don't have an option but to trust me."

"Okay then." My eyes flutter down at my leg that looks rotten. I've seen worse at crime scenes, but it still isn't pleasant to look at.

He puts on some gloves and sits on the chair he was sitting on to exam my leg before I woke up. I notice the small table filled with gauze, needles, tweezers, and viles of medications.

"I need to realign the bone as best as I can to help your tibia and fibula heal. Then I will clean the wound and stitch it up before attaching a stent to your leg to keep it from moving."

I nod. His words make sense, but it isn't any more reassuring.

"It's going to hurt. Worse than before.

I swallow hard.

"I can give you some numbing shots to your leg, but it will

only work on the surface. Or I can knock you out again with the drugs, so you don't feel anything until I'm done."

"Also so I don't remember anything either."

He nods. His eyes glare into mine waiting for my decision. Before I would have said give me the drugs. Make the pain go away. Make me forget.

But now, I need to be awake. I need to watch what he does to my leg because if he fucks it up, I want to remember what he did when I finally make it to a doctor.

"Give me the local injection."

He doesn't wait for me to tell him I'm sure I don't want to be unconscious. He takes the needle and carefully jabs it into my shin.

It burns slightly and then warms as the liquid fills my skin. He moves the needle to several different places, always slowing down his movements as the needle pierces my skin. I don't know why he cares if it hurts me. He could be using this against me, to torture me to find out where Nina is, but for some reason, he isn't.

He sets the needle back down on the table next to him and then gives me a look that tells me to brace myself.

I fist the sheets I'm lying on. My heart races but not in anticipation of the pain. It races when his hands touch my skin.

"Tell me something about yourself. What do you do for a living? Where is your favorite place to travel? What are your hobbies?"

My mouth drops open. He can't seriously care about any of the answers to those questions.

He waits. No longer touching me or preparing any of his supplies.

I sigh. "I'm a prosecutor. I deal mostly with murder and rape cases. I prosecute the bad guys and lock them away forever."

He smirks.

"I don't have a favorite place to travel. I've turned into a bit of a homebody since everything that happened with Nina. And my hobbies, I used to enjoy paint—"

He rips my leg off. I know it. The pain sears through my leg and then cascades through my body like a hurricane does a city. Shattering everything in its path and leaving nothing left untouched. My entire body is screaming for relief from whatever trauma he caused. I shouldn't have trusted him.

"Motherfucker!" I scream as I bend down to grab my leg, hoping to bring it some comfort. The spots return over my eyes, and my head is so light I'm afraid it's going to drift away from my body.

"Eden, breathe."

I can't.

The voice is crazy if it thinks I can focus on anything as silly as breathing. I can't exist.

Hands rest on my shoulder and chest as I'm gently pushed back down on the pillows behind me.

"Take a deep breath," the voice commands, again more sternly.

I can't. Why can't the voice get that?

"In...," his hands press against my chest reminding my lungs to breath. The traitors take a breath.

"Now out..." his hands guide my lungs again as I slowly exhale.

"In..." I take a breath in.

"And out..."

I open my eyes that I didn't realize I had shut and the pain is still there, but manageable. I don't feel like I'm about to die anymore, more like slow torture that may never stop.

"Tha—" I stop. I'm not going to thank him.

He slinks back from me to his chair. "I hoped taking your

mind off what I was about to do would help. Apparently, I was wrong."

I bite my lip.

"The worst part is over. I'll rinse out the wound and then close it with stitches. The novocaine I gave you earlier should make it, so you hardly feel a thing."

I nod.

He begins to work, cleaning out the wound, flushing it with a clear liquid. When he gets the needle out, I close my eyes and grab the sheets again, preparing for a sharp sting. It never comes.

I open my eyes, shocked as I watch him thread the needle through my skin as easily as he would cloth. He's done this before. He's too experienced not to have.

"I can't feel a thing."

His lips curl up a little, in what could be a smile if it wasn't for this menacing glare.

"I used to stitch my brother up on an almost weekly basis. I got skilled at it. Now I'm always working on one of the guy's wounds. It beats paying a doctor's bill every other week, and most of the time, the wounds couldn't wait until we got them to the doctor anyway."

I continue to watch him sew up my leg. Not sure what to say or how to feel. My emotions are all over the place. *Should I be thankful? Angry? Upset?*

I feel everything and more.

He finally stops sewing and leans back to take a look at his work.

"If it isn't significantly better in a week, I'll take you to the doctor myself."

I'm shocked at his words. "Thank you," I say without thinking.

His mouth drops open.

Moments pass while we both sit staring at each other without speaking, hardly breathing. I have no doubt now he will keep his word and take me to the doctor if my leg doesn't heal. But he's done such a good job I'm not sure I can even hope for that to happen. Even if I were to go to a doctor, I have little hope for escape.

He clears his throat. "I'm going to attach this stent to your leg to help keep the bone in the correct position and to remind you not to move your leg."

I nod and watch as he removes his gloves before he attaches the stent to the side of my leg with gauze. His hands are rough and calloused as they graze my skin causing tiny goosebumps to pop up.

When he's finished, he places a pillow under my leg so that it's raised. Then he walks behind him to the closet and comes back with a thick blanket to drape over me.

I gulp when he stops just inches from my body.

"You should get some rest. I'll bring you some food and more pain pills soon."

I nod, not willing to say thank you twice. Not to him.

He turns and walks away. And the ache deep in my stomach grows stronger. I don't need any other physical comforts right now. He's made me entirely comfortable on his bed. The physical pain is all but a distant memory. But I still have needs, questions that haven't been answered, and I won't be able to get any rest without him answering.

"Why did you save me?" I blurt out.

He pauses and turns his head, but not his entire body.

"Because you weren't Armas' to take."

"Why didn't you rape me?"

He hesitates. "Who says I won't?"

I swallow. Because he would have already raped me if that

was his plan. He couldn't even if he wanted to. No man that would spend that much time fixing my leg would hurt me.

I narrow my eyes and firm my stare. "You won't."

He laughs, and it sends chills down my arms, the only part of me not covered by the covers. "Don't mistake me for someone who cares about you. I don't. I'm cursed with the ability to heal, that's all. And you're mine. I wasn't about to let another man touch you. Don't think I won't rape you, I will. Unlike Armas, I prefer my woman to have the ability to fight back."

"What happened to Armas? Will he try to come after me again?"

"No."

His lips are tight, his jaw set as he speaks, but he doesn't offer me up a further explanation.

"I'm going to need more assurances than that."

He frowns as he runs his hand through his hair and finally faces me squarely on. His eyes peer into mine, and I stop breathing again. My body reacting to him unwillingly.

"He's dead," he says, deadpanned like he was telling me the weather.

"How?"

"I killed him. Beat him to death for touching what is mine. I'll make sure everyone else in his family is either dead or made to believe Armas deserved to be killed. No one will ever take you again. You're mine."

My nipples harden, my lips part, and I feel a stirring deep in my belly begging to feel the erection I swear I see when I glance down at his crotch. If he notices me staring he doesn't comment. Instead, he turns and strides out of the room, not bothering to tie me up or even lock the door. I couldn't get far anyway, not with my leg the way it is even if I tried to crawl.

My body continues to ache, and I throb between my legs, needing relief.

The trauma from the car accident and rape must have fucked with my mind. That or the painkillers are making me delusional. There is no way I want to fuck Matteo. No way is that ever happening. I don't care if he's turned into the world's greatest saint. There is nothing he can do to make me forgive him for what he's done to me.

10

——

MATTEO

Fuck this woman.

Eden's turned her charm on, and I don't know how to stop my cock from falling for her ridiculous mind games. She thinks she can manipulate me into giving her back her freedom.

She's wrong.

There is only one way for her to earn back her freedom. By telling me where I can find Nina. Otherwise, I'll keep her trapped forever.

11

EDEN

Four weeks.

That's how long it's been since the rape. That's how long it's been since my life changed forever.

My leg healing was the easy part. After watching Matteo work, as I suspected, it has healed magnificently. The swelling has gone down. The skin has fused together where it was once open. And from what I can tell, my bones have begun the long road of healing as well.

My mind is haunted. Armas may be dead, but he still has control over me. I don't sleep without having a nightmare of him raping me. I jump at every loud noise or movement. I hate being alone with any man, even the servants who are only bringing me food.

Matteo hasn't visited. Not once since the night, he saved me. The staff and men have brought me food, books, and pain pills, and have told me he's busy working. But I know it's a lie. He's staying away because I wasn't the only one who changed when I was raped. He felt something too. *What? I'm not sure, but it changed.*

I hear the familiar creak of the door as it opens. I expect one of the men, Maximo, or Dierk, or Paul to be coming in to check on me. One of them normally does around this time of day. The interaction is always brief; I'm sure Matteo gave them orders not to stay long. But it's at least something to look forward to each day.

I hope it's Dierk. He lingers the longest and will sometimes make jokes or tell me about the outside world. Mainly the weather and a few current events, but it's heaven when I don't even get to look out the window or step a foot out of bed. I should try walking soon, but I need help. And I don't trust any of the men to help me. Not to mention I need a bath, a change of clothes, and a walk outside to remember what fresh air smells like again.

My jaw unhinges when Matteo walks into the room. He doesn't look at me. He seems lost in thought as he pulls his gray T-shirt up over his head. My eyes travel over his chest, six-pack abs, and down the v that disappears into his running shorts.

My mouth waters, both from glimpsing his body and from jealousy. He can run outside, while the only thing I can do is turn over in bed.

I clear my throat, and he stops, examining at me like he forgot I was still in his room. Or I exist at all. His lips tighten together, he's going to go about his business, go shower, or whatever he came up here to do, instead of engaging with me.

"Have you tried walking yet?" he asks, surprising me by speaking.

"No." I plead with my heart to stop racing in my chest. He's just a naked man. I'm excited because it's been so long since I've experienced the pleasure and release that comes with a great fuck. That's all.

He takes the shirt in his hand and wipes the sweat from his forehead.

"You should be able to walk by now. If not, we should call a doctor out here."

"I haven't exactly had too many opportunities to walk. I don't trust if I try to get out of bed by myself, that I won't fall and hurt myself all over."

He raises an eyebrow as he edges closer to the bed.

"You? Afraid of falling?" He chuckles. "I didn't think you were scared of anything, let alone a little fall."

I narrow my eyes as the anger rolls through my body. I let it escape though, as swiftly as it came. I'll prove Matteo wrong.

I throw the covers off my body and reach down and pull the gauze off my leg holding the stent in place so that I can move my leg. I scoot to the edge of the bed until my legs dangle over the edge and without thinking, I place my legs on the floor and stand up.

He claps in a slow, teasing sort of way when I stand.

My cheeks blush red, and sweat covers my brow, now more determined than ever to prove to him I'm not afraid. I take a step forward, and gradually transfer my weight to my newly healed leg. I think I have it when my knee buckles and I fall.

His arms catch me as my face and hands are about to make contact with the ground.

"Well, at least you proved you aren't frightened."

I snarl.

He laughs again. His laughter soon turns solemn as he holds me up under my arms and I clutch his shoulders.

"Try again."

I take a step forward, and this time, with his help, I'm ready to put some weight on my leg. Not enough that I'm able to walk on my own, but enough to confirm my leg is healing and gives me enough faith I will soon make a full recovery, at least where my leg is concerned.

I grin so widely I'm sure my lips reach my eyes.

Matteo grins too, in his own way. It looks as much like a smirk as it does a genuine grin.

"Take me to the bathroom. I could use a bath."

"I was going to say you stink."

I hit him playfully, and he chuckles. It's weird to be bantering like this. We seem normal. Like any two friends, or at least, close acquaintances would.

"Bathroom. Now."

He smirks, and we make our slow trek to the bathroom taking far longer than I would like.

When my feet hit the cold tile, I gaze up at the tall shower standing beyond the entrance. The shower is impressive with five different shower heads and glass surrounding all of the walls. I don't have a hope of using it again anytime soon.

"Help me into the bath. I can remove my clothes and turn the water on after you leave."

He raises an eyebrow. "No, you either strip now, or you don't bathe at all. I should receive a reward for helping you get this far. It's been a few weeks since I've glimpsed your naked body."

I blush when I remember he's already seen me naked plenty of times before.

I pull my shirt off and push my underwear down.

Matteo's eyes don't go to my body like I was expecting. Instead, his eyes stay on mine.

I raise an eyebrow.

"I thought you wanted to ogle at my body."

"I do."

I swallow hard as my breath catches in my throat and my body shivers from the cold.

He runs my arms up and down instinctively, warming me.

He's different. Kinder somehow.

His eyes drift down my body, and I bite my lip squirming a little in his arms as he studies my curves.

"You do not need to be embarrassed. You have an amazing body, even if it's a little beat up at the moment."

"I'm not embarrassed."

"Then why are you squirming and your cheeks are blushed?"

I frown. "Because I'm naked standing in front of a man who kidnapped me. I think I'm allowed to blush."

He holds my hand, keeping me upright while he leans over the tub and turns the water on to hot. The steam from it begins to fill the room.

We are both silent for a moment while we wait for the bath to fill. I don't like the silence. In the quiet, that's when Armas creeps in making me unsafe. So I don't let the silence stretch like I usually would.

"Why do you always keep the blinds closed? I've been living in a cave for weeks. I asked the men to open them for me, but it was one of the things they wouldn't do for me no matter how much I asked them to."

He chuckles. "A misunderstanding. They think I like the darkness. I often sit in my office with all the blinds closed. Every time I've allowed anyone into my personal space, it is always jet-black."

"Why?"

"Because that's what I want them to see. I want them to think I'm nothing but a monster that lives in the night. I do like the dark when I need to focus and think, which happens to be often. I'll make sure the blinds are open from now on."

My mouth is dry as he speaks. I nod instead of saying thanks.

He reaches over and turns off the faucet. I glance over at the tub filled almost to the brim with water. I take a step toward the tub, forgetting I can't walk on my own, and my leg gives out.

Matteo holds me up though. He's always holding me up. *Saving me.*

He holds my arms as I carefully take the two steps over to the tub and step in. He doesn't let me go until I've sunk into the warm water. I close my eyes as the liquid warms my body and starts melting the dirt caked on me. Along with anything remaining of Armas.

I keep my eyes closed for a long time trying to push Armas out.

I can't.

The warm water can't do it.

I should wash and get clean. Maybe, being clean will do the trick. I open my eyes and Matteo is still standing there.

"You just going to stand there and creepily watch me?"

He removes his shorts, and my heart stops. He's going to join me.

My eyes try to stay on his chest, but I can't help but sneak a peek at his cock again. His cock is hard and thick, wanting me.

My cheeks flush as I breathe and tear my eyes from his erection.

I can't.

I don't know what's wrong with me; it's like I've never seen a cock before.

"Are you just going to stare at me creepily? Because I'd be more than okay if you were."

I attempt to smile like I'm not bothered, but he knows me well enough to realize the smile is a lie. By now my cheeks are bright red as I finally meet his gaze.

His face is smiling brightly at me. For once, he doesn't seem as serious or dangerous. He seems human.

He starts walking toward me though, and I'm not sure I want him in the tub with me. My nipples may have hardened, and my sex may be aching for his cock, but it's not what I want. I don't want to have sex with a man as cruel as him.

At the last second, he turns and steps into the all-glass shower, flipping the water on.

I exhale.

He's not going to touch me.

I try to ignore him as I take the bar of soap and begin scrubbing my body thoroughly. My eyes fluttering up to his naked ass any chance I get to take a glance without him noticing.

He doesn't glimpse my way though. He showers like I'm not two feet away and naked.

I've washed every piece of skin I can find on my body, and I still don't feel relaxed, though it helps the ache in my leg. I'm clean again. I should be calm, but I'm not.

I dunk my head under the water washing off the last pieces of dirt. I don't have any shampoo to wash my hair, but dunking it in the soapy water does enough.

When I resurface, Matteo is standing over me. Naked. His body dripping with water.

My bottom lip quivers, both terrified and excited. *What do I want from him?* I don't know. *What does he want from me?* He doesn't know either.

He extends his hand to me. I take it, and he pulls me up. He hands me a towel, and I take it wrapping it around my body. I lift my leg to step out, but he scoops me into his arms, a motion I've started to get used to and enjoy.

"I don't want you overworking your leg. I'll teach you some exercises you can start doing to increase your leg strength slowly, so you don't injure it again."

I nod, still unable to speak. Nothing but a towel separate my body from his.

He takes me back to his bed.

"Why do you always put me in your bed instead of one of the other bedrooms? Why give up your bed to me?"

He gently lays me down as he stands over me, not at all embarrassed he's naked. Not that he should be.

"Because I want you in my bed."

He says it so simply like it's obvious. He grabs a pillow and places it under my leg, lifting my leg up. Then he reaches for the towel clutched to my body. He snatches it out of my grip and pulls it off my body, exposing me again.

My breathing speeds when the cold air hits, touching my warm skin. I close my eyes making an effort to calm my breathing to keep Matteo from thinking I'm into him.

Armas.

Armas' face smirks down at me. His cock resting at my entrance.

"No."

He pushes in any way. His cock burns inside me, ripping my insides apart as he rapes me. My body isn't *mine* anymore. It's *his.* He bites down on my nipple, and I cry. It hurts too much.

I can't escape him. It all hurts, but having his cock inside me is too much. His thrusts never end, and my body can't take the intrusion much longer.

"No. Please, stop."

He doesn't. Not until his cum is spilling into me. It feels like lava. I want it out.

"Eden," Matteo's voice calls out, saving me from my nightmare, as he saved me from that day.

I open my eyes, and his arms are on my arms, concern in his eyes.

"Eden, what's happening? What's wrong?"

I pant, not wanting to talk about it. Maybe if I do, I'll feel better. Armas will finally be gone.

"Armas. I can't escape him. Every time I close my eyes he's there. Taunting me. I can't stop reliving that day. I can't stop reliving him raping me. His dick tearing me open. His teeth ripping my skin. His cum—"

"Wait, he came inside you?" His eyes widen.

I swallow needing to face my fears. "Yes, he came. He was close to coming again when you stopped him."

His eyes drop to my body like he's seeing me for the first time. He notices the tiny scars still on my breasts where he bit me. And he sees my sex that is no longer mine. It's Armas'.

I don't think I can ever have sex again. It hurts to think about it.

I touch his face because he looks like he needs comforting. His somber eyes come back to mine.

"What do you need?"

I shrug. "I don't know."

"Come on. There has to be something I can do to help. Bring you ice cream, take you to a movie, give you a massage. Something to help."

The word leaves my mouth without understanding what I want myself. "You."

His face juts back like he doesn't believe what I said.

"I'm sorry. I didn't mean it…"

I grab the covers to cover myself up along with the embarrassment. His hand pushes them down before he grabs my chin and turns it toward him.

"You meant what you said."

I nod.

"You want me to make the memories go away?"

"Yes, it's stupid. It probably won't even work. You can't make the memories go away. You can't replace them. I don't even think if I was in love with you could you make the memories go away."

"I can make the nightmares go away." He says it like he believes what he is saying, and it almost makes me believe him.

I glance down at his rippling chest, preventing my eyes from going lower. I can feel him grinning at me.

"And you can't deny you want a taste of my body. What hurt would it do to try?"

I swallow. *A lot.* If it feels like he's raping me, instead of pleasuring me, I'm not sure how I will survive. I'll die of insanity if I have to deal with both Armas and Matteo haunting me. Matteo has done some bad things, but nothing like Armas. This could make it worse.

He sighs and starts to get up sensing my hesitation. He's going to leave me alone with my nightmares. I can't handle that.

I grab his neck and pull him to me, kissing him firmly on the lips. His mouth tastes delicious, and he smells heavenly like a musky soap he used in the shower. I pull away, gently trying to give my brain time to think, because there is no way I'm going to be getting any thinking done with my lips locked with his.

I keep my eyes closed as I rest my forehead against his. "I want you. Fuck me, make me forget. I trust you, don't lose that trust. It might be the only way you have a chance to get Nina back."

He exhales like he's judging my words.

"Promise me you won't hurt me. You won't rape me. If I say stop, you'll stop."

I open my eyes to wait for his response, needing to see his eyes as he says it.

He doesn't say anything. Instead, he grabs my neck and kisses me again profoundly. His tongue sweeps into my mouth, and I forget about waiting for him to promise not to hurt me. I just feel. His tongue dancing with mine as our lips and moans collide.

He pushes me back as he climbs on top of me, our lips still locked together. I close my eyes and immediately realize it's a mistake.

"Stay with me, pretty girl," he moans against my lips. "I don't want you crediting someone else with my sexy moves."

He grins against my lips as he says it and I open my eyes, smiling a little back.

We both keep our eyes open as we continue kissing; our eyes moving deeper into each other's souls as we kiss. His eyes tell me to trust him, though he hasn't promised he wouldn't hurt me yet. I don't have a choice but to trust him.

Even if I did have an option, I would still be here, trusting him. I would choose anything over my nightmares.

His eyes change. That's what I notice first, and then a mischievous grin as he pulls away.

"What?" I ask, laughing, because it's clear he has thought of something funny.

"Nothing."

I raise an eyebrow, but he never answers me.

"Take a deep breath," he says.

I'm suspicious, but I slowly inhale, trying my best to trust him. He grabs my hands and shoves them over my head in one fluid motion while he kisses my neck.

"Matteo," I cry out, not liking my hands not having control. Even though being able to move my arms wouldn't be enough to stop Matteo if he wanted to rape me.

He kisses my neck, and I come unglued from the way he is sweetly kissing, lapping over my neck, making all the nerves in my body tingle.

"Tell me you don't like it. Tell me you want me to stop."

I moan loudly as his kissing turns to nibbling and then biting.

"Stop," I moan, but my cry isn't compelling.

He grins against my neck.

"I don't believe you."

I swallow.

His mouth drops to my hardened nipple, and I freeze thinking of the last time a man's teeth were there. How rough and terrifying it felt and how it was the final step before he plunged inside me.

He doesn't hesitate at my anxiety. He takes my nipple into his mouth, swirling his tongue around before biting, hard.

I yelp at the sudden pain, but it's not pain. Not like when Armas bit me, although I'm sure they both bit me equally hard. There's a difference; one I can't figure out.

"Tell me to stop," he says again, with his teeth still tightened against my nipple.

"Stop," I say, but it's softer than the first.

He moves to the other nipple, giving it the same treatment, my back arches against his lips, wanting him to take my nipple into his mouth deeper, to bite harder.

I feel his cock against my stomach as I arch my back, diving into my belly, pressing harder, as his erection grows. It should scare me, the feeling of how large his cock is growing. He wants me, badly. And if I genuinely begged him to stop, he wouldn't. He would hurt me worse than Armas. Both physically and emotionally.

"Grab the bars on the bed," he commands as he pushes my arms up.

I do.

"Don't let go," he orders, his eyes threatening before he releases my hands. I keep my hands on the bars like they are tied up, and I can't move them, though I can.

His dark eyes dip down as his lips travel down my neck, breasts, and stomach. His tongue tasting my skin, sending chills through my body and an ache I'm not familiar with deep in my belly.

I close my eyes, trying to gulp down my fears that are sneaking in. I know what happens next. Next, his cock drives in me. He's not a nice man. He's not going to wait for my body to adjust. He's not going to wait for me to come or even attempt to make me feel good. He's going to get what he wants and hopefully not hurt me too badly in the process.

I hold my breath, and Armas starts creeping back in while I wait for his erection to be pushing at my entrance.

Instead, I feel something much lighter and wetter. It traces slowly over my lips between my legs as hands gently push my thighs wider. His tongue laps over me and my eyes fly open to watch him.

I've never had a man lick me so intimately like he is. Most men I've been with use their fingers to get me off. It's ecstasy. Any man I'm with after this will be required to lick me if he wants me to have sex with him.

His tongue continues over my folds until he finds my clit. He flicks it fast as my juices fill my sex. He licks them up, spreading them over my clit as I moan and arch my back.

I pull at my hands wishing I could touch him. Wanting my hands free to play with his thick hair.

His eyes tease me as he looks up at me and then he plunges his fingers inside me while he keeps licking my exterior.

I expect pain. But it's nothing but pleasure. An experience I haven't felt with a man before.

His fingers slip in and out quickly while my legs begin to tighten around his head and my eyes roll back in my head. My toes curl as he continues licking me and I scream.

"Jesus," I cry as I come on his fingers, his tongue not slowing down until he's pulled all of my orgasms out of me.

My body needs to rest, but he doesn't let me rest. Not until he gets what he wants. His fingers pull out of me, and I feel my legs being pushed wider as he kneels between them, pushing his cock nearer my entrance.

He doesn't wait for permission. He pushes his cock inside me, making me cry out from the intrusion.

But I don't feel pain. Not one drop of it. My eyes widen as he smirks, holding my legs but not moving while he waits for me to realize how much my body is aching for him.

He raises an eyebrow, asking if I'm ready and I bite my lip in response.

"I got you, beautiful."

He rocks in and out of me, and my body comes alive like it had been dormant all these years, waiting until his cock reached inside and brought me back to life. I can feel everything. Every magnificent craving inside my body. Need. Excitement. Lust. It all takes over, pushing out the negative emotions I've been living with for months. Far too long to understand what's happening.

I forget about everything except being here with him. I'm willingly having sex with my kidnapper and enjoying it. *What's wrong with me? And why didn't I make him fuck me sooner?*

He thrusts, and my body responds.

"Oh my god!" I cry when he rocks deeper, hitting a sweet spot I didn't realize existed within my body.

"Tell me to stop."

I chuckle as he brings my body higher. There is no way I want this to stop.

"Tell me to stop!" he demands, his voice harsh.

"Stop," I whisper.

"Louder. Scream it."

"Stop!" I scream, and my body comes at the same time he does. Pouring his seed into my body.

I close my eyes and then open them with a goofy grin on my face while Matteo's cock still rests inside me. When I finally catch my breath again, I ask, "Why did you want me to yell stop?"

He pulls out, and the emptiness is instant. I want him again. Now.

He stares at my hands, and I realize I can let go. I'd forgotten I could let go, that they weren't tied above my head.

"Because I wanted you to realize you have more power than you think. You have control over your body. You have control of your memories. Only you have the power to get rid of the nightmares."

I swallow hard, listening to his words. He stands up, and pulls the covers over me.

"Now sleep."

"Wait."

He stops.

"Sleep with me. You're right, I have the power to make sure my nightmares don't come back, but your arms holding me might help."

I think he's going to say no. In fact, I expect it. He doesn't speak.

He walks around the bed, pulls the covers down, and climbs in still naked. He reaches down to my leg, making sure it's propped up on a pillow, and wraps his arms around me. I close my eyes, and for the first time in a long time, I don't think I will dream of Armas. Because my body is consumed with Matteo.

MATTEO

I WAKE up with Eden's arms wrapped around me. My body is far too warm, but I won't dare move her. I like her skin against mine too much to care about something as silly as being too hot.

What's gotten into me?

I've become a wuss in a matter of moments. Ever since I rescued Eden from Armas. Although, I didn't arrive there fast enough like I thought I did. I thought I stole her back before the worst happened. I was wrong.

I think I helped her now though. She didn't wake up in the night. No thrashing or apparent night terrors. And she's still asleep now, despite it being well past eight in the morning. We've been sleeping for over ten hours.

I saved her from Armas, but she should be equally terrified of me. I thought fucking her again would stir up the memory of me raping her.

It didn't.

I'm not sure what I want more. Her to remember me raping her and be afraid of me, or her to forget about it forever.

Her sultry eyes eventually open and she grins when she gapes at me.

"Good morning," she says, smiling like I'm her favorite person in the world.

I stroke her hair automatically. "Morning."

She bites her lip.

"How are you feeling?" I ask.

"Good. Really, good. I didn't have any nightmares."

I nod.

We both stare at each other, not sure where to take this from here. For one, I need food and coffee in my system to think straight, and then I have to get to work. I can deal with Eden later.

"You hungry? I can have one of the servants bring you some breakfast. I don't think you should walk all the way to the dining room until your leg is further along in the healing process."

"Eat with me here."

I raise an eyebrow. "Why?"

The covers slip, and I'm rewarded with a view of her perky breasts and nipples, which I can still taste in my mouth.

She doesn't cover up. Instead, she blushes.

"I know you aren't the rainbows and hearts kind of guy. I know you are still evil. But I have a proposition for you, and I think we could both use some coffee first."

I frown.

She's still my prisoner. I don't like her thinking she has any power over me. I have the control, not her. But I guess I need to listen to whatever she thinks she gained yesterday so I can put her back in her place.

I step out of bed, sensing her gaze on my ass.

I smirk.

She still wants me. I walk over to my dresser and pull out a dark pair of boxer briefs and put them on. I walk to my closet, pull a pair of sweatpants out, and put them on before walking back out.

She's biting her lip when she gawks at me.

"Coffee no sugar, extra crispy bacon, and eggs sunny side up?" I ask, although I know it's what she wants.

She nods with a grin.

Damn that grin. It's beautiful. Just looking at it makes me happy.

I dash down the stairs to put in our order and impatiently wait before I carry both of our breakfasts on a tray upstairs.

When I return, I place the tray on Eden's lap before climbing into bed next to her and taking my coffee off. I start drinking it while I wait for her ridiculous proposal I'm going to say no to.

She takes her time and drinks her coffee while nibbling on the bacon on her plate. I made sure the cooks prepared plenty of bacon for her since it's her favorite part of breakfast.

"So you going to tell me what your proposition is or what? I have a lot of work I should be doing."

She sighs and twirls the piece of bacon between her finger.

"Fine. I would like to make a deal with you."

"I figured that. What kind of deal?"

She sucks in a breath. She's nervous. Her hand is shaking slightly, and her breathing has sped up.

"The kind where I get more sex like last night."

I laugh. "Nina tried the same thing. You can't seduce me and get me to fall in love with you to help you escape. If I fell in love with you, it would only make you more trapped. Remember how it turned out for Nina?"

She blushes. "I'm not trying to convince you to fall in love with me. That's not what I want."

"What do you want then?"

"I want more sex like last night. Sex that makes me feel good but in control. I don't want to be raped. I want the kind that makes me feel stronger afterward."

I shake my head. "Not going to happen. Last night was a one-time thing. I did it because I don't want another guy in your head. Now I can talk to you. Question you. Torture you. Or rape you without worrying you are thinking about any man but me."

She laughs, but it's nervous. "You won't rape me."

I raise an eyebrow and inch toward her, watching as the breathing in her chest becomes weaker. "I won't?"

"No, you won't. I believe your story. You love Nina or are still obsessed with her or whatever your feelings are toward her. I believe that to be true. If you want to have a chance at having Nina back at the end of all of this, then you won't rape me. You know she would never forgive you for it. She'll forgive you for kidnapping me, but not rape. That's how I know you won't do it."

I frown. "Fine. But that doesn't mean I'll fuck you. I have plenty of women at my disposal to fuck when I want."

She smirks. "You might. But they aren't who you want. You want Nina. And me. Admit it."

"No. I like hurting women. Raping them. I don't fuck often. Not for a woman's pleasure."

"Fuck me, and for every time I let you fuck me, you hold off looking for Nina for one week."

I narrow my eyes chuckling softly. "That sounds like you get two things you want and I get nothing."

Her eyes hide behind her lashes. "I said fuck me how you want. Rough, dirty, filthy. Do what you want to me, and if I don't stop you, then Nina gets one more week of freedom."

"You think fucking you last night was that good for me?"

"Yes," she breathes.

She knows me too well. I don't understand it, but fucking her last night made my top five all-time fucks. Nina, making up the other four.

"I'll never get Nina that way. Why would I follow your plan? Why wouldn't I just hurt you until you talk?"

She smiles, her face light and airy because she thinks she's won. "Because you love Nina. That's why you won't hurt me because you can't hurt her. I believe you love her. I think your love might be a lost cause. But it's also the only way you can ever have her. I won't talk if you torture me. As you can see, that hasn't been working out well for you so far. I might talk if you gain my trust. Show me I'm right in my realization that you love her and will protect her. You are the better man for her and I'll tell you where she is."

I stare into her brown eyes intently. She's lying. Nothing will ever make her tell me where Nina is. Or at least that's what she thinks. I can think of several ways to get her to talk, now that I know her better.

Now, though, I don't want Nina. I need to deal with the aftermath of Armas' family. I need to make sure Clive and Erick are taken care of. That they won't come after us as soon as I get Nina back. Until then, I don't want to know where Nina is. It puts her at risk.

I won't shake her hand or promise her a deal though. That way when I want the agreement to end, it can, without renegotiating or breaking my promise. It will be like last night where I promise with my body and that has to be enough for her for now.

I want to fuck her. And she's right I don't want to deal with Nina finding out I raped Eden repeatedly. But I will, if that's what it takes to get her to talk to me.

This way I get to rape her with her permission. I don't plan on going easy on Eden. I plan on making her pay for not telling me where Nina is. Because I'm more desperate to get her back than she knows.

"Finish eating your breakfast," I say. Other than the one piece of bacon, she has hardly touched any of her food.

She bats her eyelashes at me as she lets the covers fall

further down her body until only her pussy and legs are covered.

"Or...we could..." She grins, licking her lip.

I shake my head as I ignore her and continue eating my breakfast. I can't help but chuckle, though, when I see her pout out of the corner of my eye.

"Eat. You're going to need your strength."

Her eyes light up like I just told her the most exciting news. She will regret the deal she made with me. Because last night was nothing. I enjoyed fucking her, but it's not what I crave. I seek the darkness, just like I do during the day.

I drink the rest of my coffee, watching her as she digs into her food as frantically as she did after going without for several days when Dierk fed her. I watched the security tapes last week and saw her with him. She used her big eyes and seductive smile to get Dierk to do whatever she wanted. She's not going to be able to do the same with me.

She finishes her food and looks at me with eager eyes.

I glance down at my coffee, letting her know she can't rush me.

It doesn't stop her from trying. She leans into me, her lips purring, begging me to make her feel as good as last night.

I slowly, deliberately, drink the rest of my coffee and then set my cup on the tray still in her lap. She practically shoves the tray into my hands as I set it down on the nightstand next to me.

"So eager," I mumble.

She reaches her hand to grab my neck and kiss me. I seize her hand, stopping her. Her mouth parts as she stares at me, holding her wrist a little too tight. I can see the realization hit her. This won't be like last time. This time, I will be taking full advantage of her body.

She takes a deep breath while I plan in my head what I want

from her body. *How do I want her? Tied up? Red? Crying my name? What do I want?*

All of it.

I want it all.

I get out of bed knowing she can't follow me, and it will drive her mad the longer I'm gone. I step into my closet and unhurriedly remove my clothes again. Taking my time and letting the image of her body, naked and tied up for me, sink into my mind. Her body red with stains where her flesh was whipped and beaten. Her eyes shed of tears all but spilled from her pain.

That's what I want. Her defeated and mine. I want her to feel like she did after Armas, but because of me.

I thought I could be kind, but the kindness has dried up.

I walk to the shelf where I keep my ties and pull two off. Usually, I would prefer something much stronger, but this will do for what I have planned.

Finally, when I know her pussy is dripping and her heart has sped to an unmeasurable speed, I step out.

Her eyes mix with concern and arousal as she looks at me.

I glare back. Her eyes reflect more worry than excitement. Her eyes drift down the ties I hold in my hand, and she grips the sheets trying to hide herself again.

"You can't hide from me. Not now."

"I'm not hiding. I made the deal remember?"

"And you are going to regret it."

"Not likely, if it keeps my friend safe for another day."

"And gives you another orgasm, right?"

Her cheeks blush her response. She wants me to fuck her as much as I want to fuck her. She just doesn't want what I have planned.

"This is your last chance to back out. You don't get a safe word. I won't stop once I start. I'll ask you beforehand each time, but once you say yes, that's it."

The fear disappears as I speak. Like my words give her confidence instead of panic.

"Fuck me, Matteo. Do your worst."

"I will."

I snatch the covers and jerk them off until her entire body is exposed and ready at my disposal.

I unroll one of the ties as I storm toward her, my gaze never leaving her and she's fighting back just as strongly, telling me she is ready for anything.

I grab her healing leg, digging my fingers deep into her skin.

She screams at my sudden touch.

My fingers continue holding pressure, loving the sounds she's making.

"You asshole."

I smirk. "Didn't think I would fight fair, did you?"

"No," she growls. "I thought you would slowly transform into a monster, not become it as quickly as I can snap my fingers."

I bend her knee, so her thigh is pressed against her stomach.

She cries again. Her leg hasn't been used to bending that way in weeks.

"I didn't need to transform. I've always been this way."

I clutch her wrist and pull it to her leg before I attach the tie around it.

She takes a deep breath. Trying not to panic. She won't be able to move when I'm done with her. She's going to remain hurting, her leg throbbing how it is, the entire time I fuck her.

I finish tying her hand tightly to her leg; then I jerk her other leg back before I grab her hand and fasten it to her leg with the other tie.

She bites her lip.

"You regretting your decision yet?"

"No, I never regret anything."

I enjoy her confidence. It will make this so much more fun when I beat it out of her.

I take a step back, admiring my work and her body tied up for me. She can't move, and there is no turning back. No words will convince me to stop, not now I've had her.

I disappear again. Needing more tools.

When I return, she's panting as she struggles against the ties, trying to break free. She freezes when she sees what I'm holding in my hand.

She closes her eyes, like that, will help her.

I hold the whip in my hand, letting my fingers tangle in the leather threads that will soon be touching her body. I doubt she has ever felt such a thing before. She would have if Armas had more time with her. But I get to be her first. I get to break her in. I get to make her mine.

"Open your eyes."

"No," she whispers.

"Open your eyes, or I'll make it extra painful."

I want to see her pupils dilate and the fear take over when the leather touches her smooth skin.

She opens them.

"Good girl."

I don't hesitate. I let the whip come down harshly against her ass that is splayed for me.

She yelps, her body swaying as it tries to adjust to the sting.

My eyes roll back as the pain I caused sinks into me, bringing me far too much pleasure.

I strike her again on the other cheek, more forceful than before.

Her yelp turns to a cry, almost a plea, that this is her limit. This is all she can take. Not a millimeter harder.

She hasn't felt anything yet.

I whip her again, this time over the most sensitive bud on her body.

She cries, and I finally see the tears streaking down her cheeks. This is what I want. This is what I crave. To see women in pain, terrified of me. I want them to feel powerless, so I feel more power. I need the darkness.

"Please," she whispers behind her tears. She doesn't say stop. She doesn't dare show she's weak so quickly. But I can still see it. I know it won't take much more for her to say it.

I crack the whip again, hitting her ass again.

Her body lurches from the contact before she rocks gently on her back, trying to calm the sting. My eyes deepen when I'm rewarded with the red mark I've left on her ass. I want more. Something permanent.

I strike her again with all the force I have. More tears spill, but she barely cries this time.

"Had enough?"

She glares at me but doesn't say anything. My cock aches watching her. She might get lucky. I'm usually a patient person, but I can't wait much longer to fuck her. My cock is growing closer to her with every moan from her body.

I hit her again, purposefully striking her pussy, needing her to tell me to stop. Needing to know I'm breaking her. That this feels like I'm taking something from her. Raping her.

She cries loudly, but her cry turns to an enduring groan.

I throw back my arm, coming down with all my strength, expecting this to be the moment she cracks. The moment where her new nightmares form that I caused.

She doesn't cry.

Or scream.

No tears fall.

Instead, she grins before her mouth falls open in ecstasy. A deep growl leaves her throat, and her body opens up more for me to hit her again.

I do.

Her toes curl, and her back arches and she pushes into the strike.

My mouth falls open. She likes the pain. She wants me to hurt her. It turns her on.

And I can't wait any longer.

I grab her ass as I stand on the edge of the bed and pull her to me, my cock plunging into her tight cunt. She's dripping and easily allows me in.

I spank her ass as I drive in and out of her. It only makes her wetter.

"Harder," she cries.

I fuck her harder.

"Deeper."

I fuck her deeper.

I don't know when I gave up control, and she took over, but I don't care. I would give her control every time if it felt this good every time.

I pound into her, loving how her body tightens around me. I lean forward so I can grasp her nipples and twist them between my fingers.

She bites her lip and like it's the most glorious thing I've done.

I stare into her eyes trying to find the woman who was raped by Armas, was so broken only a few hours ago. The woman who would have been equally shattered by me after I raped her, if she had retained her memory.

She's gone.

And in her place is a woman more powerful than any woman I've ever met. She's thriving being tied up, in pain, and in pleasure. She controlled this by making the deal. And in doing so, it gave her power over what she felt as well.

I won't last much longer, though I want this feeling to last forever. It feels far too pleasurable, and I plan on fucking her again as soon as I arrive back from work. And every day until I've had enough.

I move faster about to push my cum deep into her belly when her lips brush against mine.

My eyes fly open as I take the kiss further. My tongue sweeping into her mouth, tangling with hers. I'm not opposed to kissing her, but I wanted to deny her any pleasure. Now that I know that's not possible, why deny myself any?

I kiss her, taking in everything she feels as I fuck her.

"Oh god, Matteo!" she cries as her orgasm escapes her.

"Fuck," I growl as I shoot my load inside her.

Our eyes connect as our orgasms slowly subside. Our bodies wrench as I collapse on top of her. Neither of us understands what the hell happened. We both know that should have terrified her. It should have ripped her to pieces instead of building her back up.

"Why do I crave you?" she asks.

I smirk.

She laughs.

"Because you're fucked up. You like the darkness. The evil you have been fighting all your life is tucked inside, and you just started to let it free. You're no different than me."

13

EDEN

OH MY GOD, the sex.

The fucking sex.

Why does he have to be so good at sex?

The kissing is incredible.

His tongue massages mine in a way that makes me melt every time.

The way his hands grip my body makes me come undone.

And his cock, the way he knows exactly how much my body craves it, along with the sweet sensation of pain. I lose control with him, but also gain it. It doesn't make sense, but it's how I feel.

Sex with Matteo is *life-altering.*

He thought it would break me. Honestly, I thought it would too. I thought I would be flooded with memories of Armas. Or new painful memories with Matteo would be all I could think about.

Matteo is all I can think about. Not the nightmares. Instead, it is sweet, sweet dreams that make me forget everything else. I can't function without thinking about him. All I want is sex.

I'm an addict. One who can't survive without my drug. Sex with him has changed me. I'm not sure if it is for the better.

I feel stronger, but also less in control. I should be focused on getting free and protecting Nina. But all I can think about is sex.

Good thing every time I'm having sex with Matteo, I'm protecting Nina. I'm just not getting any closer to being free.

"Hurry up. You are using all the hot water, and you need to get dressed," Matteo says as he throws the bathroom door open.

I frown as I stand under the steaming water of the shower. I don't want to move out from under the faucet. I love the hot water and showers so much more than baths. I will never take showering for granted again.

"No! I'm enjoying my shower. Leave me alone or join me."

I expect him to join me. He likes the sex as much or more than I do and hasn't passed up an opportunity to fuck me any chance he's gotten in the last month.

His hand reaches into the shower, and he turns the faucet off.

"I mean it. Out now."

I frown. "Why?"

"Because we are going to the ball Armas' family is throwing."

My heart stops. I grab the towel and wrap it around my body not understanding what is happening or why we are just now talking about it.

"His family is still holding a ball even though Armas is dead?"

"Yes, they are arranging it in his honor."

I step out of the shower, keeping the towel wrapped around me snuggly.

"Why are you going?"

"*We*. We are going."

I frown. Matteo's never let me off the property before. The

only time I've left since he kidnapped me was when Armas stole me.

"Why are *we* going?"

He folds his arms across his chest as he leans against the counter.

"Because we are letting his family know Armas deserved to die. We are making sure they understand that."

My stomach flips. "And how does going to the ball help? Couldn't you go talk to them with some of your men?"

He shakes his head. "That's not how things work. Appearances are everything when it comes to rich families."

"Why am I going?" I ask, needing to know the answer, even though I'm excited at the thought of getting out of the house and having a chance to escape.

"Because I need a date. And I want to see what you look like in the dress I bought for you."

He nods to the dress hanging on the hook at the rear of the bathroom and my mouth drops. It's sparkly and red and divine. It's been a while since I've worn anything this fancy before and I desperately want to wear it. I want to feel pretty, which this dress would definitely help me achieve. I would also be able to seduce Matteo or any other man at the ball I want to. Possibly even make Matteo jealous.

I run my hand over the fabric already imagining it on my body when I get to the bottom of the dress and see the shoes sitting underneath. Tall, spiky heels the kind only models and women who hate their feet wear.

"I can't wear those heels."

He smirks. "If you want to go to the ball with me, you're wearing them. And preferably with no underwear underneath."

He playfully swats my ass, but there is nothing playful about it.

"I'm serious. My leg has hardly healed. I can walk, but not in heels like that."

"Fine, then I guess I'll have to find a last minute date."

I glare at him as he starts to strut by me.

"Fine, I'll wear them."

He grins. "Good. Be ready in twenty."

"Twenty minutes! I can't even do my hair in that amount of time. And did you get me any makeup?"

He nods toward one of the drawers. I pull the drawer open, and it's filled with the most expensive makeups money can buy.

"I mean it. I'm leaving in twenty so be ready, or your ass is staying here."

He shuts the door, leaving me alone in the bathroom to get ready. It's going to take a lot longer than twenty minutes for me to do my hair and makeup. And I'll make sure Matteo thinks it is worth the wait.

"Eden Marie! Get your ass out here now, or I'm leaving you," Matteo shouts.

It's the third time he's shouted at me. I apply my lipstick before I answer back. "How do you know my middle name is Marie?"

"I don't. But every American's middle name is either Elizabeth or Marie. Marie sounded better with Eden."

I smile. I like it when Matteo's relaxed with me. He's funny and charming and *human*.

I walk to the door and open it. I take two steps out before I see Matteo standing with his hands in his pockets in the most glorious tuxedo I've ever seen. It fits him snug, and his five o'clock shadow makes him appear rugged, despite how clean cut he looks in his tux. His eyes and grin are what make me weak in the knees though.

He's seen me naked dozens of times now, but he's never looked at me the way he is looking at me now. He makes me feel special, like we are going out on a proper date instead of him bringing me to a job.

"What do you think?" I ask, because I want to hear him say I'm beautiful and to fawn all over me. I like the attention.

I take a step forward so he can get a better look and I trip in my damn shoes.

He catches me.

"Why are you always catching me?" I breathe into his chest, as his cologne sneaks up my nostrils.

"Because you're always falling."

I laugh.

"You're in a good mood," he says.

"I guess something about getting out of this dark mansion and doing something fun for a change makes me happy."

His eyes narrow and I expect him to realize I could escape. After tonight, I could no longer be his slave. He doesn't say anything though.

Instead, he holds out his arm, and I take it. For once, I'm not going to worry about anything other than enjoying myself. I'm his date. I'm not his slave.

He leads me out of the house and out to a waiting limo. He holds the door open for me, and I climb in. But the limo isn't empty like I expect.

"Uh...hi..." I say staring at the two strangers already sitting inside.

"It took you long enough. We were supposed to leave thirty minutes ago," the woman says, who has a striking resemblance to Matteo.

"I'm sorry. Your brother only told me to start getting ready twenty minutes before he wanted to leave."

Gia smiles when I call Matteo her brother. She glares at Matteo when he enters and swats his leg.

"What were you thinking not telling her earlier to start getting dressed? You know it takes women longer than twenty minutes to get ready, especially for a night like tonight."

Matteo shrugs. "I thought she was my slave and she would do what she's told."

Gia hits him harder.

"Fine. I'm sorry. Next time I'll give her more time. Happy?" Matteo says.

"Yes," Gia says, smiling.

I watch the exchange happily. I can't believe Gia got Matteo to apologize. He's not usually the type of guy to give apologies, but I guess Gia might be the only one who has him wrapped around her finger.

"I'm Gia, but you already figured that out," she says.

"I'm Eden."

"And this is Stephen, my date for tonight."

The good-looking man nods at us, but otherwise doesn't seem interested in our conversation or Gia. I hope he isn't the guy she got her heart broken for.

Matteo puts his arm around my back, and I lean back into his arm. Gia stares at us intently, looking back and forth between us.

"What? Is my makeup messed up? It's been a while since I've applied makeup or done my hair."

Gia laughs. "No, you're beautiful."

I smile hesitantly, still not understanding why she is gazing at me so weirdly.

I stare out the window trying to relax until I realize where we are going.

"You didn't tell me the ball was going to be at Armas' house."

I turn to Matteo waiting for an explanation.

He shrugs again. "Must have slipped my mind."

I frown, not liking the idea of being back in his house again. Armas may be gone, but that doesn't mean he doesn't have a brother or a cousin who is as bad or worse.

The limo parks outside the house, and the door opens. Gia and her date step out while I stare at the house, not sure if I want to go inside anymore.

Matteo steps out and holds his hand out to me, commanding me to step out without pushing me.

I grab his hand, feeling calm radiate through him to me as he helps me out of the car.

I continue to hold onto his hand, grasping it for dear life, as we step inside the mansion. I expect to feel nervous, anxious butterflies flickering in my belly. I expect hauntings and terror to cloud my head. But Matteo smiles at me like he knows a secret he's sharing with me, and it all stops. I can't think about anything other than enjoying the night with him.

"You okay?" he asks, raising an eyebrow.

I smile. "Never been better."

He laughs because we both know what I said isn't true.

"Good. Now dance with me."

He pulls me to the dance floor in a large room toward the back of the house that seems it was built entirely for this purpose. With so many people laughing and enjoying themselves, and this room feeling so far from what it was like in Armas' room, it doesn't even feel like I'm in the same house.

Matteo wraps his arms around me, and we start dancing. The music is slow and classic, not what I'm used to dancing to, but Matteo is practiced and patient with me. His hands guide me until we are moving together to the music.

I step on his foot at least three times and each time he growls and laughs. I almost want to step on his foot again on purpose to make him laugh because I love hearing him laugh so much.

"Don't even think about it," he whispers in my ear.

"Think about what?"

"Stepping on my foot again."

I grin, surprised he was able to guess my next move.

He doesn't smile back. Instead, he's focused on something off in the distance.

I turn in the direction of his stare, and I see a man who looks almost exactly like Armas, but a few years older from the gray in his hair.

I swallow hard.

"Sorry, the fun needs to end. Time to get to work," he says.

My heart stops. As he hooks my arm into the crook of his and we start walking toward the man.

He pats my hand calmly, letting me know things are going to be okay, as we stroll without saying a word.

But I have a feeling everything is *not* going to be fine. My stomach is in knots, and so far since I've been captured, my gut feeling has been right. Every time.

The man strides outside to a balcony, and we follow. My throat tightens when we step outside, and we are joined by the entire Espocito family. Armas' parents, his older brother, and a younger brother, who looks to be fifteen. All are standing, staring at us like they want to kill us. They probably will. We are out numbered, and they have a vendetta against Matteo.

We are dead.

And just when I was finally accepting my new life and wanted to live.

I hear heels behind us, and see Gia, and her date walk up next to us. We are now four against four, but I still give them the better odds. The only person who would be useful in a fight on our side is Matteo.

"You had some balls to show up here tonight," Armas' older brother says.

"Why? We were invited, Bruno. It would be rude not to show up," Matteo says.

I clutch his arm tighter as I stare at the man who terrifies me with the same eyes Armas had.

"You fucking—" the young boy says, starting to run at Matteo.

I flinch, but Bruno holds his younger brother back.

"You destroyed this family when you killed Armas and don't pretend you don't know what we are talking about. You are on the security tape," Bruno says.

"Then, you know Armas deserved to die for how he treated Eden," Matteo says.

The older brother smirks and the parents hold onto each other like they can't stand this much longer.

"No. She deserved what she got and worse. And don't act like you don't treat her worse. We all know what she is - a slave," Bruno says.

I stare at the man defiantly. I'm tired of being called a slave. Matteo senses my frustration and tries to pet my hand again to calm me. It doesn't work. I want to rip his tongue out for saying I deserved what happened to me.

I glare over at Gia who appears bored with this conversation. Not the least bit worried we are all about to get shot.

"You need to drop this Bruno. All of you do. I'm more powerful than your entire family put together. I have more resources, more men, more money. Don't start a fight you can't win," Matteo says.

"I didn't start the fight. You did. I don't care what resources you have or how much money you have. We are going to make you pay for what you did to our son," the father says, breaking his silence.

Matteo ignores him, thinking he doesn't have the decision making power.

"This is your last warning. Stop this now. Go back to being old families who rule this town no matter the beef between us," Matteo says.

"No, this is not something we can forgive. This is war. So get ready because—"

Shots are fired. I duck down protecting my head as the bullets ring out around me. I don't realize where they are coming from until I see Matteo holding a gun.

I stare at the Espocito family as they begin dropping to the floor one after the other. First the mother. Then father. Then Bruno.

My eyes widen hoping he won't shoot the young boy. He's a boy. I see the fire in the boy's eyes though, and I know Matteo won't leave him standing either. He shoots him between the eyes, and he drops dead, instantly.

I can't breathe.

I've never seen a person die before. I've seen plenty of crime scene photos. I've imagined how Matteo killed Armas in my head hundreds of times, but I didn't get to witness it. I was too out of it at the time.

But this...this is like nothing I've ever imagined. I thought I would feel more, watching innocent people die. I thought it would feel cold. I thought I would feel sad or heartbroken.

I don't.

I feel nothing.

Maybe it's because this experience has changed everything for me. My heart has hardened. I no longer feel pain for other people. Because if I let the pain in, I'll never be able to survive.

Whatever the reason, I feel nothing as Matteo stores his gun and types a message on his phone.

"Time to go," he says to Gia and me.

I don't know how he will get away with killing the entire Espocito family, but I'm sure he will. He stopped the threat. Armas' family will no longer come after us because they are all dead.

We all climb back in the limo Matteo must have summoned with his text message and begin driving home in silence. Matteo hugs me to his body.

"You're safe now," he says, kissing my hair.

I smile weakly, because in my heart I know I'm thankful for what Matteo did. He killed them to protect not only himself, but me too. And for that, I'm incredibly grateful. Too thankful.

Tonight, I lost another tiny piece of myself. I lost the part that cared about innocent strangers more than I care about myself. I don't know how I can go back to work after this. I don't know how I can have any resemblance to my normal life again after this. This changed me as much or more than the rape did. I've become a monster the same as Matteo.

———

Matteo wanted sex tonight, but he respected my space when I made it clear I wanted to sleep. I wanted to fuck him, but I couldn't bring myself to do it, not when people died tonight because of us. I couldn't be that cruel to celebrate their deaths, no matter how much I wanted to.

So now I'm in his bed, his arm draped over me, as he snores and I can't sleep.

The minutes tick by, but all I can think about is the boy he killed. The white leaving his eyes as the blood spilled out. Matteo is more dangerous than I imagined. He walked into a party with over a hundred people and killed four by himself, without backup. He murdered four wealthy, well-known people in this town, and tomorrow the cops won't come knocking on his door because he paid them off.

I made a deal with the devil, and now I'm as guilty of the crimes he commits. I could have continued to fight. To hold my ground. But I caved because I wanted sex and an easier way. Now I have to live with the consequences.

I carefully slide out from under his arm and sit on the edge of the bed as my stomach grumbles. We left so early I didn't eat much, and I couldn't eat when we got back, but now I could use some food. It might help me sleep.

I stand and tiptoe over to Matteo's closet putting on a pair of his boxers and T-shirt. I have clothes in my closet, but I prefer the smell of his. It comforts me, even though it shouldn't.

But I guess I've gotten comfortable after sleeping with the devil for this long.

I walk over to the small kitchenette in his quarters that usually has at least some basic foods.

I open the fridge and find nothing but beer and moldy cheese. I open the cabinets and find it empty except for a few crackers.

I frown. I need something more substantial than crackers.

I glance over at the door that leads to the rest of the house, as I munch on a couple of the saltines. It's always locked with a key he puts in a safe, when he sleeps, with a code I don't know the password to. I'm sure it's locked, but my grumbling tummy wants food.

I walk over to the door and rest my hand on the doorknob as I glance over at Matteo sleeping. I'm sure he's going to catch me trying to get out and think I'm trying to escape rather than getting food.

My heart beats fast as I wait to ensure Matteo is still asleep before I try the door. I turn the knob and pull. Surprisingly, the door creaks open. It always makes a high pitched sound when it opens, but this time seems worse than usual.

I stare over at Matteo. He doesn't move. So I slink out between the crack before letting the door close slowly, so it doesn't make a sound.

The hallway is pitch black. I assume I'll be met with a guard right outside the door, but I'm not. I know he has security cameras, so I know it is only a matter of time before someone comes to drag me back to Matteo. I don't wait for them to come. I storm down the hallway to the kitchen.

I open the fridge and pull out leftover pizza someone left. I grab two slices and place them on a napkin before walking out to the dining room where I plan on eating before heading back to Matteo's room. I could go back and eat in Matteo's room, but I like having a moment to myself. I like having the freedom. I like that I'm being a bit of a rebel.

I freeze in the door when I find the dining room already occupied.

I wasn't expecting anyone. Least of all Gia. She has her own wing of the house, and she never bothers coming on this side. I know nothing of her life, other than she had a boyfriend who hurt her.

She's sitting at the table with tears running down her cheek and a gallon tub of ice cream sitting on the table.

"I'm sorry, I didn't realize anyone was here. I'll go back to my room," I say.

Gia chuckles. "You mean my brother's room."

I nod.

"Or I could join you?" I ask, not sure what I'm supposed to do.

She pulls out a chair next to her, and I take a seat with my cold pizza.

I start eating it, and her eyes widen and dry a little as she looks at me.

"We have an oven you know? That would taste much better warmed up."

I smile and hold out a piece to her. "You've never had cold pizza? It's an American tradition."

She wrinkles her nose and sticks to eating her ice cream.

"Are you upset about what happened tonight?" I ask, not sure if I should be asking her anything, but I might as well.

"No, I knew what was going to happen when we went. The Espocito family deserved it. I would have killed them myself if Matteo didn't."

I force the bite of pizza in my mouth down. She's as ruthless as Matteo. I need to remember that. I'll need to watch out for her and not get on her bad side.

She raises an eyebrow at me, wanting to know how I feel.

"I'm not upset about tonight either. It needed to happen. I feel guilty that I feel okay it happened."

Gia smirks. "Your first kill?"

I nod.

"You'll get used to it. The first time changes everything. Next time the guilt won't eat you anymore."

My eyes widen. I hope there isn't a next time, but I don't say that to her.

"I'm here because I'm starving and couldn't sleep, the guilt and all. Why are you down here instead of in your wing?"

"I'm all out of ice cream on my side."

"What's the ice cream for?"

She sighs. "Because I'm in love with a guy who doesn't love me back. It's ridiculous to be crying about it, I know, considering your situation, but it's the truth. I'm a hopeless romantic, and I don't know how to get over him."

I smile. "Good to know that at least one Carini has a heart."

She smiles a little.

"You want to talk about him?"

"No."

"If you ever want to, I'm here. I don't exactly have anywhere else to go."

She laughs and looks at me soberly. "Why haven't you asked me to help you get free yet?"

I frown. "You're a Carini. If I know one thing, it's that Carini's are loyal to each other. I knew it was a hopeless endeavor. Plus, I'm not sure I wanted to put siblings in that situation."

She holds out her spoon to me, and I dig into her ice cream. It's rocky road, complicated like her.

"Want to talk to me about you and Matteo?" she asks.

I chuckle and take another large bite of the ice cream. "No. What's to talk about? He stole me to get my best friend back because he's in love with her. I won't tell him where she is because I don't trust he won't hurt her, and Nina ran for a reason."

"Because of our father, not Matteo."

"What?"

"Arlo and Nina ran because Enrico is still alive. Although, I've heard he is barely hanging on in a coma or something, somewhere in Northern Ireland. They are safe from him. Matteo wants his brother back and a chance to get the girl he thinks he loves back."

I consider her words, but considering who they are coming from, I don't trust her any more than I trust Matteo. This could all be a trick to get me to talk.

"Thank you for telling me." I put the spoon down. "I guess I should be getting back. I need some sleep. "

She smirks. "Yes, you'll need some sleep to be able to keep up with my brother. "

I blush.

"He cares about you too, you know."

I freeze as I'm standing up. "What?"

"Matteo, he cares about you. He would never admit it to you or anyone, but he looks at you differently. Even differently than how he looked at Nina."

"He cares about me because he likes to fuck me and I'm his best shot at getting Nina back. That's all."

"Maybe, or maybe he's falling in love with you."

"Even if he is, it doesn't change anything. I don't love him. I don't want this life. I want to go back home to my old life."

"You sure about that? Because it would seem a woman who wasn't falling for him would try a little harder to escape, especially when given such a glaring opportunity tonight, instead of rushing back to his bed."

I ignore her and go back to Matteo's bed, but her words stay with me. I'm not falling in love with Matteo, and he's not falling in love with me. We hate each other. Sex won't change that. Killing for each other won't change that. Not even kindness will change that.

14

MATTEO

SHE THINKS SHE'S WINNING.

Ever since I killed the Espocito family, she has gotten cocky. At first, she was scared, hesitant. She didn't like that she was accepting I killed Armas's family. But now, she's fearless.

I tested her, leaving the door unlocked giving her a bit more freedom. And every night since the night I killed the Espocito family, she has snuck out.

Every. Single. Fucking. Night.

At first, I thought she was planning on finding a way to escape. I thought she was sneaking out to test my security, to find the weak points so when the timing was right, she would run to freedom.

But that's not what she was doing. It seems that merely leaving my room whenever she wanted was freedom enough, at least for now. She's happy with her life, though she will never admit it. And I can't have her happy. Happy means I'll never get what I want.

I close my eyes pretending to sleep like I always do. I wrap my arm around her naked body after fucking her earlier in the shower. She thinks I was rough then; she felt like she was drowning as she laid under the water while I fucked her. Tonight, I have even darker plans for her.

She waits for my breathing to become slow, I even fake snore for a while, so she thinks I'm fast asleep. My arm weighs her down, and I think for once, she might not sneak out tonight and my plan to tame her happy thoughts might be squandered.

But she sneaks out like I knew she would.

I grin as I throw the covers off. I'm going to enjoy tonight.

15

EDEN

I SNEAK INTO THE DARKNESS, not for any other reason than I can. I enjoy the little bit of freedom Matteo has decided to give me. I spend the night eating, walking, reading, or sitting quietly in a new room in the house. It's hard for me sometimes to pull away from his arms. I like sleeping with him wrapped around me, and I still sleep plenty with him. I don't spend more than an hour or two out of bed. And I have plenty of time while he's working during the day to nap if I'm tired.

I let the door close slowly behind me, planning on only reading for twenty minutes or so in the library and then returning to Matteo because I enjoy snuggling with him in bed.

"What are you doing out of bed?" Maximo says, as I freeze in the hallway.

"Just getting some food to bring back to Matteo. He's hungry," I lie.

"No, you're not," he says as Dierk and Paul walk up behind me.

"Matteo gave us strict orders to punish you if you ever broke his rules," Maximo says.

I smile, trying to keep it together. "I'm not breaking his rules. Ask him."

"We will," Maximo says pulling out his phone and dialing Matteo's number.

Shit.

"Matteo, we caught Eden out of bed. What would you like us to do?" Maximo says.

Please let him say take me back to his room.

Maximo grins. "Done."

I swallow hard, trying to keep the fear down. Whatever Matteo told them to do I can handle it. It won't be bad.

"I'll go back to Matteo..." I say.

"No, you'll be coming with us," Maximo says, grabbing my arm.

I elbow him as hard as I can instinctively, not liking his hands on me.

He ducks though, prepared for it this time, and I panic. More hands go on me. More hands than I'm prepared to handle. I try fighting back, but I know at least three guys are holding onto me, and there is no use fighting.

I let them hold onto me and carry me into a room. I feel the bed beneath me as they toss me. My initial thought is to panic. Fight. I'm on a bed with three men standing over me. I should be afraid. Terrified they are going to rape me. But I'm not. If Matteo has made anything clear, it's that he doesn't share. The consequences of sharing me are enormous. *Death.*

So I try to calm my breathing as they stretch my limbs wide and tie me up. Each limb. One by one until I can't move.

Deep breath. In and out. *They can't touch me. They won't touch me.*

I feel hands on my clothes though. Clothes are being ripped from my body. My shirt is torn in half, exposing my breasts. My pants are cut off.

I'm naked. In front of three men. Men I now hate. Men that had no right to try and embarrass me like this.

They all stare down at my naked body hungrily, and I'm what they are hungry for.

"You're disgusting. All of you."

Maximo grins. "We are about to get a lot more disgusting."

He holds a blindfold in his hand and ties it tightly over my eyes so I can't see.

"We won't cover your mouth. We want to hear you scream. We want you to fight. It's music to our ears. That way we know we are doing a good job when we break you. You'll be speaking about Nina by the end of the night," Maximo says.

I keep my lips closed. That's what this is about. It's what this is always about. Nina.

A fear tactic to try and get me to talk. It won't work. Nothing will work.

I've endured worse. Whatever they are going to do to me is nothing.

I still don't believe they will rape me. They might beat me though with whips and bats, anything to get me to speak.

I have to prove to them I can't be broken. I will never speak, and they will stop.

I feel the strike I was anticipating on my stomach, but I don't flinch. I'm used to the pain. I imagine Matteo doing it instead of Maximo.

I'm whipped again on my breasts, and the sting against my nipples makes them harden. Begging the attacker for more.

Next is my thighs, arms, and pussy. Each strike is hard and perfect from the hands of someone experienced with a whip.

"You're sick. You like the pain, don't you?" Maximo says.

I focus on breathing. I should try meditation after this is all over. I can see the benefits.

"You're like Matteo. Dark, sick, and cruel," he continues.

I hear the whip crack again as it hits my stomach.

"Let's see how dirty you like it." His tongue licks the side of my face, and my lips curl in disgust.

I don't want to feel him on me. I don't want him touching me.

I feel more hands. On my breasts, my stomach, my arms. They are everywhere. Exploring my body, touching me places no man should touch without permission.

"Stop," I let slip from my lips.

I bite my lip again hating that I spoke.

"You want us to stop, huh? I thought having three men at once turned you on?" Maximo says.

I deeply exhale as I feel hands twisting my nipple and I can't help but get turned on a little.

Lips on my neck send chills down my throat, and an erection is pushing at my entrance.

No.

I won't be raped.

Ever again.

But that's precisely what's happening at Matteo's orders.

I take a deep breath in again, letting the musky scent of whichever guy is on me. *Matteo?*

I try not to react. I take another deep breath as the cock pushes in. A very familiar cock to go with a very familiar scent.

The asshole was messing with me. Trying to make me think I was being raped when I wasn't.

Two can play this game.

"Stop," I scream again letting it all out as his cock pushes deeper inside me.

The other guys may have their hands on me as well, but it's mostly on the outskirts. Holding my arms and legs down, and saying dirty things to keep up the appearance they are raping me, while Matteo does the dirty work himself.

"No," I cry out as he roughly takes my breast.

"You don't get to speak," Maximo says as something covers my mouth and nose so that I can't even breathe.

I pretend to panic, my arms flailing as best as I can with everyone's arms on me. I don't panic though. I know Matteo is here and he is the one in control and if sex with him these last few weeks has taught me anything, it's he knows my limits and won't hurt me. So when my lungs start burning and aren't able to breathe, that's when the hand is removed, and I suck in a deep breath.

The hand covers my nose and mouth as Matteo thrusts inside of me, hitting the sweetest spots making me come alive like only he can.

I can't breathe as he thrusts, but it only makes it more invigorating. The fact that three other men are watching with their hands on me should embarrass me, but it only turns me on more that Matteo will let them participate to intensify the experience.

I feel my orgasm growing, and now I can't hold on. I can't keep up the ruse that this is hurting me, and I no longer care. I want my orgasm to explode out and give me freedom and pleasure.

The hand is removed so I can breathe, but I can't breathe as my orgasm explodes through my body.

"Matteo!" I cry out as I come around his dick as he explodes into my body.

No one speaks or moves. Eventually, I feel hands slowly leaving my body until I know it's just me and Matteo left in the room.

I grin widely and bite my lip as he slowly removes the blindfold.

"When did you figure out it was me this whole time?" Matteo asks.

I smirk. "The second you touched me basically. I know your scent, your touch, and I know what your cock feels like. You can't fool me."

He grins. "I thought I would teach you a lesson for sneaking out every night. I guess I need to try harder next time."

I shake my head. "Lesson learned. But I wouldn't sneak out if you locked the door."

He leans down and kisses me hard on the lips. I don't know why he kisses me. It's a gentle after fuck kiss, the kind that lovers or people who care about each other give. Not us.

"Let's get you back to bed," he says when he stops the kiss, like nothing happened.

I nod and let him undo the ties on my arms and legs before he carries me back to his bed and climbs in next to me before snuggling close.

I don't understand what we are or even what I want. But maybe that's the point. He's messing with my head completely confusing me, so I don't know how I feel or what I want. I need to get my head cleared now before I let any more confusion cloud my judgment. Or like Gia said the other night, fall in love.

16

MATTEO

I SHOULD BE FOCUSED on the new client we are delivering weapons to today. This client is enormous, and if this first delivery goes well, it could continue to be extremely lucrative for the Carini family in many ways.

But I can't focus on the trade. All I can focus on is Eden.

Damn it.

Fabio said words and I have no idea what. And now he's waiting for me to respond.

"Exactly," I say.

He smiles happily at my response. Hopefully, I didn't agree to give him double the number of weapons for the same price.

I pull out the piece of paper and slide it across his desk.

"Have your team meet us at this address in ten minutes." I stand up and walk out of the office and out to my car where my team is waiting next to their own cars.

"It's on," I say.

The men nod and get in their cars. I do the same and start driving fast to the trade location. The car ride gives me plenty of time to lose myself in ways I can fuck Eden. On the balcony, the pool, my car. Tied up, from behind, in the air. Every way makes me want her more, grow more desperate for her.

My cock can't stop thinking about her. My brain can't stop dreaming of her. And I don't just want sex. I want to drive her in my car and show her all Italy has to offer. Take her to drink fine wines with me and delicious foods. Explore the city and countryside.

I don't understand what is wrong with me. Or why I feel this way. It's been a while since I've gone on a date. Perhaps I need to invite one of my old girlfriends to do something fun with me this weekend instead of spending all my time on work or Eden. That was my father's problem. Work started consuming him until it was his entire life.

I hear the danger before I even arrive. I'm the fifth or sixth car to get to the location, but I know that we are being ambushed. And I know it isn't our new client. He was far too eager to do business, and although he is wealthy, he doesn't have the experience to launch an attack like the one I'm witnessing.

I don't hesitate, I park the car and jump out with my gun out, firing off shots into the woods at our attackers. Some leaders don't get involved in attacks like this. They hang back and let their men do the fighting for them. Carini's don't hang back and let others fight our battles. If I'm going to ask my men to fight, I better be willing to take the risk equally as much.

We are outnumbered. I know that much from the bullets whizzing past my head, but that doesn't mean we are going to lose.

I see my number two, Maximo, to my left. And I give him a look, telling him what I'm thinking without having to say anything. We've had plans like this for weeks after the last almost ambush.

We're ready.

But it's risky.

Maximo takes some of the men and starts moving them to the left side while I stay with some of the men in the middle. We need to draw them to us so that Maximo and his men can attack from behind.

I move forward out of my hiding spot so Clive and Erick's men will focus on me. I'm their target anyway. They want to take me out. Make me feel pain. They don't give a shit about my men.

They think if they can take me out, my men will switch their loyalty to them. They don't realize to join my ranks you have to be loyal. Too loyal. So loyal you'd die rather than join anyone else.

I see Clive hiding behind his men, not even bothering to attack. Letting his men do the dirty work for him.

I aim at him trying to take him out, but he's too far away. A bullet grazes my shoulder, but I keep shooting, sticking to the plan. Another hits my leg; I kneel on the ground still shooting. Not stopping until I the plan succeeds.

Another hits my hand knocking the gun out of my hand. I start to reach for it, but one of Clive's men knocks it out of the way.

A gun is pressed against my head, and I hold my hands up, not that I will surrender. I won't. I would rather die than surrender.

I glare at Clive and Erick, my body red with rage, as they walk over. They are the reason everything started in the first place.

"Ready to give up yet?" Erick asks.

I don't give him a response. He doesn't deserve one.

"Don't worry; we aren't going to kill you yet. What fun would that be?" Erick says.

I frown. The only reason they wouldn't kill me now is if they had bigger plans they thought would hurt me worse. "You can't hurt me. Arlo and Nina are gone. And I know you won't hurt Gia. So there is nothing you can do to hurt me."

Clive smirks. "Oh, there is certainly a way to hurt you."

"No, there isn't."

"There is," Clive looks to Erick both smirking at me. "Eden, your new slave toy. Except, she isn't a slave. You love her."

I growl. I don't want them threatening Eden or telling me I have feelings for someone that I don't. I will never love again. Love only makes things worse.

"My slave is nothing more than property to me. If you steal her, it would be the same as if you stole my car. I would be pissed and kill you. So go ahead and try. I'll enjoy hunting you down."

"We will. The only way to stop this is to turn over Nina, but I bet you won't do that. I think your feelings have shifted."

I open my mouth to respond but I see the gun coming down on my head, and I know it's useless anyway. I close my eyes to control the darkness before it comes. But then I don't have any control at all. I'm lost to the darkness.

———

I open my eyes and find Eden's. She's staring at me, looking at me worriedly, and I'm sure I'm still dreaming. She can't be worried about me.

I close and open my eyes again to try to force myself to wake up, but when I open them again, she's still sitting on the foot of my bed staring at me with her big eyes.

"How are you feeling?" she asks.

I frown. "Like hell."

She nods. "You want some pain meds?"

"In a minute," I say, sitting up and examining my body. My

left shin is sore, along with my right shoulder and right hand. And my head is pounding like I was knocked out.

"Don't worry; I didn't stitch up any of your wounds. You wouldn't be alive if I did. Maximo had the doctor come and remove the bullet fragments and stitch you up. He said you should rest in bed for at least a week, but you probably wouldn't listen to his advice."

I nod.

"How long have I been out?"

"Since yesterday afternoon," she says, tucking a strand of hair behind her ear. "I was worried you wouldn't wake up, but the doctor said I shouldn't worry. It was impossible not to worry though."

I grin. "You were worried about me? I figured you would be praying for me to die so you could be free."

"Nah, I figured you had something written in your will that I would go to some long-lost cousin of yours or something if you died."

I smirk. "It's not written in my will, but it gives me ideas."

She laughs, but it's nervous.

I reach out my hand and take hers in mine, wanting to calm her nerves.

"What's wrong?" I ask.

She shakes her head, but I can see the tears in her eyes.

"Nothing, I just...I'm really glad you are okay." She wipes her tears. She must be on her period or something because there is no way she should be crying over me almost dying. The sex isn't that good.

"Anyway, is there anything I can get you to make you feel more comfortable?" she asks.

My eyes turn mischievous as I grab her neck and pull her into a hasty kiss that is meant to show her exactly what I want. My cock pushes into her belly as she falls on top of me.

She pulls away. "We can't. Your doctor told you to rest, and the sex that you usually are into requires far too much of you."

I pout, and she grins.

"No," she says again.

I pull her back into a kiss, and I know she won't be able to resist me. She's horny, and I'll have her tied up in this bed in no time.

Her leg hooks over my body as she sits on my lap, kissing me, as my cock hardens against her groin. Her hips grind over me making me harder and I pull her body too me. She grabs my shoulders to keep her balance.

And I groan in pain.

She pulls back.

"I'm so sorry," she says, holding her hands over her mouth.

I wince, holding my shoulder.

"I told you it wasn't a good idea," she says.

I growl. "No, it's a very good idea."

I grab her, pulling her back to me, despite the pain in my arm. All I feel is the ache in my groin.

"It's worth the pain," I say.

She smiles, but her smile doesn't reach her eyes. It's not genuine.

I kiss her trying to make her forget about anything but having me. She moans against my lips, and I think I've convinced her when she pulls away again.

I frown. "What now?"

She bites her lip in the most adorable way, and it melts my insides a little. "I have an idea," she says.

I raise my eyebrows.

"Do you trust me?" she asks.

"Are you going to let me fuck you?"

"I'm going to fuck you."

I narrow my eyes not fully understanding the difference, but

I'll go along with whatever at this point if it gets me laid. My wounds are minimal, although she thinks I almost died. But regardless, my cock deserves sex for what I've been through lately.

She continues to straddle my lap while she looks around the room searching for something.

"Be right back," she finally says as she hops off my lap and runs to my closet.

I sigh.

I guess I understand how she feels every time I tease her and make her wait for sex.

She runs back, holding a couple of my ties in her hand.

"What are those for? Do I get to tie you up?" I ask.

"No, I'm tying you up. That way you won't hurt yourself, and we can still have sex."

I frown, not liking her logic, but as she hops back on my lap and my cock strains against my pants, there is no arguing with her. I want her. And if this is how I can have her, fine.

"Hold out your right arm," she says.

I do.

She takes it and begins tying the tie gently around my wrist before attaching it to the bed.

"I can get out of that you know."

She smiles. "I'm aware. I mainly want your injured arm out of the way, so I remember not to touch it."

She glances back at my leg. "Do I need to tie your leg up too?"

I grab her waist, pulling her to me as I sweep a kiss hungrily on her lips, not letting her stall this any longer.

She kisses back, just as hungrily, forgetting that I'm injured or that she needs to be careful. Her hands grab my neck and tangle in my hair, holding me to her.

I tangle my one free hand in her hair, keeping her lips locked with mine. We don't always kiss when we fuck, but when we do, it's like fireworks go off. Lighting strikes our bodies, and we can't stop kissing. No matter what.

I reach for the hem of her shirt needing her T-shirt off.

She grabs the hem and lifts it over her head, tossing it to the floor giving me access to her perfect tits. I massage the soft flesh of her breast as it fills my hand.

Her moans are like honey. Sweet and sultry and beautiful. I love the sounds she makes with her throat. Sounds that I cause.

Her fingers rake down my chest, feeling every muscle in their wake.

She's fierce as she moves her hands over my body, knowing exactly what she wants, and not being sorry for it.

I try to pull her pants down, but she swats my hand away.

I frown.

"You need to learn to be patient," she says, grinning and enjoying herself far too much.

She stands, and I pout, as I try to grab her and pull her back to me. She fights me off.

She very slowly lowers her pants like she is putting on a show for me. Wiggling her hips as the pants fall slowly to the floor.

I growl at her naked body that is a few feet away that I don't get to touch.

I pull at the tie that is barely holding me to the bed.

She wags her finger back and forth at me.

I growl.

She grabs the covers and pulls them down, before grabbing my boxer briefs and pulling them down my body, as I lift my hips to help her.

I want her on my cock now.

She winks at me, knowing exactly how desperate I am for her.

She takes my cock in her hand and pumps it up and down slowly. So, so slowly. I can't handle it.

I grab her hand, moving it faster over my cock.

"No, I get to be in control. Not you," she says, pushing my hand off.

She lowers her head, and her lips wrap around my cock as she moves just as slowly up and down, teasing and taunting me.

My eyes roll back in my head, and I let my head fall back on the pillow, at how good her lips and tongue feel over my cock.

But I'm not patient. Not with her.

I grab her hair, moving her head faster over my cock.

She grins when she can finally breathe again.

"I knew I should have tied both of your hands up."

I smirk. "No, you shouldn't have."

I grab her, as she climbs on top of me and finally sinks her pussy on top of me. My cock drives into her, and she moans against me as her hips climb up and down on top of me.

I won't last.

And from the moans she is making, she won't last either.

I thrust, and she sinks down on top of me, our eyes meeting and our tongues tangling.

"Yes," she moans, as she comes on my cock, drenching me.

Her moans take me over the edge, and I come right after her.

She grins as she climbs off me and slowly unties my arm, which is just beginning to ache again, now that the adrenaline is slowly leaving my body.

I watch her body, now flushed and glowing, as she puts her baggy T-shirt and sweatpants back on.

I get up to go shower and get dressed. I need to go to the office and make a plan for how to deal with Erick and Clive. I'm not going to let them make the next move. I won't let them hurt Eden or anyone else.

The only way to defend ourselves is to take out Erick and

Clive. Destroy them and their business. I need them dead. Only then will Eden be safe. Any of us be safe.

"What are you doing?" Eden asks, staring at my naked body, as I start walking toward the bathroom.

"I'm going to shower and then get dressed. I have work to do."

She frowns and chases after me as I walk to the bathroom and turn on the shower, before stepping in. The water is chilly at first but quickly turns warm within seconds of me standing under the water.

"You are not going to work," Eden says, stripping before stepping into the shower with me.

I smirk, enjoying having a naked woman in the shower with me. I grab the bar of soap and begin running it over her body, over every one of her curves.

Her eyes close as she enjoys my hands on her body. She shakes her head, realizing that I've gotten her under my spell again.

"You are not going to work! Your doctor told you to stay in bed for a couple of weeks. You were just shot. Three times and knocked unconscious. You aren't going anywhere."

I cock my head to the side and hold down her flailing arms.

"I'm going." I glance down at my wounds that are healing well and barely ache. They are nothing compared to the pain I feel knowing that Erick and Clive want to take what is mine.

I stare at Eden. "Trust me. I'm fine. This pain is nothing."

She pouts. "Stay..."

I narrow my eyes at her. "I have to go."

"Why?"

"Because I protect what's mine."

She takes the soap from me and begins scrubbing my body with it, as she contemplates what I meant by my words. I rinse off and then turn the water off when I'm done before stepping out. I hand her a towel and take one myself before I walk to my closet to get dressed.

Eden follows me to the closet, watching me dress in jeans, a shirt, and jacket.

"I don't need you to protect me. I need you to stay alive," she says, her voice soft.

I raise an eyebrow. "You'd miss my cock that much if I was dead?"

She swallows. "Something like that."

I stare at her a moment before I make up my mind. "Get dressed. Jeans, a nice shirt, and jacket. None of those sweatpants you usually wear."

"Why?"

"Because you are coming with me."

Her face lights up, and she runs to her closet to get dressed before I even step out of the closet.

She looks gorgeous in her dark jeans, red shirt, and black leather jacket. She chose red heels to complete her look.

"I'm not going to have to hold your hand to keep you from falling in those all day, am I?"

She laughs. "No, but you can hold my hand all the same."

I do hold her hand. I hold her hand in the Ferrari as we drive with the top down on the way to the warehouse we use as an office building and storage facility.

I try to relax knowing that Clive and Erick won't launch a second attack again so soon. I spoke with Maximo before we left and I know that their team was severely injured. They don't have the manpower to launch a second attack again so soon.

So Eden is safe, for now.

I stop the car outside the building that is my whole world. The men inside are not just men. They are family. Family that relies on me for an income. For keeping them safe. And for providing them a family.

I hold Eden's hand as I lead her into the building. When we step inside, all eyes are on us. Everyone has wide eyes or shocked expressions on their faces. I've never brought anyone here that wasn't my family or an employee.

No one expected me ever to bring Eden here, yet here she is.

"I need a team ready to discuss what our plan of attack is to take out Clive and Erick in five minutes," I say to Dierk.

He nods and runs off to gather a team while I lead Eden to the long table at the far end of the warehouse.

She smiles at the men. "Hi, guys. Is Matteo working you too hard?"

"Not any worse than usual," Paul says with a wink.

"I'll put in a good word to try and get you some time off," she says back, smiling.

I pull her to me. "You know that you don't have to flirt with every guy here?"

She smiles. "Why? Would it make you jealous if I did?"

"Yes, very jealous."

"Good. You don't have to worry though. I've just gotten close to a few of the guys that have been helping me out."

"I know. Going against my rules, feeding you, and taking care of you."

She grins. "Go easy on them. I'm charming."

I kiss her on the lips, claiming her in front of everyone. "I know."

We both take a seat at the long wooden table, as several of my men start taking a seat at the table surrounding us. When the team of about six of my most trusted men arrive, all sitting down at the table, I start.

"As you all know, we are here to talk about how to handle Clive and Erick. I'm done with their games. They threatened my life. They threatened this company and all of your lives." I don't add that they threatened Eden's life. "We are going to put an end to them and their business."

"I think we should set up an ambush similar to how they attacked us," Dierk says.

I nod along just listening, not shooting down anyone's ideas yet.

"That will never work, they will be expecting that," Paul says.

"They are going to be expecting every kind of attack. The only thing they won't be expecting is one where we do nothing. So unless we plan to do nothing, then we are going to lose our element of surprise."

"What do you think sexy?" Maximo asks, running his hand up and down Eden's arms. "I know you have some brains in that head of yours. What do you think?"

I glare at Maximo, not liking him touching Eden. I don't like how she shivers at his touch. I don't like him even talking to her. I immediately regret bringing her here.

Eden looks from me to the men as I can see her brain turning, thinking of a solution to our problems.

"You use me," she says.

I frown. Yep, definitely shouldn't have brought her.

I laugh. "You're crazy. Erick and Clive don't give a fuck about you."

She raises an eyebrow at me, as do most of the men.

"They are after Eden? Why?" Dierk asks.

"Because I look like Nina. The Carini's stole my best friend from them, and now they want revenge. They think I'm the new Nina. So they want to steal me. Use me to draw them in. Use me as bait, then attack," Eden says.

Realization hits every one of my men as they listen to her speak. They like her plan. And there is nothing I can say to convince them otherwise. The only leverage I have to put an end to the plan is my claim as the leader. Their boss. Tell them they don't get a say in decisions that affect their lives too.

"No, we aren't using Eden," I say, trying to end the conversation. They know that if I say no, that's the end of it.

But instead, chaos erupts. Men start talking over each other trying to throw out plans and convince me why Eden should be involved in the plan.

This is not what I expected. At all. I thought we would come up with a plan that involved a carefully crafted attack. Not one that would involve using Eden as bait.

I glance to my right and see Maximo, with his hands on Eden. I've had enough.

I punch Maximo in the face. "Touch her again, and you're fired," I say, grabbing Eden's arm and leading her out of the warehouse.

Maximo runs after me blood pouring down his face. He grabs my arm, and I think he's going to punch me. Instead, he says, "I'm sorry."

He looks from me to Eden.

"Apology accepted," Eden says.

"Eden, go wait for me in the car," I say, tossing her the keys, knowing that she could jump in the car, take off, and I could never see her again.

She takes them with wide eyes and walks out to the car.

"I don't need your apologies. I need you to focus on work instead of on my woman. Understand?" I say.

Maximo nods. "I understand. But I need to be blunt with you. Your feelings for that woman have blinded you. Clive and Erick want Eden, don't they?"

I don't respond, giving him his answer.

"That's what I thought. So the only way to take them out is to use her as bait. She knows that. The men know that. And —"

"I know that," I say finishing his sentence.

He pauses. "So what are you going to do? Are you going to lead us into an ambush even though you know it will end in us all dead or will you use the girl?"

I glare at him. "She's not a girl."

He takes a step back, assuming I'm about to hit him again.

I glance out the window to where Eden is sitting in the car. "I'll use Eden."

17
———

EDEN

THE DAY MATTEO took me to the old warehouse, where he runs his business, was the day that everything changed.

I don't know what changed. And I don't care. But my life is much easier now.

Matteo never locks the door to his bedroom. He lets me freely explore the house and the grounds whenever I want.

He even let Gia take me shopping the other day.

It's like we are a couple. Well, almost.

Minus the fact that I didn't enter into this relationship willingly. And the fact that he never takes me on dates. And when we fuck, it's borderline rape every time, somehow pushing the line, but crossing it. And I don't have access to a phone.

Otherwise, we've developed an easy relationship with each other. We may not talk about mundane things, like how our work day went, or the weather, or anything like that, but none of that stuff matters anyway.

We know how each other feels with just a glance. We know what each other craves with just a touch. We know what each wants with just a kiss.

We both like fucking each other too much. I'm not sure it's

195

healthy. Actually, I know it's not. I'm addicted to his body. I'd willingly have sex with him multiple times a day, and it has nothing to do with saving Nina.

I'm afraid that if given a choice between returning home immediately to freedom, or getting a day full of sex with Matteo but having to stay his slave forever, I might choose the latter.

I'm sick. And Matteo is my cure.

This can't keep going on like this. It's not healthy for either of us when we both know this sexual relationship has a time limit on it. And the longer we go, the harder it's going to be when we stop.

Neither of us cares or think about that though. All we care about is the next fuck. Like a drug addict only caring about his next fix.

Matteo won't be home for hours, which means I'm going to have to handle the familiar ache between my legs myself. He's at work, trying to figure out a plan to deal with Clive and Erick, the same single focus he's been worried about for weeks.

He hasn't brought me back to the warehouse since he first took me there weeks ago. He also won't even talk to me about using me as bait. He won't even consider it.

Which means he either cares, or he really thinks of me as his property.

He's fooling himself if he doesn't think I can help though. I know what Clive and Erick want. Me.

Matteo can deny it all he wants, but it doesn't matter. I know the truth he hides behind his eyes.

I head to the bathroom and turn on the faucet in the tub. I might as well take a long bath since I have hours to kill and nothing to do until Matteo gets home. I have free range of the house and could watch TV, read a book, or go for a run. But none of those things can hold my attention.

It seems that only Matteo can hold my attention.

I turn the water off when it fills the bath, drop my clothes to the floor, and then climb into the bath, sinking all the way down until the water hits the tip of my chin.

It's warm and relaxing. But I didn't draw the bath for relaxing. I drew it to get rid of the aches that consume my thoughts.

I let my hand drift down between my legs, rubbing gently as my bud slowly starts to awaken. I close my eyes and my thoughts immediately go to Matteo. I try to think of past boyfriends, hot celebrities, and imaginary men. Anything to make me stop thinking of Matteo. But despite trying, it never works.

Matteo is what my body wants, even when he isn't good for me.

I picture his hand replacing mine. I picture him climbing into the tub naked, as his cock drives against my stomach letting me know he wants me as much as I want him. He pinches my nipples, making my hard peaks come alive. And then he sweeps his tongue into my mouth, claiming me in a kiss that is primal, hungry, and sexy as hell.

I purr, the kiss feeling far too real.

"You wouldn't be trying to get yourself off without me, would you?" Matteo asks.

My eyes fly open, and I grin.

"No, you were there in my dreams."

He smirks. "I bet."

He climbs into the tub, still fully clothed, and I squeal from the excitement of him being here.

"Why are you back so early?" I ask.

"We figured out a solution."

"Really? What is it?"

He shakes his head and then kisses me again. "Does it matter?"

No, it doesn't matter. He's kissing me and that only means one thing. He's going to fuck me.

He reaches behind me. "I have some fun toys to try."

My eyes darken as I see the nipple clamps in his hand.

He kisses me again, and I feel the cold metal against my skin. My nipple hardens against his touch, and then he places the clamp firmly on my nipple.

I moan from the pain and the pleasure.

He does the other one, and I can't focus on anything but my breasts. It's like all my blood and focus go there. He grins as his hand goes down between my legs, tearing my focus between my nipples and the ache between my legs.

I let my head roll back and rest against the edge of the bath, no longer caring where my focus is. It's his. Just like my body. He can do whatever he wants to me, and it doesn't matter.

I feel his cock slide into me, and my body feels whole.

I open my eyes to see him still clothed except for his cock. He grabs my shoulder as he thrusts into me, sliding me down deeper into the tub. I don't care. I let him. I trust him completely with my body. Despite the fact that with each thrust, my mouth falls further beneath the water threatening my oxygen supply.

I can't breathe after a few thrusts, because my face is covered with water. His lips come down on mine giving me breath and a sweet release. I come on his cock as easily as breathing.

He grins pulling out of me and pulling me back up out of the water. He stands and then pulls me up too. He tugs at the nipple clamps, turning me on again before he pulls them off and I'm left with nothing but ecstasy and emptiness, missing his cock.

He helps me out of the tub and hands me a towel, while he finally undresses and wraps a towel low around his waist.

"I want to try something. Trust me?" he says, but all I hear is a command to my soul to which I can't say no.

I nod, my mouth dry. I love when he wants round two so quickly afterward.

"Go lie down on my bed, face down."

I don't bother to dry off all the water from my body. I walk to the bed, laying the towel down first to not completely soak the bed, and then lie down on my stomach as he asked.

He takes his time before he finally walks to the bed. I don't hear him, but I can feel him standing at the base of the bed.

I don't turn to look. I don't need to. I trust him and whatever new thing he wants to try.

He climbs on the bed behind me and gently lifts my hips up placing a pillow under my stomach.

"I'm not going to tie you up, but you can't move. Understand?" he asks.

I nod.

"I need to hear you say you won't move."

"I won't move."

"Good girl." He pushes his cock inside me without warning into my ass. He's fucked me in the ass before, but usually, I get a lot more warning and preparation. Not this time. This time he wants me to feel the pain.

Tears sting my eyes, but quickly subside when his fingers play with my most sensitive bud, and he starts thrusting, making me feel like I'm floating on a cloud.

He kisses my neck, and I moan. I love it when he kisses my neck before he nibbles. I love feeling his lips anywhere on my body.

"Take a deep breath, baby," he whispers into my ear before sucking on my earlobe sweetly. He's acting far too sweet, which means it's time for the pain. The part where I don't know if I can handle it right before I come but want more and more of the pain I thought moments before I couldn't tolerate.

I suck in a breath.

Pain.

I feel searing pain in the back of my neck as Matteo stabs me with something. I know he's drawing blood from whatever he's doing.

This.

This is my breaking point.

I can't handle more of whatever this is.

"Stop," I beg through tears.

He kisses my neck, and the pain disappears. Just like that. Did he listen to me? Or did I blackout?

He thrusts inside, and I'm back to the real world again. The world where he worships my body in the worst ways.

"You got this baby. I need this," he says, and then I feel the burning pain again against my neck.

I don't know what he's doing or why. I take his words and play them in my head again and again. He needs this. He's using my body to please himself. And as screwed up as it is, I'm more than okay with that.

The tears still sting my eyes, but less this time. My body jolts as the stabbing continues, but this time he thrusts, I focus on what his cock is doing to my body instead of the pain in my neck.

"You're mine, beautiful," he moans as he continues.

"Yours," I whisper back, knowing exactly how true my words are.

I don't care about being a lawyer again.

I don't care about returning to my old boring life.

I care about him. Because he's the only one that has made me feel alive.

He's protected me against Armas. He's taken care of me when I needed help the most. He's done everything for me. More than anyone else in my life ever has.

I can see myself painting again here. I can run. I can study history again. I'm stronger here. No longer afraid of anything.

Because I know I can handle any pain or nightmares. I'm stronger than I ever realized.

Matteo showed me that.

I'm more alive here than I ever was back home. Matteo is my new home. I don't ever want to go back.

I might even love him.

It's a crazy thought.

One I shouldn't have.

I probably have Stockholm syndrome. I just fell in love with my captor, and when I get free, I'll realize how crazy these feelings are. But I don't think so.

I've seen other women who had feelings for their captor. This is different. I still despise him for taking me against my will. I won't ever forgive him for that, but I can't ignore the caring man he can be when he's not pretending to be a monster.

All the feelings in my body intensify. The pain. The pleasure. The heartache. It all comes to a head.

"Come, Eden," Matteo commands.

I don't think it's possible. I can't when I'm in this much pain. But I feel the tightening of my body. My toes curl, my breath catches. And I come like I haven't ever before.

I come hard on his cock as the pain slowly subsides and the kisses on my neck stop.

I come, and it's an experience I never want to forget. It's the first time I've come while in love. And I want to remember it forever.

Matteo doesn't let me collapse against the bed. He grabs my arm and drags me off the bed and into his arms. I'm too exhausted to walk. He knows, so he scoops me into his arms to carry me to the bathroom, most likely to clean up.

"Look in the mirror," Matteo commands, and he brushes my hair off my neck.

I glance in the mirror, out of the corner of my eye.

My eyes widen when I see the marks he left in black ink.

Matteo Carini's.

It's a crude tattoo. Blood is oozing down my back, and the lettering isn't perfect or dark, but I wouldn't have it any other way. It's a perfect way to mark how I feel.

He doesn't wait for me to respond. He doesn't speak any other words either. He simply kisses my forehead and then carries me back to bed.

He didn't say I love you. I didn't either.

He didn't ask if I liked the tattoo or if it was okay.

I didn't want him to anyway.

He marked me as his. And it's exactly what I wanted.

Even though our relationship will never last, I'll never remain his forever. Someday another man will fuck me and have to look at his name on my neck with his name on it.

I may love another man one day. A man that treats me nicely and lets me make my own decisions in my life. A man that isn't dangerous enough. A man that won't remind me of Matteo in any way.

When that day comes, I'll be more than happy to have Matteo's name etched on my skin.

18

———

MATTEO

"You ready?" I ask Eden.

She raises an eyebrow. "I'm always ready for you." She throws her arms around my neck and kisses me hard on the lips.

I smirk. "I meant ready to go."

Her eyes widen as she falls off my lap. "You were serious? You're taking me on a date?"

I nod.

Her face lights up, and I really wish it wouldn't. She's wanted to go on a date for weeks, despite never asking me to take her. I've wanted to take her on a date too. Today's that day.

But as much as I wish this was just about going on a date, it's not. It's playing double duty. I've given into what Eden wants, in more way than one.

"You have five minutes to get changed."

She darts off my lap in the main living room and starts running toward my bedroom.

She pauses in the hallway. "What should I wear?"

"Jeans and a nice shirt. And make sure to wear your hair up!"

She grins and then disappears. She better fucking listen to

me, for once, and wear her hair up. I need to see her tattoo today.

I thought she would make a big fuss when she finally saw the tattoo. I thought she would yell and tell me I had no right to do it.

She didn't. In fact, I'm pretty sure she likes it. More than she should.

I don't even know why I did it. It was an impulse thing. I had the equipment. Not the fancy tattoo guns that you get at the shop, but the kind that barely gets the job done, although in a more painful way.

I just knew that I needed her marked. Especially before today. I may be giving in to Eden and my men's plans, but I'm going to let the world know she's mine while I do it.

Eden leans against the wall of the living room. "Does this work?" she asks beaming, knowing how fucking sexy she looks.

I stand and walk over to her. Taking in her dark jeans, her cleavage-revealing yellow halter top, and her matching spiked heels. And her hair pulled up in a clip.

I kiss her on the lips, sweeping her off her feet, reminding her who she belongs to tonight because I'm afraid this plan is going to fail. I think it will work to take Clive and Erick out, but I'm worried I might lose Eden in the process. She might finally find a way to escape. Although, the heels she is wearing makes it a little less likely. But she can run fast. Even in heels.

"So where are you taking me?" she asks, grinning far too brightly.

"Dinner."

"It's two o'clock in the afternoon? What are we doing before dinner?"

"Whatever you want."

She bites her lip. "Anything?"

"Anything."

"How about horseback riding?" she asks, her cheeks flushed.

I laugh. "You want to go horseback riding, in that?" I look down at her heels.

She frowns. "I didn't realize we could do anything I wanted when I picked this outfit out. But yes, I want to go horseback riding. I think it will make me feel free. And then I want you to take me to a local bakery. Buy me something sweet and coffee, and then make out with me as the sunsets, before taking me to dinner. That's what I want."

"You are such a girl."

She puts her hands on her hips. "Well, what would you have us do then?"

I shrug. I hadn't really thought about what we were going to do before dinner. I just wanted out of this house with her. That was the plan.

"I guess, drive fast in my Ferrari with the top down. Then take you to one of my favorite wine bars to get a drink, and then I guess I could show you my favorite spot to watch the sunset before dinner."

She thinks for a moment. "Damn it. I like your idea better."

I smirk, surprised that she would be so agreeable to my plans.

"Let's go," she says, holding out her hand to me. I take it, and we run through the house, like two teenagers sneaking out of their parents' house.

We make it to the garage. "Which car should we drive?"

"The red one," she says, knowing that one is my favorite, despite not knowing the name of the car.

"Good choice."

We climb in, and then I spend the next hour racing through the countryside of Italy. Enjoying the twists and turns, occasionally taking a turn too fast just to hear her squeal.

Then I take her to my favorite wine bar, where I let her taste various wines and explain to her why her tastes in wine are wrong. She laughs but eventually comes to see things my way.

Lastly, I take her to an old bridge that looks out over the river to watch the sunset. I take her in my arms, wrapping my hands around her waist, while we watch the sunset. Kissing her neck, just to the side of where I carved my name into her neck a few days before.

Just as the sun is about to set fully, she says, "Why did you give me the tattoo?"

I swallow but don't immediately answer.

"Why are we on this date? Why give me the perfect day? What's going on?"

I kiss her again, giving her one more perfect moment, not wanting this to end.

"I'm giving you what you want."

She cocks her head to the side, not understanding. "You're giving me my freedom?"

I suck in a breath, not liking her response, but of course, that's what she wants - freedom from me. I'm not ready to give her that yet. I can't give her freedom.

"Using you as bait to draw out Clive and Erick."

She tucks a strand of hair behind her ear.

"Is that still what you want?" I ask, thinking I made a mistake.

She nods. "Yes, I want to help."

"Good. Because it's going down tonight. That's what this date tonight is about."

"Oh..."

I study her soft expression, but I don't understand what it means.

"What's wrong?"

"Nothing. I just thought... never mind." She smiles too brightly. "What do you need me to do?"

"Nothing. I just need you to pretend you are on a date with me and let me and my men do the rest."

She nods.

"Can you do that?"

She nods again.

"Don't be afraid. I won't let them take you. You're mine."

She melts against my side as we start walking the three blocks to the restaurant we picked out. I made reservations at the restaurant a couple of days ago under a fake name, but I know the owner likes to run his mouth, and he's good friends with Clive. He would have told him that I was coming in and bringing a date. I'm positive Clive will take the bait once it's confirmed that Eden is here with me.

He will try to steal her. And I'll take him out when he does.

We walk into the restaurant, and we are guided toward a booth at the back that overlooks the river. This is one of the most upscale restaurants in town. And I'm the wealthiest sucker in this town, so I always get the best table. They bring over a bottle of my favorite wine without me even having to ask. They pour us both a glass, and I notice Eden drinking hers faster than usual.

I take her hand in mine and try to come up with something funny to say to distract her, but I can't. I can't even distract myself. Clive will give us one look, and he'll know that this is fake. A setup.

I stand up and slide into her side of the booth draping my arm around her shoulder. I may not be able to make her laugh right now, but I can make her forget.

My hand slides up her jeans, and I silently wish that she had worn a skirt instead of pants. She shifts as her cheeks finally flush pink.

I tilt her head toward mine and kiss her firmly on the lips. She melts in my arms, instantly forgetting about everything. I continue making out with her in the booth, not caring that this is a fancy restaurant and this is simply not done. I want her calm. She doesn't know that my men are all around, waiting for the signal to attack.

Food is set in front of us. The restaurant has a fixed menu so course after course will be brought to us.

The first is soup, bringing us both back to the night I fed her soup by holding the bowl up to her lips.

She laughs when I pick the bowl up to her lips, but it doesn't stop her from drinking the liquid from it.

The rest of our meal is pretty uneventful. We talk, we laugh, we eat. Clive nor Erick have made an appearance, nor any of their men. We've been eating dinner for almost three hours now, well past the time that a normal dinner would take. They aren't coming.

"I need to use the restroom before we go," Eden says.

I nod, get out of the booth to let her out, and then take a seat again, watching her ass sway as she walks away in her jeans. Loving that we are both wearing jeans, despite this being a fancy restaurant where everyone in it is wearing dresses and suits. The staff hasn't said anything to us. They know better.

I pay the waiter while I wait for Eden to return. But ten minutes pass and she still hasn't returned.

I glance back at Dierk at one of the tables a few back. He has a concerned look on his face as well.

Shit.

We both dash up, drawing our guns, as we run toward the back exit.

I find Eden with a gun pointed at her head in Erick's arms.

She doesn't look afraid though. She looks mad. And I know that she has the skills to break free from Erick's arms any moment she wants to. I don't know what self-defense classes she took, but they were good. She's taken out plenty of my men before. She won't right now. She's acting as bait. But she will when the time is right.

"Let her go," I say, acting scared. Although it's not an act. I am scared. I hate him touching her or having a gun pointed at her. Even if the plan is working.

"Nah, I think we will keep her. You seem to care about her. I think we will enjoy playing with her a bit first," Erick says, nuzzling Eden's neck. Her eyes turn to rage, matching my own.

Patience.

Don't let him goad you into doing anything stupid, I tell myself.

I sigh. "Fine. Take her. She's nothing to me." I put my weapon down pretending I'm done fighting.

Clive laughs. "You can't fool us. You love her. You won't let any harm come to her."

I swallow. I don't love her. But damn, do I care about her more than I should.

"Fine. You got me. Now make a trade."

Clive raises his eyebrows. "What kind of trade?"

"Me for her."

He laughs. "No way, what use are you to us?"

My men are in position. The only man that ran out with me was Dierk, and that's because he was acting as my usual security. Clive and Erick and the dozen men they brought with them don't know that I have more men here.

"What do I have to do to get her back?" I ask slowly and deliberately, giving Eden a look that she needs to break free now, as I give my team the cue words to attack.

Erick's hand drops just a tiny bit as he grows tired of holding the gun. Eden takes the opportunity to knock the gun out of his hand while she elbows him hard in the nose. He lets go of her immediately, grabbing his nose. She runs toward me as shots from my men ring out around us.

I start shooting as well; I won't ever leave my men to fight a battle for me.

"Get her out of her," I say to Dierk as Eden reaches me. I grab her hand and sling her over into Dierk's arms. He grabs her arms and starts pulling her. He'll get her inside.

I have a job to do. I need to kill these bastards and keep my men and Eden safe.

I glance to my right to make sure that Eden is safe after Erick & Clive's men start returning shots, but Dierk has barely made it to the door and Eden is in his arms, fighting him the whole way. I give him a look and then turn my attention back to Erick who now has his sights set on me.

He fires, but I'm faster. I hit him hard in the chest watching him fall to the ground. Most likely dead, or he will be soon enough.

I hear Eden scream, and I feel the bullet in the back of my arm. I try to spin to turn and shoot my attacker before he gets another shot off but I know I won't be fast enough. I can only hope that he doesn't have great aim and hits me in my extremities instead of my head or chest.

The shot has gone off, but I make it all the way around before I realize what happened.

Eden.

She took the bullet for me and is lying on the ground at my feet.

I aim my gun at the guy that shot us both, and hit him in the head, watching him drop dead instantly.

And then I fall to the ground, scooping Eden up in my arms before I run. I never run. I stay and fight with my men. Maybe I would have in the past, but not now that I'm their leader.

But tonight is different. Eden could be dying in my arms, and I need to save her.

I run as fast as I can to my car, toss her in and then start driving, not thinking about anything other than getting her to a hospital as fast as I can. She took a bullet that could have easily killed me. She saved me.

I stroke her lifeless face as I drive. I'm pretty sure she stole more than a bullet meant for me. She stole my heart.

Erick may not be right about many things. But he was right when he said that I love her. I do. I love Eden. I would do anything for her.

I only hope I get the chance to tell her and earn hers in return. Because there is no way, an angel like her could love the devil in me. I need to give her her freedom and hope it's enough to keep her.

19

EDEN

I WAKE up and immediately know I'm in a hospital. It's far too bright to be anywhere in Matteo's home. The only other place it could be is heaven, but I know that the bullet just barely grazed my arm, so that can't be it.

Although, why I'm in a hospital is lost on me. I can tell from how my body barely aches that I'm not injured enough to be here.

I look over and see Matteo holding my hand like I'm about to die, staring at me with relieved eyes when I open mine. He exhales deeply, reaches over the hospital bed, and hugs me.

"I'm so glad that you are okay," he says.

I scrunch my nose. "Did I miss something? Because I don't feel that injured."

I move my arms and legs around, realizing the only part of me that is even taped up is my arm, and it barely hurts. I have an IV that could be feeding me pain drugs, but they wouldn't make me feel this much better.

"You were shot in the arm."

I smile. "You brought me here because I was shot in the arm?"

He nods, still frowning and not understanding while I'm smiling.

"Yes, you were also passed out, and I was afraid you might die."

I bite my lip to keep from smiling brighter as I stroke his cheek.

"You do know I survived an injury to my leg that was a lot worse than this without going to the hospital?"

"That was a mistake," he says coldly.

I raise an eyebrow. "Did the doctor say that something was wrong with my leg?" I'd be surprised if he did. My leg feels amazing.

"No, he said it seemed to have healed nicely."

"Then, what's the problem?"

He sighs.

My heart falls in love a little more, seeing him risking losing me to bring me here.

"How did...?" I ask, not being able to ask how many men he lost when he saved me instead of staying and fighting.

"Clive and Erick are taken care of. We only lost two men. It's going to be hard for the men to lose them. But their sacrifice wasn't in vain. Just like yours wasn't."

I swallow. I hate that anyone died, but I'm glad it's over. We're safe. For now at least.

I hear the knock and look up to see a doctor walk in smiling at me brightly.

"Can I have a moment alone with Eden?" she says, looking at Matteo.

"No, I'd like to be here for whatever you have to talk to her about," Matteo says, glaring at the woman for even suggesting that he leave my side for a moment.

I don't care if he stays or leaves, but I like that he wants to stay.

The woman gives him a snide look back. "I'm not asking. I have private information that I need to discuss with Eden, and I will not have you here when I talk to her."

He doesn't budge. "I'm her husband."

She laughs. "No, you're not. Now get out of here, before I call security and have you thrown out. I don't care if you are the king of Italy, I want you out."

He looks from her to me, and I nod, encouraging him it's okay that he leaves.

"I'll be right outside the door if you need me." He kisses me gently on the lips and then storms out, flipping off the doctor as he does.

The doctor ignores him and walks over to my bed. "I'm Abigail Faustino. I've been looking after you while you are here. How are you feeling?"

"Great actually."

She smiles. "Good. I know that you were involved in a gunfight with Mr. Carini. I'm not here to ask questions or get involved. But I am here to help if you want a way out. Do you need a way out?"

I swallow. I may never get another chance like this again. She's offering to help me. I should take it. My heart thumps loudly. I can't.

"No, I don't need your help," I finally say.

She nods. "I figured you'd say that. Mr. Carini seems to be especially fond of you, so I hope he treats you well."

"He does."

"Good, well now that that is out of the way, I have some news to share with you. When you were admitted, we ran some regular tests and well...you're pregnant."

I gasp and then I can't breathe. I can't move. I can't think. Of all the things she could have said, that was the least expected.

The door is thrown open, and Matteo runs in, clearly having heard what the doctor said.

The woman sighs but doesn't object as Matteo runs to my side and holds my hand.

"I think she might be in shock," the doctor says, coming to my side as Matteo stares at me.

I suck in a breath as the doctor puts her hands on me.

"How far along?" I ask, coming to.

"We don't know for sure without an ultrasound, but it could be a couple of months."

I swallow, staring at Matteo, silently telling him that it could be Armas' baby.

Matteo frowns. Grabbing my cheek and forcing me to look at him. "It's mine."

I swallow. It should make me feel better. It should make me feel happy to know that it's most likely Matteo's, but it doesn't. I don't know how he will feel about having a baby. I don't even know how I feel. Should I get an abortion? I shouldn't have a monster's baby while I'm captured.

But I haven't really been captured in a while. He has given me freedom without actually telling me I was free. I just turned down freedom. He's shown me he loved me without telling me.

And I know I love him. Is this the worst thing? Maybe him having a kid would change him. Make him softer, get out of this life and live a whole new life with me.

"Could you leave us alone for a few minutes, doctor?" Matteo asks.

The woman nods and leaves.

I stare at Matteo, still not understanding how I feel. Matteo smiles at me softly as he holds his hand over my stomach.

"We are going to have a baby," he says, giddily kissing me firmly on the lips, seemingly happy with the idea.

I take a deep breath and close my eyes as he kisses me. He's happy to have a baby with me, so I'm not going to fret. Not immediately anyway. I'm going to just be. And see what happens.

I open my eyes though, needing to talk about so many things. But what I see when I open my eyes isn't the Matteo I've gotten used to these last few weeks.

Instead, a darker Matteo is here with much darker intentions. His hands are on me touching me without permission. His cock burns inside me, and his eyes see red.

I close my eyes and open them again, and I'm back in the hospital room instead of the couch in his room. It was a memory. A memory I had forgotten or tried to push out of my head. Whichever it is doesn't matter.

What matters is that I remember. I remember the worst of Matteo. And I realize I should have taken the doctor's offer to help me escape.

20

MATTEO

Eden's pregnant.

That should send my heart into a panic.

I've stolen a woman, made her mine, and now I've knocked her up.

She hates me. There is no way she will want to carry my baby. Even if she does, there is no way that afterward, she will stay. That she won't try and steal the baby away from me.

Eden deserves to be free. I can't keep her trapped. Not anymore.

But I can't let her go. Because if I do, if she gets that chance, she will never stay. I won't ever see the baby.

And this baby is already mine. I need an heir. I need a family to continue my legacy just like my father needed me. And more than that, I want a family. I want someone to love and take care of. That's who I am. I take care of people, and I want to take care of a family.

I stare at Eden. I have no idea how to keep her. I have no idea how to set her free, but convince her to stay. I have to try though. And it starts with telling her how I feel.

"Eden I—"

She slaps me hard across the cheek before throwing the covers off and stepping out of hospital bed. She rips the IV out of her hand before she starts gathering her clothes in the corner of the room and starts putting them on, one by one.

"What was that for?" I ask, trying to keep my anger out of my voice.

She pulls up her jeans before grabbing her top and jerking it on before she answers me.

"You raped me," she says.

I freeze. The one thing I didn't want her to remember is rushing back into her memory. I stare at her, not sure how to continue. I don't see fear when she looks at me. I don't see the same broken woman I saw with Armas.

Instead, I see a strong, fierce woman, that won't put up with my crap.

"Eden, let me explain."

She laughs. But it's not a funny laugh. It's a 'you're ridiculous for trying to explain rape to me' laugh.

"I don't need you to explain. I was there. I remember. You raped me."

"I stopped!"

"You stopped because you were interrupted. And stopping doesn't matter anyway. You should have never started!"

"I'm sorry! Okay? Is that what you want to hear? I'm fucking sorry."

She shakes her head. "You can't just apologize for rape. That doesn't make it any better. It doesn't take away any of the pain."

She starts walking toward the door, and I grab her arm.

"Where are you going?" I ask.

"I'm leaving," she says, before realizing her mistake. She doesn't have freedom. She doesn't get to leave because she wants to. I tell her what she gets to do and what she doesn't.

She freezes, as does my heart because I know what I have to do, and it risks losing her and the baby forever.

I reach into my back pocket and pull out my wallet. I dig out my cash and my credit card along with my cell phone and hand them all to her.

She takes them hesitantly, not understanding what I'm doing.

"You're free. Use the money, the phone, to get you wherever you want to go. Tell Dierk to take you if you prefer. But you're free to go. You're not my slave or my captive. You're free."

She studies me for a moment and then she walks to the door.

"I love you, Eden. I love this baby. I still want you to be mine," I say.

She doesn't hesitate at my words. She simply walks out, leaving me alone.

I thought raping her would break her. I thought it would change her and force her to give me what I want.

Instead, she broke me.

———

One week after Eden left, I could barely get out of bed.

Three weeks after she left, I was so drunk all the time I couldn't even think straight.

Six weeks after she left, and I'm now a broken man, not worth anything.

"I found her," Dierk says, while I lie on the couch staring out the window.

"What?" I ask, sitting up abruptly.

"I found her," he says again.

"Did she go back to her condo in Los Angeles? Or did she get a new apartment?"

"She didn't go back."

"Huh?"

"She didn't go back," Dierk says again, getting annoyed at having to repeat everything to me. "She's staying in a hotel in the old downtown area. She's working at a coffee shop as a barista. She stayed."

She stayed.

She fucking stayed.

That must mean something. She still has feelings for me. She still wants me. She wants me to fight for her. Or she still has unfinished business. Whatever it is, I'm going to find out. Today.

I get up off the couch, needing to go to her immediately.

"Where are you going?" Dierk asks.

"To get Eden back."

He runs in front of me, blocking my path to the garage.

"You aren't going anywhere. One, you are drunk and are not driving a car. Two, Eden will not take you back in this state. You'll just piss her off further. You are going to have to work hard to earn her trust back."

I glare at him, but even in my haze, I know he's right.

I sink back down onto the couch, hating myself for getting drunk again today. It takes me far too long sitting on the couch to realize what my next move should be.

"I need you to get me the number to the florist. I should at least send her flowers," I say to Dierk, who has been standing over me to ensure that I don't do anything crazy.

He nods. "It's going to take a lot more than flowers to get her back."

"I know, but it's the best place to start."

———

After I sent her flowers every day for a week, I decide to step foot inside the coffee shop. I figure it's safer to show up during the day, instead of waiting until she goes back to her hotel room where she's alone. She'll probably shoot me without a second thought if I show up there.

The bells chime as I step inside the quaint tiny shop that only has two small tables, both of which are occupied. Most people just come in to grab a cup of coffee and then go out to the local park to drink it or head off to work.

There is nowhere for me to hide in the shop and take my time by studying her first.

She spots me the second she hears the chimes.

Her face is expressionless. She doesn't react. She must have been expecting me after all the flowers. She looks good, despite her expression. Her body is curvy, just beginning to show signs that she's pregnant.

She's still pregnant. My insides warm seeing her still pregnant. I thought she would have gotten rid of the baby by now if she hated me.

I walk slowly to the counter, not sure how to handle this. I haven't asked a woman for forgiveness, ever. I don't date. I don't know how to make up with her. I don't know how to make any of this better.

"What can I make for you?" she asks, when I get to the counter like I'm any other customer. I understand now what the expression on her face is - indifference. That's at least how she's trying to appear. Like she doesn't care about me.

But if she didn't have any feelings for me, whether it be love, or caring, or hatred, she wouldn't still be in Italy.

"I'll have an espresso."

She types it into the computer and then turns to make my coffee. When she finishes, she sets the mug down with a thud, letting a couple of drops of the coffee spill out onto the counter.

She takes my credit card and swipes it, before handing it back to me.

"Why are you still here? Why haven't you gone back to the US yet?"

She frowns. "Because they won't let me back without a passport. And since I don't have one of those, I'm stuck here for a while."

I sigh. A passport. Of course. "I'll have Dierk get you a passport by the end of the day."

I take the espresso to go drink it on the small patio outside when I see, out of the corner of my eye, the flowers that I sent her sitting in the far back of the coffee shop. She didn't immediately toss them. There is still hope for us yet.

I show up at her coffee shop every day for a week. Every day I go, I expect her to be gone. She has everything she needs to leave now. A passport. Money. I even bought her a suitcase and packed up all her things from my house so that she had whatever she needed to leave.

And yet she still hasn't left.

She hasn't spoken more than two words to me or smiled at me, either. But I figure it will take a long time for her to be accepting of me, let alone start to forgive me for what I've done.

I stole her from her life.

I've threatened her life and her best friends.

I raped her.

I knocked her up.

I shouldn't ever be forgiven.

Today, though, I have to try. I can live with myself if she leaves, as long as I've tried everything I can to keep her, while also giving her her freedom.

"I'm sorry," I say when she hands me my cup of coffee.

She doesn't look up. She keeps staring down at the cash register.

"I'm sorry for being a monster. I'm sorry for stealing you. I'm sorry for hurting you. I'm sorry for raping you. You shouldn't forgive me, ever. But I'm not going to lie. I want you back. And I'll do anything to make that happen."

Her breath catches.

"But I won't steal you again. I won't take you against your will. I love you, Eden. I don't know what that means or even how to love you, but I will work hard every day to love you more than I did before. I will become the man that you deserve."

I take my coffee, walk out, and then I pull out my cell phone. She needs a grand gesture to come back. I know that. This phone call is the first step in making that happen.

21

EDEN

I DON'T KNOW what I'm doing at Matteo's doorstep with my luggage in my hand. All I know is I won't run. I don't know what's going on between us. I doubt we can ever work through the damage we have caused each other, but if I leave without trying to figure this out, it will feel like running.

He will come after me eventually. He might be trying to change, but he hasn't changed that quickly. And he will continue to haunt my dreams as he has for the past few weeks.

Our child will grow up without a father, and I won't have a reasonable explanation as to why, other than he was a monster once and I never gave him a chance to change.

So I guess that's what I'm doing knocking on his door. Seeing if he can change. And seeing if I can forgive.

I'm not sure if one or either is possible. But the growing baby in my stomach convinces me I need to try at least.

The door opens, and I'm shocked Matteo is the one that opens the door, but then I remember he has plenty of security to tell him who is standing at his door.

"Hi," I say, my voice sounding weaker than I'd hoped.

"Hi, would you like to come in?" he asks, his voice just as weak.

I nod.

He takes my suitcase from my hand and holds the door while I step in. It's strange walking in the front door instead of the side from the garage. It was strange ringing the doorbell. His house had started to feel like home the last time I was here.

"Can I get you anything? Something to eat or drink?" Matteo asks. He's nervous.

So am I. I wanted to pretend he didn't affect me when I stepped inside this house. That's not possible.

"No, I'm fine."

He tries to be patient with me, but it's clear he can't be.

"What do you want then?" he asks.

"Let's go out back and talk."

He nods and places his hand on the small of my back as he leads me through the house to the back patio. I like having his hand touching me, even if his hand has done wrong, monstrous things.

We take a seat on couches, opposite each other. I want him sitting right next to me, touching me, comforting me, but it's not what this conversation needs.

I sit in silence, watching him squirm, trying to remain calm and patient with me. I like watching him squirm, so I take my time before I speak.

"I can't forgive you," I say.

He sucks in a breath, and his eyes turn sad.

"But I can try. Maybe I can't forgive you, but we can start from here and grow into something better. Or maybe we can't. I don't know. I just know I don't want to run. I want to stay and figure this out. I want to see if the man that sends me flowers and love notes every day is possible of actually loving this baby and me. I think he can."

"I can. I love you more than I want to keep breathing."

"I have a couple of conditions."

He nods, his eyes glaring into mine as his hands grip the armrests to keep himself glued to his seat.

"I'm not a slave. I'm free—"

"You're free. It's not something I want anymore. I don't want to trap you or kidnap you ever again. I don't ever want to hurt you."

I smile and nod. "Good. You don't get to tell me what to do or boss me around in any way. We make decisions together. Understand?"

"Yes, together," he says, smirking a little as I smile at him, giving up a little of my authority.

"And you give up searching for Nina. You leave Nina and Arlo alone."

This is the one condition I expect to be the hardest for him. I don't understand what his connection is to her. I don't know if he still wants her or wants revenge. I don't know.

When I was free, I called Nina a few times. I didn't tell her what happened. I pretended I was still back in the US and had just been busy working. But she didn't seem that shocked I hadn't called in a while. She understood I was busy with work.

"I won't go after Nina or Arlo. I give you my word," Matteo says without hesitation.

I listen to his words looking for any deception. But I believe him. I have to if I'm going to give whatever crazy relationship we have a shot again.

It doesn't mean I won't want him to continue proving it to me over and over.

But to be honest, something changed when I found out I was pregnant in the hospital. Matteo changed. He set me free. And I realized what I wanted, more than my freedom was to be with him. How fucked up is that?

"Can I show you something?" Matteo asks.

I nod.

He holds out his hand, and I take it automatically, feeling his warm grip comfort me with just his touch.

He leads me inside, and we walk to his bedroom. I smirk, he's going to show me his cock. He's such a guy.

He opens the door that isn't locked and holds it open while I step inside.

It's so bright. Light shines in through the large windows that he usually keeps hidden beneath the drapes. The bed and furniture are gone and replaced by white antique furniture with a light gray comforter and turquoise and pink pillows.

"Pink?"

He shrugs. "I had Gia help. She said you would like the pink."

I laugh. But my laughter soon turns to tears when I see the bassinet he put in the corner next to the bed. I walk over and run my hand across the white lace fabric draped over it.

I turn to Matteo who has his hands in his pockets. He does that when he wants to touch me but won't let himself do it.

"I started clearing out the room next door for a baby's room, but I thought I should wait to see if you'd come back before I decorated it. I thought you might enjoy doing that. And I had no idea what color you would want it to be."

"Pink."

He chuckles. "It can be pink, or whatever color makes you happy."

I shake my head because he doesn't understand what I'm saying. I walk over to him swaying my hips just to torture him.

"There is a reason I want it pink, and it's not because I like the color."

He frowns. "Why?"

I bite my lip to keep from laughing hysterically. He's so clueless; he doesn't even understand what I'm saying. "I'm having a girl."

I don't know how he will respond. If I had to guess which gender he would prefer, it would be a boy. A boy to follow in his footsteps and his father's before him. A boy that will become as ruthless as him. He would have taught him how to shoot a gun at the same time he learned to walk most likely.

He grabs me by the waist and twirls me around before kissing me firmly on the lips. "*We* are having a girl."

I nod. "*We*." I like the sound of that.

He kisses me again, and his hands are all over my body, feeling my curves like he hasn't felt them in years instead of weeks.

I moan because I've missed his hands just as much. Honestly, I've yearned for everything about him. Even the darkness.

I throw my hands around his neck, not thinking of anything but Matteo. I want him, and he wants me. I don't care that I haven't forgiven him yet. I don't care that I still don't know what I want and he's still the devil. I don't care about any of our problems.

I want him. Naked. Worshipping my body. Making it so that all I can think about his tongue, his hands, and his cock.

He gets the message immediately and pushes us back on the bed. We fall in a heap, our arms and legs tangling together, refusing to let go of each other.

I grab for the hem of his T-shirt, jerking it off his head so that I can see and taste his hard skin. He helps me pull off his shirt before his lips land back on mine again, not giving me enough time to ogle his body as I want, but when his tongue sweeps over mine, I forget about hot his body is. I can look later. I only want this. So much more of this.

His hands slide under my shirt, careful over my belly, and push my flowy tank up, as his hands caress my swollen breasts.

Every time he touches me it feels like more. More intensity. More caring. More energy. More love.

He pushes the shirt off my body and stands to remove both of our pants until we are both naked, our bodies pulsing with blood and filled with aches that need satiating.

"Tie me up. Spank me. Whip me. Claim me," I beg, needing to see the darkest side of him again. He might think that is one of the reasons I ran, but it's not. It's one of the things I surprisingly like about sex with him. He's not afraid to be himself with me. Even the darkest parts.

But his darkest parts allow for me to be free.

His eyes deepen, and his throat growls. At first, I think he's going to give me what I want.

Instead, he spreads my legs wide, and his head buries between my legs, licking my most sensitive of areas as he worships my body. I grab his hair, needing to touch him, as he drives me wild with his masterful tongue.

"God, yes, Matteo. I forgot how good that feels."

He grins against my lips as he continues to lick until I'm screaming his name and coming around his tongue.

My legs fall to the bed, exhausted from coming. But I know we aren't done. I need his cock, and he needs me.

"Do you trust me?" he asks.

I stare up at him with wide eyes, not sure what he's asking, but if it has to do with tying me up or spanking, then yes. I trust him completely.

"Yes," I whisper, still in my sex coma from coming once already.

He scoops up my body and starts carrying my naked body. I think he's going to carry me out of the bedroom to another room where he thinks he can fuck me better. He doesn't.

He takes me to the couch where he raped me.

I close my eyes and take a deep breath as he forces me to face the worse in him. I expect the butterflies and the pain in my heart to overtake me. I wait for the tears to pour. But they don't come.

He lays me down, ever so gently on the couch and then carefully nests himself between my legs.

"I want to fuck you. Make love to you," he says, waiting for me to respond.

"Fuck me," I respond, knowing we both need this if we are ever going to have a shot at moving forward together.

He leans down and kisses me tenderly as his cock slides into my pussy. I arch my back at the invasion, wanting him deeper as he intensifies the kiss and tangles his hand in my hair.

His eyes are open as he kisses me and thrusts inside. I keep my eyes open as well, not willing to miss one moment of the emotion oozing out of his eyes.

His eyes tell me everything as he fucks me sweetly. I'm sorry. You're beautiful. You're my everything. I love you.

I never thought that someone could say so much and my heart would melt so quickly.

He kisses my favorite spot on my neck making my toes curl before he says, "I love you, Eden. More than anything."

I suck in a breath as he starts bringing me to my climax again.

My body convulses exploding around him as he comes inside me. "I love you, too."

He stays inside me holding me on the couch for what must be hours as we both drift to sleep. The couch used to represent so much pain. He tied me up here. He raped me here. But now, I can't think of this couch without thinking about what just happened. We made loved and found the first step toward what could be a forever kind of love here. The beginning of forgiveness.

————

Our love and forgiveness continue to grow over the next month, as our baby grows large in my stomach, making it clear how pregnant I am when I'm wearing anything other than a baggy T-shirt to cover up my bump.

Our days are filled with normal things that normal couples do. Dates. Fights. Cooking. Sex. And a lot of decorating the baby's soon to be room.

Matteo painted the walls pink for me. I hated it, so he painted it this beautiful gold sparkly color. But then I saw this gorgeous crib that was a silver color that would have been perfect, and he offered to paint it again. He might have to, but for now, I've settled on gold with pink accents.

Our life has been simple. Good. But we haven't talked about any of the big stuff. I figure if we can get through the little things like what we are having for dinner and what movie we are watching on our dates, then the big stuff will come.

Am I ever going back to the US and my old life? Do I want to start a new career here? What are we going to name this baby? What life do we want for her? Is Matteo going to continue killing people? Am I okay if he does? Are Nina and Arlo ever going to be safe to come out of hiding?

I don't know the answers to any of those questions. All I know is that I'm desperately in love with Matteo. And he's equally in love with me. And both of us are smitten with our baby that's due in a few months. *What else could we need?*

It's early in the morning when Matteo slips out of bed, throws on some clothes, and sneaks out of our bedroom without kissing me goodbye or letting me know he was leaving.

He rarely does this. But he has done it a handful of times over the last month. He doesn't tell me where he is going and I don't ask. But I know what he is doing. Working.

Just one of the many topics we should discuss and be honest with each other, but we don't. I guess we aren't doing as well as I thought we were.

I try sleeping, but I know it is a useless endeavor. I can't sleep with him out of bed.

I get out of bed and put on a robe, deciding I should head downstairs to get some coffee and drink it out on the back balcony to watch the sunrise and think about how we should handle all the things we are too afraid to talk about.

I make it to the kitchen and start pouring myself a cup of coffee when I hear Matteo's voice ringing through the hallway before it drops to barely a whisper.

I frown. That's weird. He's working in his home office instead of the warehouse.

I decide to go give him a kiss, bring him a cup of coffee, and let him know I'll be out on the balcony if he wants to join me when he is finished with his phone call. I pour another cup of coffee and then carry them both down the hallway to Matteo's office.

"I have them. I know where Nina and Arlo are," Matteo says.

I freeze outside the door, my heart sinking.

"Yes, I remember our deal. I'll be ready to bring them to you by the end of the week."

I try to calm my breathing and heart, but both are beating so speedily I'm sure that Matteo can hear me lurking outside his door.

"Yes, father. You can do whatever you want with Nina and Arlo. I'll even help you kill them if you want. But you have to keep your end of the deal. I expect to be paid well for this, and you promise to leave Italy and never return. I don't want you messing with what is mine now."

I can't listen anymore. He's making me sick. I thought he had changed. I thought he cared about me, loved me. I didn't think he was ready to give up his entire life and I never asked him to. All I asked was for him to give up Nina. That's all I wanted. To keep her safe.

He told me he loved her once, but it was never about love. It was always about revenge and money. That's how he and his father both think. That's why Nina chose Arlo.

I need a phone.

I run through the house, needing to find a phone to call Nina. The thing that I've spent my entire time trying not to do, I now have to do. Matteo figured out where Nina and Arlo are. He might already have men there, ready to take them. I have to warn them.

The problem is there are no fucking phones in this house. I know because I've looked countless times.

I see Maximo round the corner. He must be on duty this morning. He's not my favorite. He doesn't usually want to help. But today, I'll force him to help me.

"Maximo," I shout.

He stops.

"I need to use your phone," I say, panting heavily.

He stares at me a moment, and I think he's going to say no. He's going to revert back to the slave talk and say I don't get such privileges.

Instead, he pulls out his phone and hands it to me.

"I need to go patrol outside for a bit. I'll make sure to buy you your own phone after I get done with my patrol. I'm sure Matteo meant for you to have a phone but hasn't gotten around to getting you one yet," he says.

Even Maximo thinks highly of Matteo. Matteo has fooled everyone, his trusty employees included.

"Thank you, Maximo," I say. I don't tell him that the new phone won't be necessary because I won't be staying. I need to warn Nina and then get out of here as fast as I can.

When Maximo has walked outside, I pull up the keyboard and begin typing the number I memorized that Nina gave me for emergencies only. I wait impatiently, pacing back and forth in the hallway hoping that Nina answers. If she answers, she's still alive.

I hear the phone click over, "Nin—"

The phone is snatched out of my hand, and Matteo speaks, "I have Eden. I've had her for the past year. If you want to save her, I suggest you and Arlo get to Italy. Fast."

"No," I shout, hoping she hears me before he hangs up the phone.

"She won't come. You won't get her."

He shakes his head, and I swear I see tears in his menacing eyes.

"Nina will come. She loves you. She will do anything to protect you," Matteo says.

He's right. And I hate him for it.

"You won't hurt her. You promised. You won't turn her over to Enrico. You can't."

He swallows. "I'm sorry."

I back up, sick and tired of his apologies.

"If you do this, we are done. I won't forgive you for this. I'll run. And I'll take our baby with me. You'll never get to see her."

"If that is what you think is for the best, then I will let you go. You won't have to run; I won't come after you or our daughter. You can be free."

I narrow my eyes, not understanding him. He's fought so

hard to get me back only to let me go now? It doesn't make sense.

"When this is all over, I'll let you go."

I see the syringe in his hand too late. I feel the sting, and then my eyes grow heavy. If this fucks up our baby, I'll kill him. He catches me in his arms, and the last thing I remember is him saying, "This is for the best. It's the only way to keep you safe."

He could have said those words. Or my brain may have imagined them because I was too desperate to hold onto the thought that he still loves me and we can be a happy family someday. He could have said those words. He could have been protecting me. Or he could not have given a fuck at all.

22

NINA

SHE'S BEEN GONE A YEAR. And I did nothing. I didn't even know she was gone.

I don't know why Matteo took Eden. The only thought I can come up with is because he is pissed at me and looking for revenge. He wants to hurt Arlo and me for what we did to him.

He's had Eden this whole time. Tortured her. Raped her. And now he might kill her if we don't do exactly what he wants.

I swore I would never go back. That Arlo and I had started fresh. We would run forever if it meant we would never have to go back. But I would do anything for Eden.

I'll go back to her in a heartbeat if she can be free.

"Can you drive any faster?" I ask Arlo, who's barely breaking the speed limit as we drive through the curvy roads of Italy.

He rests his hand on my lap trying to calm me. "Dying in a car crash won't help Eden. Besides, he won't touch her until we get there. He wants us to suffer," Arlo says.

I swallow the lump in my throat. "I was a horrible friend. I was living this amazing life with you, while my best friend was suffering in agonizing pain."

"No, you didn't know. And from what you've told me, Eden's tough. She will get through this. Just like you did."

I nod. She's made it a year. That's a lot longer than I was locked up for.

Arlo speeds up, and we finally pull up in the driveway of the Carini house. It's long and dark and equally as hauntingly beautiful as I remember.

But we aren't here to admire the beautiful architecture. We are here to do whatever it takes to get Eden back.

Arlo takes my hand as we pull up in front of the house, both of us knowing that the security team already knows we are here.

"Ready?" he asks.

I pull the gun he gave me and taught me to use, out of my purse.

I nod.

He pulls his gun out, and then we step out of the car ready for an attack at any moment.

Arlo still has hope that he can negotiate with Matteo. Get him to talk to us, and we will get out of here without a scratch. I don't think we will be so lucky.

Arlo also thinks that the men that now work for Matteo will still show him some loyalty because he used to work with them. Was friends with them. They were like family.

He's delusional. I remember what family does to each other.

We step into the house and don't hear anything. Not a person talking. Not the TV or radio on. Not even a deep exhale of breath. Nothing.

We hold onto each other's hands as we slink through the house, trying to hide in the shadows, but it quickly becomes apparent that there is no one to hide from. No one is here.

"Why would Matteo call us here and then not be here?" I ask.

Arlo gives me a dark look, and I know what he's thinking.

Dungeon.

He's in the dungeons waiting for us. I don't want to go back to the dungeon. It holds too many mixed memories for me. It's dark, and Matteo will have the upper hand. But we didn't exactly get to pick the place where the fight will happen.

It will also be harder for us to talk calmly with Matteo.

We don't have a choice. We have to go.

So we slink down to the dungeon. Trying to be as quiet as possible.

But when we open the unlocked door and it creaks loudly, we know that it was the wrong approach.

I scream as Arlo is knocked out from behind before he even has a chance to fight.

"Seems you've lost your touch brother," Matteo says.

"Matteo, please. Just let us go. I'm sorry I chose Arlo. We never meant to hurt you."

"It's been a long time. You don't understand the trouble you have caused," he says.

I drop the gun, knowing it's useless against him. My only hope is to find his weakness.

"Let Eden go. She doesn't deserve to be here. Take me instead," I say.

"No!" I hear Eden cry behind me.

I turn and see Eden locked away in one of the cells behind me. She's still alive. Her eyes are still full of fight. I exhale a little seeing her, but I don't run to her as much as I want to. I need Matteo to make the trade first.

"You're right about one thing. Eden doesn't deserve to be here."

He grabs me by the arm, and he motions for his men to pick up Arlo's lifeless body that I can barely look at. I know he's still alive, but I still hate seeing him like that.

I hear Eden continue to scream behind us, but I tune her out as Matteo walks me away from the dungeon.

"Where are we going?" I ask.

"To make you good on your end of the deal. Eden will go free, in exchange, I'm turning you and Arlo over to Enrico."

Everything stops. I would die for Eden. Do anything for her. But I will do anything not to be taken by Enrico again. He raped me. Did unspeakable things. I will not let him be the one to torture and eventually kill me. I'll die before I let him touch me again.

23

MATTEO

I HAVE Maximo take Nina in one of the cars. I can't be near her and do what I need to do.

I sit in the back of one of the SUVs while Dierk drives with Arlo tied up next to me.

He slowly wakes up. I knew he would on the way to the warehouse.

"You asshole. Nina gave you all this power, and this is how you choose to use it, by turning us over to Enrico?" Arlo asks.

"It beats running," I say.

Arlo glares. "Running kept us alive."

I smirk. "For how long. I was able to track you within a month. Even with Enrico weak and with limited resources, he wouldn't have taken much longer to find you even without my help. You were dead anyway."

"So that makes this better? We were going to die one way or another so you might as well make some cash off of this and get on Enrico's good side?"

I shrug. "You know me. Only looking out for myself. You aren't worth much to me after you abandoned me."

"Why wait so long? Why not turn us over the second you

found us?" Arlo asks, struggling against the ropes, but it's useless, he isn't getting free.

"I thought it would be more enjoyable if you and Nina had a chance to bond. Fall in love truly and all that shit. It also gave me plenty of time to have my own fun with Eden. Now Nina will die knowing that I have her best friend who also faces her same fate."

"If you love Nina, let her go. She's yours. I'll back off. You can have her. She loved you once; she can love you again. Just don't turn her over to Enrico. Keep her alive and safe," Arlo begs.

I stare at him, my brother who has no idea who I am or what I want. I laugh. "You really are clueless."

"I'll do whatever you want. Just don't hurt Nina."

"Then you should have stayed. You should have been loyal to me. Instead, you ran. Now deal with the consequences."

I pull out my cell phone and dial the number. "I have them. We are making the trade tonight. At the warehouse."

Arlo's eyes grow big as he realizes he's lost. That soon I'm turning him and Nina over to Enrico, and there is nothing he can do.

Welcome to my life brother. How does it feel to have no power and know there is nothing you can do to protect the woman you love?

24

EDEN

Nina and Arlo came. Nina was feet away from me, and there was nothing I could do to protect her.

Matteo took them, and I'm afraid it was the last time I might ever see either of them ever again.

"Dierk!" I shout to the man standing guard outside my dungeon cell.

He casually walks over to the door that has bars and a small window at the top.

"Where is Matteo taking them?" I ask.

He looks at me sadly. "To the warehouse. He's turning them over to Enrico. But if it makes you feel any better, I really think he will let you go free when this is all over. He told me not to hurt you no matter what. He wouldn't do that if he wasn't going to let you free."

What is it with everyone thinking that Matteo is a good man? He's a cruel, manipulative, monster. He wants power and money. He doesn't give a shit about anyone else.

I sink down on the floor terrified Nina is going to die, and it's my fault. I should have protected her. I should have called her

245

and told her what was happening when I was free. Now I'll never get the chance.

My body shakes and trembles as I sit on the floor, sobbing. My voice cracks, a high-pitched cry that encompasses everything I'm feeling. Heartache. Terror. Fear. Love. Useless.

"Eden, are you okay?" Dierk shouts through the bars.

I open my mouth to say yes, but an idea forms.

"No, I think...god, my stomach, I think something is wrong with the baby..."

I don't know what instructions that Matteo gave Dierk, but if Dierk thinks that Matteo still cares about the baby and me then Dierk will think he has to do everything he can to protect me.

Dierk pops the door open and runs to me holding me in his arms.

"Let's get you to the hospital," he says, helping me to my feet. "Can you walk?" he asks.

I nod as he puts his arms around me and starts leading me to the garage. He walks me to the car that is parked nearest to the exit of the garage. Just as he's lowering me into the car, I say, "I'm sorry," and elbow him hard in the nose.

Dierk falls to the floor, and I grab the keys, race around to the driver's side, and speed off. I may not be able to save Nina, but I have to try.

The warehouse is dark when I pull up, but there are dozens of cars scattered around the parking lot. I know they are here.

I don't have any weapons. Nothing to get Nina back or protect myself with. I have no idea how I'm going to get her back. But I have to find a way.

I rub my stomach reminding myself that I'm not just risking my life when I try to save Nina. I'm risking my baby's life too.

It just makes me more determined.

I choose the back entrance to enter, hoping that I can sneak in without being noticed. I do, but I hear a man's voice that brings fear to my soul.

Enrico Carini, I assume.

I slink down the hallway to the large room that serves as everything; weapons hold, meeting room, office, and now as a trading place. A place to trade my best friend for money and the promise of Enrico to leave Matteo alone.

I duck down behind a desk when I see Matteo. He's standing in the center of the room across from a man that looks twice his age. He's shorter than Matteo, but also somehow crueler looking. It's Enrico.

Behind Enrico is a dozen men on his side.

At least a dozen stand behind Matteo as well.

I search, but it doesn't take me long to see Nina and Arlo with their arms tied behind their back, standing behind Matteo with a gun pointed at their heads by Maximo and Paul.

My fingers tremble, and my legs ache as I squat down. I want to jump over the table and demand Matteo to release Nina and Arlo, but I know that won't happen. All I can do is stay here behind this dusky desk and hope that an opportunity presents itself to save them.

"You brought them. I didn't think you had it in you, Matteo, to betray your own brother, but maybe you are my son after all," Enrico says.

"I did. Now you need to hold up your end of the deal," Matteo responds.

Enrico nods to one of his men, who brings forward a large briefcase. He opens it presenting it to Matteo. Matteo flips through the cash quickly and the nods, accepting the cash.

The man closes the briefcase and sets it next to Matteo.

"And the second half of our agreement?" Matteo asks.

"You won't see or hear from me again. I won't return to Italy. I've been staying in Northern Ireland setting up a new turf there. That's where I'll be returning," Enrico says.

Matteo nods. "Good."

"Now one last thing to meet my terms," Enrico says.

"You didn't have any other terms," Matteo says, the corner of his lip twitching, upset.

Enrico cocks his head to the side as he smirks. "I always have additional terms when needed. You brought me Nina and Arlo so I could get my revenge. I'm still not convinced you've completely turned on your brother and are now on my side, however."

Matteo narrows his eyes, clearly annoyed with his father's requests. He doesn't argue though. Instead, he turns and walks toward Nina first. He grabs her chin as she struggles against the ropes, which keep her from lashing out at Matteo.

"I love you, and you betrayed me. You deserve what's coming to you," Matteo says. He tightens his grip on her chin and then kisses her lips. It's not like a kiss he's ever done with me. It's all tongue as he slobbers over her lips and forces his tongue into her mouth. Suddenly, he ends the kiss, as quickly as he started it, and then slaps her, knocking her to the floor.

I was expecting him to hurt her. I knew he hated her, but I can't stop the tears from flooding my eyes, seeing her drop to the floor in pain. And I can't stop the ache in my heart from forming when I see Matteo kissing another woman. Even Nina. Even under these circumstances. I know that he loves her and hates her. Unlike me, who is nothing to him.

Matteo turns his attention to Arlo, who is writhing with anger after watching the woman he loves hurt by Matteo.

"You're no brother of mine," Arlo says growling.

Matteo stands expressionless in front of his brother. He stands still for a long time as he stares at Arlo. I don't know what he's doing. He doesn't talk. He doesn't move. He just stands there.

Suddenly, he pulls something shiny out of his pocket and quickly jabs the object into Arlo's stomach.

I gasp at the sight of the blood pouring out of Arlo, not expecting Matteo to actually stab him.

Everyone's eyes turn toward me. My gasp was far too loud not to be discovered, but they can barely see me as I'm still crouched behind the desk.

I have two choices. Run away. Or try to save Nina.

I choose the latter.

I run around the desk and race toward Nina, hoping if I distract Matteo's men long enough, Nina will be able to escape. I'm fast, but not as fast as I used to be, now that I'm pregnant.

I run straight toward Paul, who is holding Nina back, and I kick him as hard as I can in the shin. He jumps back, and I grab her.

"Shoot her," Enrico says to his men.

I hear the shots and Nina and I both duck down instinctively.

Abruptly, I'm gripped by strong hands, and I know that my plan to try to free Nina is short-lived.

I glance up and see Matteo shielding me from the bullets. Not Nina, me.

I frown, not understanding. I thought he only had love-hate feelings toward Nina. I thought he felt nothing toward me.

"Stop," Enrico says, and the bullets stop. He chuckles loudly.

"Now, this looks familiar. Fallen in love again so soon have we? I thought I taught you better than to get attached," Enrico says.

Matteo glares at him as he slowly lets me go, realizing his mistake.

"I don't love her," Matteo says. "I was trying to protect Nina. I don't want you thinking I planned this and to renege on our agreement."

Enrico narrows his eyes and lets his lips fall as he studies Matteo and then each of us.

"Time to make the swap, then. You won't mind throwing in the bitch then will ya? An old man like me doesn't get many opportunities to taste two beautiful women in one night," Enrico says.

"It will cost you more," Matteo answers.

"Well, of course," Matteo says, snapping his fingers and more money is brought to Matteo's feet.

Matteo grabs both Nina and my arms and starts walking us toward Enrico, he glances to his right, and I swear I see Matteo wink.

And then bullets. I duck again, getting far too used to covering my head at the sound of bullets.

People start running, and my feet start moving instinctively.

Matteo's hand falls from my arm.

"Eden!" Matteo screams, but I don't stop running. He doesn't love me. He won't protect me. I can only rely on myself to keep my baby and me safe.

I run, trying to get as far away from the bullets as I can. I don't wait for Nina. She's smart, and I know that she's running back to Arlo. Together, they will be able to escape now that all hell has broken loose. I have no doubt.

I have to worry about myself.

I dart around a lifeless body and then make it to the back door. I need to make it to the car and then drive straight to the airport and never look back.

I grab the handle of the door as I feel a hand grip my shoulder, jerking me back.

"Hello, beautiful," Enrico says, tossing me into two of his

men's arms. "I came for revenge, and I got something better, a chance to ruin true love."

"You're wrong. Matteo doesn't love me. He doesn't want me."

He laughs. "Of course he loves you. He did everything he could to protect you and keep you out of harm's way, even giving up his brother and old fling for a chance to keep me far away so that I would never discover you."

Matteo loves me. I try to search for him to see if it's true. To see if I was the idiot that missed the signs, that this was somehow all an elaborate plan to save me. I can't find him. Enrico's men start dragging me away. And now I'm afraid I'll never know.

25

MATTEO

SHIT.

Enrico took Eden. I felt it the second she was gone. The bullet fire slowly started to subside, and Enrico was nowhere in sight. He stole her from me. I won't let him live.

I'm going to kill Dierk for not keeping Eden locked up where it was safe.

I race back to where Arlo lays on the ground, with Nina over him, trying her best to close his wound and undo the rope around his wrists.

I bend down and place my hands on him, but Nina tries to fight me off.

"Get the fuck away from him!" Nina yells.

"Calm down. I'm helping him."

"Get away!" she cries again.

I turn to Arlo. "Will you tell her to stop so that I can help you?"

Arlo studies me a minute and then looks at Nina. She stops screaming, and I look down at his wound. I pull thread and a needle out of my pocket I always keep with me when we are going into battle, and I start closing his wound.

"You did this all on purpose, didn't you? Why?" Arlo asks, finally understanding I was scheming this whole time.

"Because Enrico was alive after you left. And he wouldn't stop until he got his revenge. You protected Nina by running. I protected her by setting a trap for Enrico."

"By using us as the bait?" Arlo asks, his voice raised.

"Yes."

Arlo head butts me. "You put Nina's life at risk!"

"I had to; it was the only way to get Enrico to come to me. I needed to ensure that he was killed."

"You stabbed me and didn't include me on the plan."

I roll my eyes. "I barely stabbed you, and you know I missed any major organs. You'll be good as new in a few weeks."

Arlo growls, and Nina crosses her arms with a pissed expression.

"Why did you steal Eden? Why keep her so long?" Nina asks.

I wince, not wanting to answer. "I found you guys within a few weeks of you leaving. I needed it to look like I hadn't though so Enrico would think you were so off the grid, he wouldn't bother looking. So I pretended that I needed Eden's help to find you. I planned on using her to get him to think I was struggling to find you and keep you safe until I came up with a plan. But then..."

"Then you fell in love with her," Nina finishes.

I nod. "And now she thinks I hate her."

Nina places a hand on my shoulder. "You'll earn her love back."

She slaps me across the cheek. "But don't ever hurt her or stab my boyfriend again."

"I won't," I say, rubbing the spot that barely stings.

"He's headed north. We think he has a cabin he's renting about thirty miles from here," Clive says as he jogs over to me.

Nina's eyes grow big as she takes a step in front of Arlo, who still has his arms tied behind his back.

"What the hell are you doing here?" Arlo asks, looking at Clive.

Clive cocks his head to the side as he grins as Nina. "Matteo needed my assistance."

Nina and Arlo turn their gazes to me.

"I needed more help to ensure that Enrico was dead. I've been busy with Eden and the baby—"

"Baby?" Nina squeals.

I smile. "Eden's pregnant."

"Oh my god! I'm going to be an aunt!" she screams.

"Baby, that's great, and all but our lives are still in danger, and we need to get Eden back and kill Enrico," Arlo says.

Nina stops squealing.

I turn to Clive. "I found out Clive and Erick were still alive after I almost killed them in an ambush. They have doubled the size of their team, and I thought I could use all the help I could get going against Enrico.

"Enrico thinks Clive and Erick would be the last people I would ever work with, so I knew if they planned this operation, it would mean Enrico would have no clue of the plan. I was afraid some of my men might still be loyal to Enrico."

I grab Clive by the collar of his shirt. "But it seems that Enrico isn't dead. And Eden is gone. Your plan didn't work. You have one hour to fix your screw up, and we'll be right behind you. Enrico needs to be dead, and Eden needs to be safe. Otherwise, we have no deal. Understand?" I say.

"Yes," Clive smirks.

I release him, and he runs off.

"What deal?" Arlo asks.

I shrug. "It doesn't matter. All that matters is killing Enrico and protecting Eden and our baby."

I pull a knife out of my pocket and cut the ropes holding Arlo back.

"Thanks," he says, as the ropes drop from his wrists.

Then he punches me in the jaw.

I close my eyes as the pain radiates through my entire head and down my arms.

"That was for stabbing me," Arlo says.

"Seems fair."

He laughs. "I'm not done yet. I still get a jab for risking me and my fiancé's lives."

"Fiancé?"

"I haven't asked yet, but yea, I'm hoping," Arlo says.

Nina gives him look that says 'yes' and then jumps into his arms with a kiss.

I sigh. "It's good to have you back. And as much as I'd love to watch you two make out, can we please go save Eden?"

26

EDEN

My hands are tied in front of my body, and my mouth is taped shut as I sit in the passenger seat of Enrico's car. He had one of his men throw me in the car so he could drive off alone with me.

He talks nonsense as he drives. Things about honor and what it means to be a man. How his sons have both disappointed him and just want him dead. But now that he has me, he will destroy Matteo, and then go back to obliterate Arlo by killing Nina.

I can't listen.

I feel sick, and not just because he's speeding around turns far too quickly. I'm sick that I left Matteo and didn't have confidence in his love for me. He was trying to protect me in his own way. I'm sick he doesn't understand that I trust him. I'm sick I'm going to die, along with our baby. I should have been thinking about our baby first, instead of trying to play the hero.

Enrico finally stops in front of an old cabin. I glance in the side mirror to see if there are any other cars behind us. There aren't. There will be soon though. I have one shot.

My hands grab the door, and I jump out, running down the gravel road toward the street. A street we only passed one car during the entire ten plus miles we drove down it. The odds aren't great that a car will pass when I reach the road, but it's my only shot.

Enrico chases after me, and as much as I beg my legs to move faster, he catches me. He grabs my arms and jerks me backward, lifting my legs off the ground.

I try to beg through the duct tape, but it comes out mumbled. I can move my hands up enough to reach the duct tape, barely. So that's what I do. I focus on getting the tape off. I can't fight him physically, but I can fight with my words. I can hope that this man has a heart or soul in there somewhere. He might show some compassion if I could only speak to him.

He drags me away from the street and into the cabin, which isn't much more than a fridge, couch, and bed. My eyes widen when I see the bed already set up with ropes to tie me down. He will not rape me. He might kill me, but he will not rape me. I won't let him. I will fight to the death.

I finally rip the tape off my mouth.

"Please don't do this," I beg.

He tosses me to the ground, and I'm barely able to catch myself with my hands before hitting the floor.

"I'm pregnant!" I shout, pissed he just risked my baby's life. Again.

He freezes, staring at me, finally seeing the small bump beneath my T-shirt.

"It's Matteo's. He's going to be a father. You are going to be a grandfather. You can be in this child's life. But you have to stop hurting your family. Stop. Ask for forgiveness and let's move past this."

He continues to stand over me, speechless, while I take several deep breaths, glancing around me for the nearest escape. There isn't one. Unless breaking a window counts. The only door is the front door he carried me through.

He squats down to look me in the eye. This is it. My last shot.

I hold his gaze, trying to get him to see my humanity. He doesn't need to hurt the baby or me. He can change.

If Matteo can change, so can he.

He cocks his head to the side and grins. "You're not going to be pregnant for long. Not when you're dead."

I scramble to my feet to run, but he grabs my hair, jerking me backward.

He yanks me toward the bed, but I dig my feet in, making it as hard as possible for him.

He punches me hard in the stomach.

I see stars. I can't feel anything. I'm dizzy, and sick, and pissed off. If he hurt my baby in any way, death will be his preferred option when I get through with him.

He grabs my hair again and starts dragging me to the bed. My eyes are barely open, but I see the shiny object sticking out of his shoe.

He's not paying attention to me, so I quickly and quietly snatch the knife and hide it in my hands. I could stab him in the leg, but then he'd just shoot me. I have to wait for the right moment.

We get to the bed, and he scoops me up, tossing me to the bed.

His body crashes down on top of me. His weight feels like an elephant sitting on my chest. I can't breathe. If I'm lucky, he might suffocate me before he has a chance to rape me.

His tongue licks my face, and I scream, "No."

He pauses a second at my unexpected outburst. He laughs and does it again.

I scream again.

If he touches me, it won't be enjoyable for him. I'm going to scream and yell and bite and fight. Do anything I can to try and stop him.

"I like fighters. This is going to be more enjoyable than I thought." He sits back. "I'll rape you here on this white bed. Then I'll cut out your baby and let you bleed to death, before Matteo finally arrives, too late to save his one true love. It's perfect."

"You disgusting bastard! You won't touch me."

He licks my face again, simply to show his dominance. As his body presses in again, I remember the knife in my hand, the metal cutting into my grip. Somehow I must have grabbed the blade instead of the handle.

I need to turn the knife around. I need to stab him in the chest. Before he ties me to the bed.

I try to keep my pain focused on Enrico, as he continues to slobber all over my face, down my neck to my breasts. He rips my shirt open, giving him access, as his disgusting cock presses into my belly. I try to ignore him as I slowly turn the knife around, cutting my hands and side in the process.

"Your breasts are going to taste delicious in my mouth," he says, lowering his mouth.

I jab the knife as hard as I can into his stomach. He cries out, but grabs my neck, tightening around me, trying to suck the oxygen out of me. I have limited mobility, but I jab the knife into his stomach again and again, until finally, he releases me.

I roll out from underneath him as he grasps his stomach, lying on his back, holding his wounds.

He thinks I'm done. That I will try to run off and his guards will capture me. But I can't let him live.

Matteo and Arlo made that mistake before. Enrico threatened everyone I love: Matteo, Arlo, Nina, and even my baby. I gave him the chance to change, but he didn't take it. He has to die.

I don't think twice. I take the knife and jab it into his throat will all my might.

Blood spurts out and his body jerks. I pull out the knife and stab him again, blood spraying everywhere. I stab him one more time until the blood slowly stops pouring out and his body is lifeless. I stare at him a few minutes, ensuring there is no way he is still alive. Finally, I get off the bed and head to the door, still holding the knife with my bound hands.

I don't have time to untie my hands. I need to get out of here.

I throw the door open, and I'm met with gunfire.

I know I should slam the door shut, run back inside, and wait for the winner to emerge, but then I see Matteo. He sees me, and I see the pain in his eyes. I can't lose him. I can't risk his death without telling him I love him and I trust him.

So instead, I stupidly run toward him. He runs toward me with a pissed off expression on his face.

I don't see the bullets. I don't see the men dying. Only Matteo.

He catches me in his arms, wrapping them around me tightly, and dives us down to the ground as he takes a bullet in the back.

"Oh my god! Matteo!" I cry, needing him to live.

He strokes my face, and I know he's going to be okay.

"Are you hurt?" he looks down, seeing the blood covering my body. His hands start searching for my wounds, but other than the small ones on my hands and stomach, he'll find none.

"I'm fine. But..." I pause, not sure how Matteo will take my news. He was trying to protect us all from Enrico, but he was still his father. I'm not sure if he would have killed Enrico if it came down to it. "I killed Enrico."

Matteo's eyes widen. "You're sure?"

"I stabbed him three times in the neck and waited until blood stopped spewing out of his neck."

Matteo grins. "That's my baby," he says, kissing me firmly on the lips.

"I'm so sorry. I should have trusted you. I love you. I want to spend forever with you," I say.

He grins. "That's my line. I'm sorry. I should have trusted you with the plan. I should have told you."

I shake my head. "I don't care. I just want you safe."

Matteo kisses me as men continue to fight around us. We should move somewhere safer, but we can't. So instead, we lie on the ground making out, tongues swirling together as we wait for it to be over.

"I think we need to get you two to the hospital," Arlo says over us.

Matteo looks over his shoulder. "Nah, I'll have you stitch it up, and Eden is fine."

Matteo helps me up, and I hold my shirt closed, Matteo wrapping his arms around me.

"I just checked the cabin. Enrico's dead. I made sure this time. He's really gone," Arlo says.

"Eden killed him."

"Thank you," Arlo says.

I smile.

"You're safe!" Nina cries when she finally gets to me.

We throw our arms around each other, hugging tightly as tears stream down our cheeks.

"You're pregnant! And happy?" she asks, eyeing Matteo behind me.

I glance behind me to Matteo with a grin. "Very happy. Or at least we will be."

Matteo pulls me back to him. "We need to talk," he says, pulling me away from Arlo and Nina.

"Okay," I say, not liking his tone.

"We haven't talked much about our future. Whether we will be together or separate. Whether I will get to be part of our child's life or not. And how to keep our family safe, while still doing what we want."

I nod. "I don't know the answers to most of those except that I want us to be together."

"I have answers for a few."

I raise an eyebrow.

"I made a deal with Clive and Erick."

"They are still alive?" I ask.

He nods. "I needed help to try and take out Enrico. Although, apparently, I just needed you."

I smirk.

He holds me tighter against his body. "I gave up everything."

"What?"

"I gave up everything. The house. My job. The weapons. I gave up being a monster."

My eyes widen and my pulse freezes, not understanding. "But it was your whole life. You loved being a Carini, ruler of Italy, and weapons trader. What will you do if you don't do that?"

He smiles. "I'll love you, and I'll love this baby. We can live in America, or in Italy. I don't care. Although, you might have to work and I'll be a stay home dad for a while, until I figure out what I'm good at, other than killing people."

I laugh.

"I love you, Matteo, but you will always be a bit of a monster to me. The kind with a big heart."

He kisses me. "A monster that gave up everything for love."

27

MATTEO

I GAVE IT ALL UP.

Everything.

The guns. The lifestyle. The mansion. My security team and employees. Everything.

It's gone.

None of that mattered anyway. The only thing that mattered was Eden. I was addicted to her from the moment I took her. I thought I was obsessed with Nina, but it was nothing compared to what I feel now for Eden.

The only thing I kept is money, but Eden will hardly let me spend it. We moved into her condo in Los Angeles, which is beautiful, light, and airy, but it's not very big. Not when we are about to bring another life into this world.

"Matteo?" she moans on all fours, her gorgeous ass in the air, begging me to enter her.

I grab her hips and press my cock to her entrance. Eden is due to have our baby any day. But she's insatiable. I didn't think we should, but Eden begged for my cock, and I'm always happy to oblige.

"I love you, baby," I say, kissing down her back.

"That doesn't sound like fucking," she snaps back sassily.

I laugh as I begin to push my cock inside her.

"Wait...ow..." she moans.

I stop and move to her head.

"Are you okay?" I ask.

"I think that was a contraction."

I grin. Yes. Finally. I don't think I can take much more of a pregnant Eden. I love her. I want to spend my life with her forever. But her mood swings are killing me.

I help her off the bed and put a T-shirt and sweats on so we can go to the hospital in a few hours, since her contractions just started.

"Matteo, I think we need to get to the hospital. Now," she says, gripping my hand tightly at a contraction.

It shouldn't be this painful this early, should it? I think.

"Um... are you sure?"

Her look tells me she will kill me if I don't get her to the hospital ASAP.

"Okay," I say, as I grab the bag she packed, and then take her hand and lead her out of the condo, with her stopping every few feet to rest as another contraction hits her.

It takes us twenty minutes to make it to the elevator, and our car is parked in a garage three blocks away. I'm afraid we won't make it.

We step into the elevator, while I try to figure out how to call an Uber.

"The baby is coming!" she screams. "The baby is coming, now!"

Shit, shit, shit.

"Okay, stay calm."

She lies down on the floor, and I see the baby's head crowning.

"This baby's coming!" I shout.

She half laughs, half screams.

"Breathe baby. You got this. You are a fighter. You have survived much worse. Push our baby out."

I've never helped deliver a baby before, but I know enough. As long as nothing goes wrong, I just need to catch the baby and keep it warm. If nothing goes wrong.

This is us. Everything bad will go wrong. But we didn't survive everything we've been through for Eden to die in childbirth. Not going to happen.

"Push, baby," I say.

Eden pushes and our daughter lands in my arms. I wrap the baby in my shirt, and hold her up to Eden's chest.

My heart stops until I hear her cry. It's a magnificent sound.

Eden cries, as well, as she holds our daughter. I wrap my arms around both of them, knowing I need to call an ambulance soon, but right now I can't. I just want to be happy with Eden.

"That was one of the scariest moments of my life," I say.

Eden smiles. "Me too. But we're fine. And we have a daughter."

I stroke our daughter's cheek.

"What should we name her?"

She thinks for a moment. "Nora."

"It's beautiful."

I reach into my pocket, pull out my phone, and call an ambulance. Then I call Arlo to tell Nina and Gia to meet us at the hospital to meet their new niece.

Everyone is living in LA now. None of us have jobs at the moment, but we will figure all of that out soon enough. We have each other, and we are safe.

I look down at my daughter and the woman I love. They are safe. I ensured their safety by giving up my life as a criminal, and by making Clive and Erick happy, giving them my empire. I knew they would always be running after us if I didn't. We would never be safe. This was the only way.

I did everything I could to protect my family and today was still the scariest day of my life. Because I realized that sometimes we can't save people. Sometimes they die anyway.

Today we beat the odds. Eden lived. We get to keep being a family for another day.

I was afraid to love Eden because I knew what it meant. Especially after loving Nina. I loved her, and she was taken from me. Eden could be taken from me just as easily. But it is still worth it to love her.

I may live my life afraid of losing her, but that is what love is. Love is fear. But that fear can't keep us from living.

EPILOGUE

GIA

"Yes, Matteo, I'll be careful. I'm just in Paris to see friends for a few days. How much trouble could I get in?" I say, stepping off the plane.

"Don't get upset with me for caring about you. I love you. I'm your big brother; I'm supposed to look out for you."

"I know, I know," I say, my heels clicking against the floor as I walk toward the exit of the airport to a taxi.

"When will you be back? Your niece, Nora, already misses you, and Nina is due any day now."

"I'll probably be gone a month," I say, knowing he's going to be upset.

"A month? Gia! You can't be gone that long. Do you understand how much Nora will have grown in a month? And Eden needs your help."

I laugh. "Eden does not need my help. She's a wonderful mother. And as much as I love her offer to work for her at the law firm, I need to find my own way."

I hop into a cab and hand the driver the address.

Matteo pauses. "I understand."

I raise my eyebrows. My brother never understands. Eden has really changed him.

"I love you. Don't worry about me. I simply need some time to figure out what I do next, now that I don't have to worry about the Carini enemies coming after me all the time."

"Did you take security? It's not completely safe. It won't be for a while, but it is safer."

"Of course, I brought security," I lie.

"Good. Who did you bring? Because Dierk isn't bad, but don't even get me started on Paul," Matteo rambles.

"Um...oh sorry. I have to go; I just got to the airport, and the girls are waiting. Kisses. Love you. Bye," I say, ending the call before I have to lie anymore to my brother. Lying to him used to be easy. But now that he's turned into a saint, I struggle lying to him.

I ignore the cab driver, who is looking at me with suspicion after hearing my lie about arriving at the airport.

The cab driver finally parks the car in front of the Carini mansion.

"Thank you," I say, before stepping out. The cab driver gets my bags and then drives off leaving me alone in the only home I've ever known. It may have sucked at times growing up, but it was still home. It's hard figuring out what my life might be without it.

I stare at my phone in my hand. I can't keep it. Matteo or Arlo could be tracking it. They could find out exactly where I am and come after me.

I drop the phone to the gravel driveway and stomp on it as hard as I can with my high heel, watching the phone shatter.

I smile, and stomp off to the front door. I ring the doorbell, feeling strange ringing my own doorbell. But it's not my doorbell anymore. This house isn't mine anymore. I have to stop pretending otherwise.

I wait no more than a couple of seconds before the door opens, and Roman stands in the doorway.

My grin reaches my eyes, elated when I see him. He's just as handsome as I remember. Tall, dark, and beautiful.

"You came," he says with a bright smile.

"You doubted me?"

Roman shrugs and pulls me into a tight hug. "After how I treated you, yes. I didn't think you would show up."

I take a deep breath, smelling his cologne I've missed so much. He may have hurt me, but all can be forgiven if he treats me right this time. I'm tired of being alone. That's all I ever am, alone.

"When did you move into my home?" I ask, staring at Roman.

"About two weeks ago. I'm just living here while my company renovates the property for Clive and Erick to move into."

My smile falters. I don't like the thought of my home being renovated at all. I like it as it is. Darkness and all.

"You okay?" he asks.

I nod. "Of course. I'm here with you."

I reach up to kiss him, but he turns, and my kiss hits his cheek. I frown. "What's wrong?"

"Nothing. Just don't want to move things too fast."

I raise an eyebrow and step out from under his arm. "Since when?"

He puts his hands in his pockets and shrugs. "Since we want a deeper relationship."

I study him. I want his words to be true, but I don't believe him. People change. Arlo and Matteo are proof of that. But not this fast and not without a lot of help.

"Why did you invite me here? If it wasn't for sex?"

"Everything doesn't have to be about sex."

I glare at him. "I want the truth. I know you. All you see when you look at me is sex. I'm hoping that can change with time, but right now, it can't."

He blushes, and I think he's about to tell me the truth, finally. Tell me why I haven't ever been more than just a sex object to him. Pour out his heart to me and tell me how sorry he is, but he'll do better.

Instead, he glances behind me as a dozen men fill the room.

"What's going on?" I ask, looking around behind me.

"I needed money Gia. I was in a lot of debt. I got five million out of the deal."

My eyes widen, already understanding. It's the world I grew up in. But I can't fathom it's happening to me.

"You got five million for what, Roman?"

"For you. I sold you."

The End

Thank you so much for reading *Dirty Addiction*! The next book in the *Dirty* series is *Dirty Revenge* and is coming in June! If you want to receive updates on when the next book is coming and get a **FREE** book sign up here: ellamiles.com/freebooks

FREE BOOKS

EllaMiles.com/freebooks

Want to get my full length romance *Not Sorry* for **free**?

Want to get my **free** bonus novella—*Aligned: Ever After*?

Want to know when I put my books on sale for **free or 99 cents**?

You can get all of the above and more goodies here:
EllaMiles.com/freebooks

ABOUT THE AUTHOR

Ella Miles writes steamy romance with a twist. She's currently living her own happily ever after near the Rocky Mountains with her high school sweetheart husband. Her heart is also taken by her goofy four year old black lab that is scared of everything, including her own shadow.

Ella is a USA Today Bestselling author, author of the Amazon top 100 bestselling books: TOO MUCH and SAVAGE LOVE. She is also the author of the ALIGNED series, MAYBE series, DEFINITELY series, UNFORGIVABLE series, NOT SORRY, and DIRTY series.

Stalk me at:
www.ellamiles.com
ella@ellamiles.com